The Mongolian

by
Mark R. Sneller

Published by Fresh Air Press

Visit Mark's website at
markrsneller.com

This edition was prepared for publication by
Ghost River Images
5350 East Fourth Street
Tucson, Arizona 85711
www.ghostriverimages.com

Cover image by permission–Wikimedia Commons
Hamtdaa Mongolian Arts Culture Masks - 0061
Author–S Pakhrin from DC, USA

ISBN 979-8-9881588-0-6

Library of Congress Control Number: 2023906436

Printed in the United States of America
April, 2023

The Mongolian

DEDICATION

This book is dedicated to Eileen, who lived there and served as inspiration for this book.

ACKNOWLEDEMENTS

The author wishes to extend his gratitude to Lionel Montana. His lifetime of mining experiences and his enthusiastic assistance were invaluable in adding dimensions to this tale not otherwise achieved.

Grateful thanks are also extended to Ellie McAloney, whose simple suggestions helped provide a critical backdrop for this novel.

Preface

On the map, the country of Mongolia resembles an oval twice the size of the state of Texas, measuring some 1500 by 800 miles, once the rough edges of the borders are smoothed out. The country is bordered by only three other; Russia/Siberia to the north and China to the south, with its northwestern tip just touching Kazakhstan.

The country was not immune to the warfare and atrocities that occurred during the reign of Genghis Khan, or tribal, religious, and cultural wars before and afterward. Unlike the United States, the country is landlocked; no rocky shoals or shipwrecks, no oceans lapping the shores, no tsunamis, and no hurricanes. Seasonally, these are replaced by bitter cold nights, high winds, and dust storms accompanied by an overabundance of clear skies, that is, outside the sprawling capital city graced with temples and parks. An abundance of tourist attractions in the country include sporting events, fishing, hunting, cultural events, dinosaur hunting, and widespread beauty.

With a population of only 3 million, Mongolia is the least populated country in the world averaging 5 persons every square mile compared with the United States with 94 and India with 386. It is a recently modernized country in many regards, as defined by fishing and hunting regulations, women's rights, and a strong uptick in conservationist measures, including national parks and nature reserves. Mining ventures are common with other countries. A concerted attempt is made to enforce environmental laws pertaining to those ventures.

Old memories die hard. Enmity still exists between the Mongolian people and the Chinese, as well as with the Russians, thanks to the expansive empire of Genghis Khan (meaning Greatest and Ruler) some 800 years earlier.

What the Mongolian people received from both sides was communism, multi-cultural ethnicities, wholesale massacres, the Russian Orthodox Church (to the detriment of Buddhism), occasional remaining buildings designed by both Russian and Chinese architects, the Cyrillic script, vodka, a drinking population, and the abject poverty that foreign domination brought with it. Through it all, historical ties remain strong with Russia.

Finally reaching independence in 1990, the country aligned with Western capitalism and began to flourish; reaching out for assistance from whomever they believed could be trusted. This included the need for English to be taught by Americans.

PART 1

Chapter 1

Anna drove her Mercedes into the garage and pushed the remote to close the door. The lighted space would remain on for a full two minutes while she removed her groceries and wet swim gear. She shook the sand out of the swim suit and beach towel, threw them in the washing machine just inside the kitchen door, removed a matched set from the dryer, and took them back to the car.

She grabbed the bag of groceries from the back seat and with precision timing, entered her condo just as the light in the garage went out. She placed the groceries on the kitchen counter and began to put away her purchases, placing the Chinese stir fry in a large pan on the stove to warm.

She hadn't overly enjoyed her night with Brad, which was followed by a boring day with him at the beach. The man did tend to be somewhat shallow and was bent on one thing only, for which she had complied, not because she craved him, but because she was bored to tears.

She needed a night to herself without graduation parties, or celebrations cheering her on toward a new life. Her father was eternally angry at her for not having lined up a serious career job; more so, because she had no vision for the future.

Minutes later, Anna luxuriated in the warm spray of the shower, her long black hair losing the sea salt and sweat. She scrubbed herself with an actual sea sponge and ratcheted a towel around herself in an effort to return to the norm. She took the blow dryer, pausing occasionally to work on an eyebrow. Checking out her body, front and back, she noticed a definite need to tan more areas. Her friend, Debbie, was way ahead of her in that department. She couldn't let that happen.

Finally, dressed in silky evening wear, she took the dinner off the stove, suddenly remembering to pick up the mail. She threw on a pair of slippers and robe to retrieve it from the box in front of the condominium in the cool evening Malibu air. She immediately noticed a large manila envelope in the pile of junk mail and bills. The letters TAB stood out in the upper left hand corner with an address and a logo of two hands shaking. The envelope was addressed to her.

She walked to the kitchen counter, poured herself a generous portion of red wine and slit open the bulky envelope. She found an enclosed letter which read:

Dear Ms. Chan: We are pleased to inform you that you have been selected to join our international group of English teachers who will be sent overseas. We found that your resume and your experiences match our goals. We invite you attend our training program. Enclosed please find all the details of your assignment and feel free to call us at any time should you have any questions.

Thanking you, Sandra Carlson,

Chairwoman,

Teachers Across Borders

What the hell? She thought. Anna temporarily gave up dinner and migrated to the sofa, taking the packet and a glass of wine with her. Fluffing up a pillow, she soon found her mind reeling to find she would be flown to Monterey, California, for training in how to teach English—in Mongolia, no less. The training would begin two months hence in early September and would last for a two month period, after which time she would be flown to Ulaanbaatar, the capitol of the country, all expenses paid, and would remain there for a period of two years. The package also enclosed a fold-out map of the world and a map of Mongolia, along with two books: *History of Mongolia,* and *Traditions and Customs of the Mongolian people.*

Anna scratched her head wondering how this had come about; and Monterey, no less, with probably the best language training program on the planet. She knew Monterey. It was parked next door to Carmel. Only three years before, her biology class had spent a weekend up there identifying sea creatures in the tide pools. This was serious.

Completely sober, but not intending to stay that way for long, she tried to recollect. Yes, some months before, on a dare during a sorority party, she had filled out the application and sent it in.

Chuckling at her collegiate foolishness, she set the books and papers onto the floor and got up to finish eating. Picking at her food, she began to ruminate about the affair. Why would TAB choose a Chinese woman—all right, an American born of Chinese descent, otherwise known as an ABC, without any siblings——to teach in a place like that?

What was the matter with Hong Kong where she could speak Mandarin, a language in which she was fluent? They needed teachers there and almost everywhere else. It made no sense, unless they had focused on her experience teaching English to immigrants at her mother's insistence. Her mother had taught grammar in high school for years and therefore, believed that Anna should follow in her footsteps. Apparently, TAB had ignored her three years of studies in chemistry and went for the last two years of her college time when she had changed majors, all because she got caught up in a political rally and was high at the time.

Anna had always been a good student. She found it easy to grasp new material and barely studied for exams to get top grades. The major drawback to having this quality was that she had an excessive amount of free time. There existed an unfortunate spin-off to the latter. Her father, a senior engineer with Rayburn Missile Defense Systems, endlessly harped that she find something useful to do with her life. "Life is passing you by," he was fond to say, which infuriated her. What did he know of her life? Wasn't she getting the most out of every day?

Anna finished her dinner and threw all the junk mail in the trash, including the papers from TAB. She had no desire to watch TV. Instead, she lazily walked over to a bookcase to focus on a single shelf that held unread books. Selecting a hardbound by James Patterson, she took it to the bathroom, got ready for bed, and soon, lay against fluffed up pillows with the book open to the first page. By the time she had reached page 10, totally drained from a day in the sun, she turned off the light.

At some early hour, in a half-sleep, from the recesses of her mind, a stanza from a poem she had once read rattled around so much she paid it heed.

How strong I feel this inner strength
But question what I know
Hypocrisy will always be

From here I wonder where to go

At 3:13 am and troubled by her concern about where she might be going with her life, she padded over to the trash, wiped off the food from the relevant mail she sought, including the large envelope, and reread everything carefully. This time it struck a nerve.

Here was a chance for a free vacation, to get out from under her father's cajoling, to explore a new world, one that would occupy more than two years of her life, years she could spend doing other things. Which things, she would hard-pressed to define.

This took some serious thought. She wasn't so naïve as to believe she'd live in a luxury hotel, but surely TAB would watch out for her. What else did she have to look forward to; perhaps marry a rich dude, hang out in social circles, end her life with regrets over what she might have done; what she might been? What they heck? Why not confirm her acceptance. She could always say no. It might even be fun. Yeah, right.

She speed-read through their books and studied the maps. By the time she finished, she had almost convinced herself that this was a bad idea, until she had a close look at what her future held if she didn't agree to their terms. Impulsively, and against every instinct screaming at her not to do it, she went to the computer, logged in, dialed up their website, found the appropriate page, and signed her acceptance to their terms.

Those terms included her permission for the release of all her college transcripts for their review and permission for them to interview three of her former teachers.

After that, she completely forgot about the entire matter until six weeks passed when she received a notice that registered mail awaited her at the post office. The sender's address listed TAB headquartered in Monterey, California. Stepping away from other customers, she moved over to a side table and slit open the envelope where she found a one-way plane ticket from San Diego north to San Jose located some two hours south of San Francisco, and a bus ticket from San Jose down to Monterey, less than an hour's ride down U.S. 101.

The entire west coast of California had been her stomping ground ever since she could remember and it looked like things were destined to remain that way. She would be housed with the other trainees (number unspecified) a short distance from the facility. It doesn't get any better than that. TAB knew how to take care of its people.

However, the date listed for her departure was only two weeks away. Included in the letter were instructions regarding what to bring, not only for the training period, but for the two year period in-country to immediately follow the training. She would *not* be flown home post-training for a short visit prior to her overseas assignment because they had lost too many people that way for a variety of reasons.

What had she gotten herself into? She took the paperwork out of the post office and walked into the morning sunlight to flop onto the seat of her car, ruminating about what to do. What crazy impulse had made her get into this? She would not be committing a crime, but she would be punished doing time in a prison of her own making. This wasn't like choosing between boyfriends or what lingerie company to work for after school. This was real life.

If she refused, then what? She was tired of school, although her grades were easily good enough to get into grad school at USC, for which she hadn't applied anyway, so it was too late for this semester. Reluctantly, she forced herself to admit to her limbo status with only a single direction arrow.

What had her father always told her? Go with the flow of the river, which brought up another problem. She hadn't spoken to her parents about this venture because it had never seemed real until it was. Now, she had to tell her friends and family about her venture. She would be leaving for an extended period, as though she were entering the military, give notice to the landlord, bail out of a lease, get caught up on bills, go shopping, and whatever else came out of left field. As far as the lease, she did have a friend who needed a place, and money was no object.

She had enough. But everything had to be accomplished in 14 days and 14 nights, which she knew, would fly by.

She didn't need anybody's permission to make the commitment. Anna was pragmatic enough to understand she would never be the same after she returned. Nobody ever was after a journey like that. She had spoken with too many Peace Corps Volunteers who had been remodeled, not quite the idealists they had been when they joined to learn what it was to live without, to look at their own country from the eyes of another. They became like a lump of clay thrown against the wall to be sculpted by the vagaries of life over a period of time, rough edges removed, deeper grooves added.

A sense of panic and dread overcame her. The swiftly moving river carrying her appeared to be heading over the falls.

Chapter 2

Housed in a complex like a single-storied motel, 30 trainees were paired and assigned rooms upon their arrival with orientation scheduled for the following morning following breakfast. Bused to the institute, the trainees met in the conference room where the administrator, Sandra Carlson gave the standard greeting and welcoming speech to the roomful with several of her instructors standing around the periphery. She introduced them and then invited each person to look at the booklet in front of them. This booklet contained information about each class that would be taught and at what hour and at which location on the campus it would be held.

Sandra Carlson was younger than what Anna had expected. She had been to enough office parties with her father to know money when she saw it. The woman appeared to be about fiftyish, of average height, but with clean simple lines to her body and her clothing. She could have been a model in another life. Her pants-suit was light brown to match her layered hair and her eyes. She wore no lipstick, but believed in well-manicured brows. Her face was more angular than oval with cheekbones that were more European than Asian. Her on-line bio stated that she had worked as a sales rep for Boeing before starting her own company, which was amply funded through her money-gathering skills. She was married with two children, both attending Stanford University, where her husband taught.

Carlson paced slowly as she spoke, as if to add emphasis to her words. "The teaching techniques you use will vary depending on the culture you will be visiting. This will include those going to Beijing, Hong Kong, Malaysia, Nigeria, Ethiopia, Mexico City, Thailand, and one who is going to Mongolia. Social customs and dress will vary and you will need to be schooled as to what to say and how to say it in order to communicate most effectively. The person going to Mongolia—please raise your hand—yes, Anna, will be learning the Mongolian language and will be teaching deaf people using Mongolian sign."

Anna heard the words and zoned out the next moments of Carlson's speech reflecting on what she had been told. Despite her trepidation, her father only smiled when she told him the news of her upcoming event. Her mother seemed relieved as well, probably because she wouldn't have to listen to his grumbling anymore.

". . . you will also find a list of the common classes," Carlson continued, pulling Anna out of her reverie. "These will include the basic structure of the English language, teaching English to all ages, and use of proper grammar for the college educated. In Anna's case, she will be teaching at all levels with a specialization in sign language, as I mentioned before."

Upon hearing those words again, Anna felt as though she had walked into a pop quiz without having prepared. *Mongolian sign language? What the fuck?*

She spent the next two months in a whirlwind of activity in what seemed to be randomized events with little time to play. Even in graduate school, she would have free time. She found herself going to bed at 10:00 each night with breakfast between 7:00 and 7:30. Her books and classes fulfilled the promises of Carlson to learn the culture and history of the respective country. However, the bulk of each day consisted of language tapes in addition to five hour-long one-on-one sessions with two Mongolian instructors, a married couple, who alternated shifts. The wife taught sign, the husband concentrated on verbal. The last session was with both of them. Two-on-one. If Carlson had asked her to do the teaching, they couldn't pay her enough. She found the challenge to be tedious and brain-draining, leaving her exhausted each day, yet having to pick up the other books to continue learning when she returned to her room.

For some strange reason she found herself converting the 26 letters and 17 diphthongs of the Mongolian language to numbers that lined up vertically and horizontally, almost as though she were a student of Gematria, the ancient study of finding meanings within each word by converting it to a numerical equivalent. She abstained from telling her instructors about this occurrence, lest they think she had reached a stress level high enough to eliminate her from the program.

On Sundays, she walked to the beach, close enough to catch the spray of the surf crashing against the rocks, trying to let her brain heal from the week-long punishment. She had never concentrated for so long in her life. Leaving books behind, she still found herself running standard language phrases through her mind trying to become adept at a subject not of her choosing. Fortunately, she took the early advice of Carlson who recommended that all students eat right and drink an abundance of water for the upcoming ordeal.

Somehow she made it through the course without throwing her hands in the air and demanding to be sent home. Both instructors gave her glowing recommendations, which she refused to accept. In her mind, she had finished first in a class of one. To her, it was all academics, and if she knew anything, it was how to pass tests. Anyway, Mongolians were polite to strangers.

Toward the end of the course, on a Saturday evening, her language teachers invited her to their apartment for dinner with the caveat that she arrive early enough to help them prepare it. The man's name was Jargal and his wife's was Khunbish. They insisted on being called Jim and Connie. Clearly Mongolian, at least in her eyes, when Anna heard those names, she suppressed a laugh. Those names were as odd as a pale, be-freckled, red haired man wanting to be called Mataua Golumb, or a Nigerian woman who said she wanted to be called Scarlet O'Hara.

Reportedly, the senior couple spent several months each year teaching for TAB, and then returned to teach at a university in Ulaanbaatar. When in Palo Alto, the pair lived in the same complex as the students and other staff. When back home, they lived in an upscale neighbor-hood.

For Anna, learning nouns was a lot easier than discussing the facts of life and her vocabu-lary for the names of objects, both indoors and outdoors was exceptional. They had long since insisted that she call them by their first names while learning how to prepare food from Connie, who would most frequently speak to her in her native tongue. When the three sat down to din-ner, both spent time educating her on the layout of the city to which she would be sent. Lapsing into English to ensure Anna understood, Jim patiently explained that he and his wife would not be going back home until the bitterly cold winter was over, as was their habit—a winter that Anna was slated to meet head-on in all its glory. They gave her their contact information should she choose to call at some later date. Many did.

That particular evening session with Jim and Connie was almost entirely in Mongolian, which served to add layers of knowledge to her base, for the reason that she could now tie actions to words. On the other hand, as warm as the experience might have been, it did nothing to dispel the terrible panic that worsened the closer she got to graduation.

Of the original 30, only 15 remained. Par for the course. When she found this out, Anna wondered whether it was the dropouts who might be the smart ones. If she could see into her immediate future, she might have been forced to make the decision to go with them. She recalled a comedy series of old in which Oliver Hardy said to Stan Laurel, "Well, here's another fine mess you've gotten me into."

Chapter 3

It was a typical cold day when Anna's plane touched down at Chinggis Khann International Airport in a city of 1.5 million people where half the country's population resided. Numerous taller buildings appeared modernistic in style. She could read and cram and imagine all she wanted, but she would never ever forget the sights, smells, sounds, feels, and overwhelming immensity of her surrounds the moment she stood in the doorway of the plane. The freezing coal-dust, diesel exhaust-laden smog, hit her like a poleaxe.

She had read that the capital city of Yakutsk in Eastern Siberia could reach temperatures of -70° F. It is rivaled by Ulaanbaatar (Ulan Bator or UB) for the honor of being the coldest capital city in the world. The latter, however also holds the honor of being the most polluted, ahead of New Delhi, Beijing, and Taipei. Smoke stacks hundreds of feet tall churned out black coal dust, replete with trace minerals and chemical gases that covered everything with soot, fouling the air, as though one were riding a coal-driven train 24 hours a day. The heavy cold air blanket compressed the smoke particulates, forcing them downward, contrary to the intent of engineers to send them into the higher air currents.

She could look forward to another six months of winter with the average daily temperature below zero for three of those months, sans wind chill. At some point she could expect -40° F. Snow on the ground and piled against structures would remain in place, until temperatures rose somewhat above freezing for the other months, give or take.

Outlying gers, or yurts, infiltrated and surrounded the city, each burning coal, cow dung, or wood for warmth and cooking, which added to the hazardous concentration of minute particles in what was left of the atmosphere.

Only a score of passengers occupied the Canadian Jet owned by Korean Air, traveling their regular route from Seoul to Ulaanbaatar. Virtually all passengers were Mongolian or Asian in appearance, including many Koreans, save a single older man who may have been European, possibly a scientist or paleontologist.

When they had landed in Korea direct from SFO, she found the city to be vibrant, especially at night when it came to life, packed with tourists and locals, as though flies had scented bounty. People walked the streets with headsets on, or read from their phones, or patronized the endless rows of shops stuffed with the latest in electronics, many of which had not yet reached the Western world. Foolishly, she had assumed the humidity and temperature would be high, not realizing that the country had already begun its own brutal winter.

Before leaving home, a friend suggested she purchase a rugged watch, which she did. It had everything from GPS, to compass, to numerous timers. Anna mused when she saw that one could also read the time, given enough button pushes. However, the watch was obtrusive and, to her, would seem out of place. She decided to remove the straps and keep the bulk in her pocket.

When the door opened, Anna found herself in no hurry of depart. She waited until the others had done so, and, grabbing her overhead, reluctantly ambled to the door to begin her decent to the tarmac.

The plane arrived in the afternoon in later October, the sun a huge orange orb magnified and colorized by the airborne soot. She could smell it and taste it. This was not the salt air and fresh breeze of the Malibu sea coast. This was another alien world she had crossed the expanse of space to visit. At that moment she despised Carlson and TAB. They had not been honest. They had told her to expect cold. They taught her cultural values and how to teach and what to eat and what to shop for. They had locked her in a meat freezer and told her to come back in two years. Nobody had told her about what to expect at this particular instant in life.

At that moment, she wished Carlson, with all her money, to join her and share the experience. Despite her training, an instant of panic washed over her. She felt ignorant, with little expectation as to what awaited. It might be fitting if H.P. Lovecraft or Edgar Allen Poe were here to share this moment with her.

Her guts churned. She quickly glanced back at the plane's twin bathroom stalls, and returned her gaze forward into a wall of cold. She didn't look forward to the early morning hours when it got worse. At least the sun was shining, for what that was worth. Some inner strength forced her to take a painful breath and get on with it.

Reluctantly, holding onto the handrails, Anna carefully descended the stairs to find a young woman on the tarmac awaiting her at the bottom. Seeing her, Anna felt a flush of embarrassment. She, herself, was dressed in ski boots, heavy parka, long-Johns, and woolen scarf. She had removed her ear muffs. Her specific instructions in the mail had been clear. *Your luggage is limited. Only take essentials, but be prepared for very cold weather. Your luggage may be searched and the searchers may take items they personally need or can sell.* According to her reading of Mongolian history, that particular practice was something they likely picked up from the Russians.

Thus, unable to package her necessities, along with all the heavy gear she needed for the cold, she had been forced to wear it. This did not bode well on the plane when she had to disturb other passengers, while she removed her heavy clothing to place beneath the seat, but foolishly layered again when the plane landed. In the hot, humid, weather of Seoul, she sweated profusely on the trip to the hotel, unlayered to see the sights like an onion with a purpose and stayed that way until the pilot announced their imminent landing.

The young woman at the bottom of the plane's stairs held out her hand. "Are you Anna Chan?"

Anna took her hand and stared hard at the other. But for their difference in height, they might have sisters. Both possessed Asian eyes, high cheekbones, the same smooth, blemish-free complexion, and dark eyes. The other stood about average height for a Mongolian woman at 5'2" with shorter hair compared with Anna's reaching below her shoulders. Although Anna stood a full six inches taller, she could have been one of them.

Anna nodded and said, "Yes, that is me."

"My name is Narangarel. That means sunlight. You call me Nara. I am . . . uh, we will be friends together."

Nara wore European clothing, with a heavy jacket, ski cap, jeans and earmuffs, foregoing the traditional high-collared gown and head covering common to villagers. Her English was broken, but understandable.

Anna replied in her own limited Mongolian accent, "It is my happiness to meet you."

She had been taught about the country's obsession to have Americans teach their English classes, no matter how fluent their own people were, and they sure as hell weren't going to let the Russians or Chinese teach their children no matter what the fluency of their English.

Nara quickly talked Anna through customs where those Mongolians who were present were dressed in traditional colorful garb of greens, reds, blues, yellows, browns, whites, and blacks, each color representing various virtues and qualities of earth's properties. Anna had been schooled on each of the colors in detail and could better understand the personalities of the individuals who expressed themselves through their chosen colors and home decor.

The taxi Nara obtained took them on a perilous ride through the bustling wave of human traffic moving on every type of conveyance, with the exception of bicycles that, weather permitting, followed a separate bike path on the side of the main highway, notwithstanding adventurous souls who believed a shortcut via the hospital might be more to their liking. Painted buildings served as a cheerful backdrop to the pedestrians who loved their earth tones and brilliant colors.

As Anna quickly noted, driving in Ulan Bator can be extremely difficult, due to poorly maintained streets, broken traffic lights, poor street lighting, seasonal ice on the roads, a shortage of traffic signs, undisciplined pedestrians, and undisciplined wild animals. All those factors clearly demonstrated a veneer of civilization without civil obedience, poor city design, or the funds for maintenance, in turn suggesting a lack of money and proper planning.

In the taxi, Nara cautioned, "Anna, don't go street when no lights, uh, sometimes many bad dogs together and can bite. You get sick. Also, we have bad people. Be careful on bus. Cheap ride and people take from your pockets."

Anna shuddered. She thought, *Great. Right off the plane I get to deal with feral rabid dogs, along with muggers and pickpockets.* The latter two were not unique to any city, the former was unexpected. Rubbing her forehead, she decided she might not want to know more.

Some twenty minutes later, the cab pulled in front of a hotel. Anna collected her luggage while Nara paid the driver, then led Anna to the hotel entrance that was announced by an unlit hand-painted sign hung vertically next to the door announcing ROYAL HOTEL in English, now faded in pale red lettering after years of neglect. Beneath the name were two paragraphs. The first was written in Cyrillic script. The second read as follows:

I hate luxury. I exercise in moderation. It will be easy to forget your vision and purpose once you have fine clothes, fast horses, and beautiful women, in which case you will be no better off than a slave, and you will surely lose everything.

Genghis Kahn

Anna was thunderstruck. In one instant, the statement summarized her life. Had she been a slave? Are we all slaves? Questioning her core values, she had a terrible fear. As of this moment, she may have lost everything, a lone person floating in the void of outer space. She wondered, *Dear Lord, why had you brought this man from 800 years in the past to stab my heart?* She logically thought of an alternative value statement: Absent the frills of life, one would gain everything, whatever that meant.

A breeze had come up. She needed to get inside. The old Russian-built hotel seriously needed insulation. For now it would serve as a temporary headquarters for the women. In a couple of days, the two would be relocated to an apartment. At this point, whoever built it was irrelevant. She was too cold to be pissed off. She quickly followed Nara through the hotel's entrance into a cold lobby that smelled musty with lingering cigarette smoke and overall, suggested an abundance of life forms too small for the eye to see. A chain-smoking, thin, elderly desk clerk apparently recognized Nara and held out a key he retrieved from a key box behind him. Most of the boxes still retained their keys.

Smiling politely, Nara accepted the offering, gave a word of thanks, and led her guest past a non-operating elevator up four flights of stairs with Anna carrying her single heavy suitcase along with a stuffed backpack, both of which contained her life's essentials.

When Nara opened the door, the size of the room shocked Anna. A suitcase stood against one wall, likely Nara's. Presumably, it contained warmer clothing than what she now wore, a frightening thought. Two beds the size of cots were situated some eight inches apart. A brown-stained wash basin leaned against one wall with a narrow three-drawer chest next to it. The communal bath was down the hall. A noisy electric floor heater kept the chill off. To Anna, she could swear that her master closet at home was larger than the room. At first glance, it would seem TAB believed in saving money on housing, to be consistent with the small stipend they awarded their personnel each month. She fervently wished that the bitch, Ms. Prim-and-Proper Sandra Carlson could be with her at this instant.

An hour later, when the pair exited the door to their hotel, the sub-zero cold stunned Anna beyond what she had experienced. The temperature drop of some 70 degrees from the hotel room had been precipitous. She felt unbalanced psychologically. She perceived herself to be in a fictional flip-flop universe in which nothing matched her past experience, certainly well beyond the norms she was accustomed to. *This is such incredible bullshit. I'm done with this,* she thought for the nth time, as though it were a mantra.

Nara led her guest through the heart of the city. Their excursion took them past an Internet Café and glittering outdoor and indoor lights of American, Korean, Japanese, Chinese, Italian, and Mongolian restaurants, all busy in terms of sit-down and take-out. To maintain her sanity, Anna remembered her Yoga teacher speaking about proper breathing in order to relieve stress. She told herself, *Relax, this is just another city in the winter where people speak a different language and dress in their native garb. It could be Amsterdam or Iceland; never mind the numerous four-legged creatures looking for garbage to eat. Is that a rat running in that alley? If that were the case, it could be New York City.* The comparison did not give her comfort.

An American pizza franchise restaurant beckoned Anna. To be on the safe side, she pointed to it. Happily, Nara complied, following her into the brightly lit establishment. The menus were printed in both English and Cyrillic lettering. Other than language differences in the menu and the toppings offered on the pizza, reading the menu was a welcome sight for a weary traveler. Nara ordered an Asian pizza topped with stir fry beef, veggies, won ton strips, and goat cheese, which Anna ate with some reluctance, washing it down with a Coke. Soon, sated with an ample supply of grease, carbohydrates, protein, and sugar, Anna felt physically better. Her psyche had a long way to go.

The women quickly bonded, albeit each struggling with the other's language. Finally completing their dinner, the women browsed the shops. This wasn't Seoul or Las Vegas, where the residents stayed home and the tourists contributed to the welfare of the city. The vast majority of those Anna could recognize as foreigners beneath their hoods and hats were there for business and not because Ulan Bator was at the crossroads of the world like Amsterdam, Jerusalem, Istanbul, or Delhi. Just because the Trans-Siberian Railway connected Moscow, some 3700 miles to the west, curving downward through UB to Beijing, some 730 to the south, did not necessarily designate Ulan Bator as a must see for visitors from either capital city.

Nara took her to the bars where they could choose from a wide variety of imported liquors. Sorely tempted as she was, Anna made the wise decision to stay out of trouble, and eschewed drinking, although she desperately needed to slam down a couple of shooters. Keeping her fingers crossed, she permitted Nara to choose their drinks, and two minutes later the waitress brought over two glasses of some room temperature drink that resembled and tasted like sour milk. The drink bespoke Anna's mood. A juke box played Elvis Presley.

Outside again. Into another store. Outside again. Three hours after arrival, physically beaten and mentally numb, Anna crashed hard. Filled with the glitter of the night life, such as it was, the pair climbed the four sets of rickety stairs to their room only to find that the stand-alone heater had died.

Nara volunteered to go downstairs to report the problem to find the night clerk absent. When she returned upstairs, Anna lay in her bed, stripped down to her long-Johns with her socks still on. Nara unplugged the heater from the wall and examined the back of it. Unperturbed, she pulled out a pocket knife, unscrewed a burnt wire, cut off the end, stripped it clean, rewired it, and plugged it back it. The heater turned on, but it was too late to play catch-up with the cold.

Morning found Nara checking out several marks on her skin while Anna, not having slept at all and shivering all night, arose to find her body covered with welts. "Bed bugs," Nara contributed.

Nara stripped down Anna's bed with a bemused look, clearly failing to grasp the look of horror on the face of her new friend. She took out all the bed sheets and coverings into the hallway and shook them out. She returned moments later and piled the sheets and wool covering onto her own bed and pulled the shallow mattress from Anna's, scraping along each edge with a fingernail.

Once that task had been completed, she marched downstairs and retrieved a teapot full of boiling water in one hand that she had obtained from somewhere and a second heater in the other. She poured the hot water along the frames of the bed then repeated the process on her own bed. "That will help," she announced with great enthusiasm, having been informed that many untraveled Americans were likely to be naïve about the ways of the world.

While Nara worked and cleaned, Anna plugged in the new heater. When the coils glowed red, she picked up the heater by the handle and waved it over her body until she felt toasted enough to dress and to survive a trip down the hall to the communal toilet.

She had been advised not to bring her own computer. It might not survive customs. When she returned, she told Nara she was going to the Internet Café they had passed the night before. She needed to make good on her promises to contact friends and family to let them know she had arrived safely. Her goal was to accomplish the communiques without the use of foul language, or besmirching the country. As inexperienced as she was, she knew without a doubt such an attitude would not be a good way to begin a new life. It could only lead to bad luck, and she'd had her fill.

Chapter 4

Within two days, as promised, Nara shifted them to an apartment building significantly better than the hotel, with a room ready for them as per TAB request, close to another pizzeria. This one also served yak steaks and mutton dishes.

Anna washed her hair, drying it the best she could. She announced her desire for another pizza, promising to bring one back. Although, she had enjoyed the meal with her instructors, she wasn't quite ready to dive into the local cuisine. Nara thought a moment and said, "All right. Don't get lost."

Twenty minutes later Anna returned with the pizza, but the cold had caused her still damp hair to freeze like a rock. When she tried to untangle it, Nara said, too late, "No, don't."

Anna's mane broke off at the point where she grabbed it. She was left with few options. One of them was to go into a hissy-fit crying tantrum; however, Nara wasn't a girlfriend who would understand. Not wanting to appear to be a weak-kneed foreigner, she decided to go the other route. "Well, look at that will you," she declared, to which Nara replied, "When that happened to me, I cried."

She permitted the room air to thaw the remainder of her hair, took a few minutes to trim it with Nara's help, who said, "Anna, you look like today's modern Mongolian woman," and then shared a cold pizza.

As her newly assigned friend, Nara was obligated to accompany Anna on the bus to The Health Sciences University, one of 39 universities in the city, where she had been provided a classroom for her teaching duties. As the days wore on, Nara attended all her classes, including a late afternoon sign language class, one of the few in the city, catering to some 30 students of all ages.

Despite her daily misadventures, Anna found herself enjoying her role and soon gained respect as a member of the staff. Students would remain after class or approach her during lunch in the commissary to ask questions, both in English and Mongolian. The questions centered on the sex lives of American movie stars, the wages paid to workers in various professions, and the kinds of sports Americans enjoyed. The latter Anna found difficult to explain because it required a different vocabulary. The fact that she knew next to nothing about sports in general didn't help, so she simply told them the truth.

Out of politeness, she found herself a dedicated listener hearing the latest data on the national sports of wrestling, horse and camel racing, and soccer. She found herself having to swallow her disgust at the unsanitary conditions of native life in general, which served to give her more appreciation for the school where she stayed after hours more often than not.

On weekends and after school, Nara worked language drills with Anna. She found that her student's interest in the language enable her to learn quickly, including written script. "When holiday comes next month, you will come with me to see our ger and meet my family," Nara offered.

The gers (gairs) are occupied by half the population of the country. The 30-foot diameter circular tent is supported by stakes to give it an interior floor space of over 700 square feet. It is weighted to resist the wind. The structure maintains warmth in the winter and coolness in the summer. To Anna, the latter would amount to an average winter day in Southern California. Nomadic tribes may dismantle the ger within an hour when it is time to move on, depending on a number of factors, many of which revolve on weather and feeding conditions for their livestock. After pulling up stakes, the earth will be smoothed over to return it to its natural condition. The ger has only a single room.

Many extended families live together in what can only be described as crowded conditions. The nomadic families take down their ger two or three times a year, place everything on a truck and move some miles away to set up again. The gers are constructed of a latticework of wood layered with wool and cotton which provides for incredible efficiency in terms protecting the occupants from all manner of inclement weather.

A flat-top stove stands at each ger's center, as though it were a deity, with an opening at the top for the long chimney to exit the smoke. This opening is surrounded by a larger opening that can be closed. An accompanying fuel box sits next to the stove.

In the northern quadrant of the ger, religious symbols and family photos are mounted. Men's quarters occupy the western quadrant that includes an area for sleeping, saddles, and a bag of fermenting mare's milk. Women reside on the east where cooking utensils are located. Water is brought from nearby streams and toilet facilities are taken care of outdoors in a dug latrine, a somewhat challenging task considering the climate. Money is garnered from the sales of milk, cheese, meat, wool, cashmere, and hand-crafted items.

Now mid-January, some 10 weeks after Anna's arrival, the daily temperature averaged 7 degrees above zero with nighttime temperatures at 20 below. Other areas of the country did not fare much better, but would improve to comfortable conditions once late spring and summer arrived. Moving outward from the city center in their cab, the limited number of paved roads devolved into gravel, then icy dirt roads, which, in turn, devolved into trails leading through grassland spreading out like veins.

As they drove into the hinterland toward Nara's home, Anna's mind reeled when their taxi began to enter the outer ger district occupied primarily by nomads, or those who were forced to move into the city in an attempt to find employ. *What's less than this, living in caves?* Anna thought.

As Anna's vocabulary increased, so did her appreciation for the basics required for human life to go on, and they did not include 2000 square-foot-homes and color television sets that got larger each year. In general, she was loath to describe her lifestyle and her home to anyone, except to her wealthy students, who could identify with her descriptions. In the case of Nara's family, she needed to tread lightly. She tried to look at her own lifestyle through their eyes. Perhaps they saw the evident flaws in having too much, in always wanting more. She also understood that Americans had built what they had from nothing but ingenuity. At the same time, when you live in a windswept freezing wasteland, it's difficult to develop a work force to harvest raw materials necessary for industrialization.

Comparisons and reflections came with the territory, which, to Anna, still meant she could go home. Thinking about it, though, and leaving self-deprecation aside, these people probably had family members who lived in the city whose children took the bus to school, went to bakeries, and enjoyed TV at home. Many had a family car and parked it in a heated garage. There are poor and rich everywhere.

It might be nice to hook up with one family of wealth, she considered. TAB wouldn't have to know. Maybe on the way back she would talk to Nara about how they could make the move to an upscale house.

Anna was still deep in thought when, an hour later, they had reached Nara's family's ger to the far west of the city with some 20 or more gers in a tight community, all within easy walking distance of one another. "That's our community health center." Nara pointed to a ger with a flag in the front. "We have the good fortune of being in an area where we get city water, even though it is polluted."

Only short brittlegrass separated one home from another. An occasional motorbike could be seen parked next to a residence. Smoke arose from each and every chimney, and sunlight abounded, as it did virtually every day of the year, in the most sunlit country in the world.

Nara paid the taxi driver and dismissed him.

"How are we going to get back?" Anna queried.

Nara grinned and pulled out a cell phone from a pocket inside her Deel. She had converted to traditional native clothing. Anna felt embarrassed for asking such a foolish question. Walking up to the ger, she asked, "Is this your parents'?"

"No, it is my husband's and mine. He is out with our herd and will return before dark. My children will be inside. My mother is teaching them."

"You never told me you were married." Anna said, taken aback at the news the revelations piled onto her.

"My job is to take care of you. It is not about me."

Anna made a mental note to contemplate Nara's statement at a later date.

Before Nara could lead her guest through the wooden door to her home, Anna noticed two stand-up solar panels outside and remarked about them.

Nara shrugged and looked at Anna as though she thought she was joking. "That's for electricity for our TV and lighting. A lot of times the city power goes off. We like to watch world news, sports, and soap operas. We have a lot of sunlight."

"I thought you folks were . . . ," she wanted

to say, "more like savages," but came out with, "less than advanced."

Nara replied, "Anna, we have 96% literacy rate in this country with almost everyone bilingual and trilingual. My sons already speak two languages. A news report we saw on the TV said that 55% of Americans had only a 6th grade vocabulary, which might include some of your elected officials. Who is more advanced than the other? Your country has been in five major wars in the last century and twice that number of skirmishes and ongoing battles, all on foreign soil, not including all the years you spent in Afghanistan. Who is the more civilized?"

Nara's vocabulary became markedly improved when she got serious about it. Anna reflected that she'd better do the same with hers as quickly as possible, and not when she was merely excited, or needed something badly.

Looking up, Anna queried, "Nara, what in the world is that on the roof of your home?"

"Those are wrapped mutton legs. We're keeping them safe from wolves. We like to eat them in the winter for the fat. My husband will take one down maybe next week," Nara replied, casually. "Hope you like beef dumplings in vegetable soup," she added. "Unfortunately, it's out of season for rancid mare's milk with butter served on the side with hard curd."

"Oh, darn, I was so looking forward to eating those," Anna quipped, while thinking, *Poverty is always a relative term. No matter who you are, there are always going to be people better or worse off than you. Besides, there are many ways to enrich oneself.* She chided herself for lapsing into philosophical thought, something she seemed to be doing a lot of lately.

She tried to absorb the surrounds of Nana's family ger. Her husband appeared and two young sons were giggling at almost everything Anna said. The sons were considered to be pluses, rather than minuses. The parents would be able to receive a dowry, likely a number of animals, if all went well, rather than have to provide them, if the children were females.

Not accustomed to the sarcastic side of American humor, Nara said, "Don't worry. We'll have plenty for you next time you come."

Chapter 5

The paint on the frosted glass of the heavy oaken door read:

KHALED AL-YAMANI
CEO
GROEBELS MINING, INC.

David Alday knocked at the door, waited a beat, and went in. Al-Yamani, the diminutive Palestinian, sat behind a large desk. With the exception of a file folder in front of him, the desk was clear of clutter with two land lines available, one on the right and one on the left. Without standing, he said, cheerily, "David, either you've gotten taller or I've gotten shorter. Take a seat, please."

Al-Yamani, born in Gaza and raised in Egypt by an uncle, took no sides when it came to business, especially when empire building was at stake.

David had graduated high school eight months early and worked various aspects of the phosphorus mining business until he turned eighteen. He joined the New Zealand army where he served two tours in Afghanistan. When he returned, he spent the next five years in college, working various mining operations in both Morocco and Spain with his father when he could find time away from school.

At 6'2" and 220 pounds, David wore a full well-trimmed beard of black hair that matched his dark hair that he combed straight back. Constructed like his father, albeit 20 pounds less in weight, he enjoyed the rugged look. His dark eyes held humor and presented a sense of intelligence through eyes that were somewhat narrowed, giving him the appearance of always being suspicious, always wary, despite his open candor. His strong forearms and general demeanor bespoke of an educated man who had learned about life inside and outside the classroom.

Taking the proffered seat, he unabashedly stretched his back and took a moment to stretch his broad shoulders. The flight from Casablanca, Morocco, to Cologne, Germany, had been rough.

Groebels mined a dozen ores and a score of rare earths in as many countries, including Israel, to the chagrin of many of Al-Yamani's associates. To him, politics was one thing, business was quite another. Keeping it in the family, David's father, Josh Alday, was heading an operation with his best friend, Draco Harwood.

Al-Yamani went on, opening the file in front of him. "I have your school records here . . . "

"How . . . ," David began, and then grinned. The man in front of him could obtain records from the inner workings of the Russian politburo, if he chose to do so.

Al-Yamani ignored the slight interruption. "Quite impressive. A Bachelor's degree in Mining and Geological Engineering and an Associate degree in Business Administration. You also have an avocation of drone operations, it says here. Is that right?"

"That is correct," David responded. To him, there was more to him than what had been recited. Under his father's tutelage, by the age of fourteen, he had sledged pins into rail base plates, learned how to shore a mine tunnel, and had learned the basics of properly using dynamite. Just as importantly, he had learned about how to adjust his attitude, and that of others, if it came to it.

"It must have taken you a while to obtain degrees as diverse as these?" asked the man across from him.

"Longer than I would have liked. What can I say? I have wide ranging interests," declared the visitor.

"Don't we both? I'm curious, though, how does a person get interested in these drone creatures? How did that come about?" Al-Yamani queried.

David found the use of the man's terminology, amusing. He replied, "People who fly
them are pilots, those who like to play computer games, or are interested in flight in general.
They're a step up from model planes. When I
was very young, my father gave me one for my
birthday. It was an in inexpensive little thing,
but I got quite good at maneuvering it and I began to read on the subject. Years later, I guess
I was about twelve, my father and uncle Draco suspected that somebody wanted to blow up
the mine they were working at. They thought
the men were hiding in the nearby hills, so they
bought an expensive unit with infra-red and other features and turned me loose to find the men."

"And did you?" asked his host, now captivated by the tale.

"Indeed. They waited for the men and did
them great harm when they entered the mine,
which considered to be it a home away from
home. I picked up a lot about blasting and mining from them, but it doesn't show on my school
records."

Al-Yamani nodded in apparent approval of
the reply, and then said, "David, the reason I
asked you here is to discuss a particular issue
with you. Aside from your school records, your
résumé says you worked at an alga farm in Morocco during your college years. Tell me what
you know about the life forms and then I'll tell
you why I am asking."

David felt relaxed, comfortable, and conversational. Al-Yamani was family and he had known him most of his life. Ever since his father had save the lives of the man's young sons in a boating incident years before, his father, mother, he, and his younger brother were taken into the Easterner's household.

Certain the man knew more than he was letting on, he began, "Do you want the good news or the bad news first?"

"You choose."

"The bad news is that algal blooms are taking over the world's waterways, including coastlines, and fresh water lakes. Several species produce a neurotoxin that is killing millions of salmon, along with crustaceans and the sea life that eats them. It grows so thick in many waters that ships' propellers won't rotate. The reasons for this growth are warming waters, fertilizer and raw sewage runoff, and lots of rainfall. When they die, they create a terrible stink and attract a world of flies. In my humble opinion, there is nothing we can do about it, at least at the present time. The world has other issues. As for the good news, we can use these life forms for our benefit. I won't go through the chemistry of it, but the difference between the amounts of biofuel oil we can get from algae compared with the amounts of ethanol we get from fermenting corn or soy grown over the same space is monstrous.

"Many countries and companies all over the world are heavily invested in growing these life forms outdoors; many use various species of seaweed. Indoors, many others use single-celled species. The outdoor ponds I worked at were a foot deep and lined with plastic. The species we used produced about 50-60 percent dry weight in oils, which is what is processed for fuel. We got a million gallons of oil a year off a single acre after about six harvests.

David continued, "Algae are also rich in protein, carbohydrates, and antioxidants. A number of species are currently being used as a source for Omega 3 fatty acid, carotenoids, fertilizers, bioplastics, dyes, fiber, vitamins, pharmaceuticals and whatever else we can invent, which in my view, is almost endless. Millions of tons of are grown each year in a score of countries. The growth is skimmed off, dried, or freeze-dried, and sent to plants where all the extractions take place."

David recounted what he had heard about the incredible nutritional values gained from eating dried and prepared crickets and locusts. In his view, if algae could be combined with crickets as food, also rich in amino acids and minerals, nutrient bars could be made with this combo and astronauts sent to Mars would not need anything else except water for sustenance.

He continued, "You need an average daily temperature of 60-80 degrees Fahrenheit and lots of sun, although there are ways to grow it without sunlight or even without ultraviolet, but that's the best way. An acre of land is a little more than two American football fields including roadways around the perimeters of each pond for trucks and walkways.

"What I was doing with drones was to use infrared scanning to determine peak harvest times of each pond. This saved repeated daily testing by technicians and saved man hours. The drone technique proved to be extremely accurate. Still, once I pinpointed the mature pond, we sent someone out to confirm the finding. Each pond will mature at a different rate for a lot of reasons, so you have to stay on top of it. That's a short summary."

Al-Yamani leaned back in his chair and nodded slowly. David queried, "Why the interest and why me?" He knew enough not to ask why the man was interested in a field that was outside of mining. At Al-Yamani's world-class level of business, you have to diversify in order to survive—cut old losses, take new risks.

"I'll answer the second question first." Al-Yamani leaned forward and tapped a finger on the manila folder in front of him. "Why you? Because of this. Because you're family I trust you implicitly. And you speak English, Arabic, and Spanish, so apparently you have a propensity for languages. The first part will take some explanation."

"The Arabic I speak is Moroccan with an Egyptian dialect," David interjected.

"Mine is Gazan with an Egyptian dialect. Both are Arabic nonetheless."

David had heard rumors about Al-Yamani's uncle who ran a chain of stores in Egypt that specialized in opium dealing on the side. The pair had concocted a plan to frame the ill-mannered hierarchy of Groebels, when the nephew was vice president. Once that plan succeeded, the unsuspecting board moved Al-Yamani to the top position.

"Languages in general are one area of my concern," the Palestinian continued. "How's your Mongolian?"

David shook his head, narrowing his eyes further.

Al-Yamani spoke to David in Arabic to which David replied. They conversed for a few moments until Al-Yamani waved a hand. "Permit me to get to the heart of the matter," he began. "About four years ago, a representative from the Mongolian government approached me on a matter of his concern. In the end, we partnered with their government to create just such ponds. We each put up $10 million to not only create the ponds and indoor growth facilities, but to pay for the processing of one of their byproducts. The country is not interested in vitamins, skin conditioners, fibers, or nutritional supplements. They are quite happy to digest mare's milk, mutton, rodents, and fresh vegetables for that. However, they are interested in biofuels. After the oil is extracted and sent back to them, they'll sell the rest on the open market to offset costs."

David's gears turned, but he showed no impatience, permitting Al-Yamani to continue, wondering where this was going. "The biofuel component has enormous consequences for them, not for use in a few scooters and public buses, but as a substitute for hundreds of thousands of tons of dirty coal they burn each year. Most of the good quality Anthracite they sell to China. I have no say in that.

"They use coal to create power for the industrial grid. We can't do anything about that, nor can we do anything about vehicular pollution; they don't exactly specialize in catalytic converters over there. To their detriment, coal is used off the grid, as well, where the real problem lies. This pertains to a high percentage of the gers. It's destroying everyone's lungs and the lungs of their unborn children. It's severely shortening their lifespan. We can't do much about their smoking habits, or the liquor the Russians bring in, but we can make a big difference in the pollution aspect.

"The Gobi includes a large part of Mongolia. We've got the operation set up in the southern portion of the country fairly close to China. It's so huge that I'm told it encompasses about half the size of Mongolia itself and has 33 different ecological zones."

David knew next to nothing about the country. He pictured rolling sand dunes as far as the eye could see.

Al-Yamani answered David's question before he could ask. "It's a desert because it gets maybe 2-4 inches of rain a year, maybe less in some parts, maybe a little more in others, not because it's hot. In fact, it happens to be the coldest desert in the world. Most the time the place is either cool, cold, extremely cold, or shirt-sleeve weather. Occasionally it boils. I need you down there with a drone because our personnel can't get the harvest timing right. In short, their yield is not maximized.

"We have both indoor and outdoor operations with a couple of problems. For one, the Chinese keep sticking their noses into the operation."

"How so?" David was surprised at this new wrinkle.

"We have a large staff. They're all smart and sharp. We thought we had everyone accounted for, but I'm getting reports about occasional conversations in Chinese being heard, but nobody's been able to pin it down to any of them."

David shrugged. "So what? Just about everyone is multi-lingual, except for most Americans."

"Granted, except that when we interviewed for the jobs, we specifically asked each person the languages they spoke or understood so we could pair them and house them together. Nobody mentioned Chinese. There's only one reason we're being infiltrated and that's to steal cultures or our secrets, of which there are several."

"I don't think I can help with that part. I don't speak, what, Mandarin or Cantonese?" David replied.

"It's Mandarin over there. In any case, you're sharp enough to keep a watchful eye out and fly the drone for us."

"With all due respect, I don't get it. So what if the formulas get stolen? It's not like they're nukes. It'll be good for the world in the long run," David concluded, feeling as though he was missing a point.

"No argument there, except they'll sell it back to the Mongolians at a fraction of the cost, or give it to them free; no, almost free."

Seeing the quizzical look remaining on David's face, Al-Yamani continued, "Typically the Chinese go into a poor nation such as Venezuela, or some African or South American country and offer to loan them the funds to build them a port, or a power grid, or a transportation or communication system, or all of the above. But the nation is poor, not because they lack resources, but because of nepotism of unparalleled graft and rampant corruption in the government. If you want to become wealthy, aspire to be a politician. In many cases, that's why people want to get into politics in the first place."

"The pinnacle of that condition is a dirt-poor dictatorship like North Korea with everybody starving, but somehow the top dogs find the billions to make all the rockets and nukes they want," David interjected.

Al-Yamani ignored David's statement as a non sequitur in order to finish his thought. "In the end, they can't repay the money, so the Chinese now own what they built. It's the same thing in our case. They'll offer to provide free biofuel, falsely claim to clean up the environment, but trade out for their utilities, or seats in their legislature. There's less muss and fuss doing it that way as opposed to sending in troops and murdering everyone, including monks and destroying monasteries, like they did in Tibet."

David felt humbled. He had idolized the head of Groebels for many years. Now he found himself elevated to the man's trusted inner circle. Almost in a fog, he listened to the man speak. "David, I need a man with character and a business background to manage the entire operation. We have a boatload of great minds down there, but none have managerial skills. Our joint investment is suffering.

"Presently, a man who goes by the name of Batu Gansukh runs the operation. He and his associates are very good scientists, but I also believe he will step on his dick, sooner or later, and could blow the entire enterprise. I've seen it happen before."

Al-Yamani visibly relaxed in his desk chair, awaiting an answer. David's plate was full, or so he thought. "When do you want me to leave?" he asked, with a placid face. When the man says he needs your help, you say 'yes, sir'; nothing complicated.

Did David see a glint of pleasure in the man's eyes when he answered, "Let's say a week from today. That will give you time to pack and prepare, especially when it comes to proper clothing. Mongolia is not Morocco. You'll need to stop first in the capital city of Ulan Bator, before you take a plane down to your worksite, I want you to meet someone."

Preparing to stand, David asked, "Okay, is that it?"

"Probably not, but I'll let you know, Al-Yamani replied, dismissing him with a wave of the hand. Watching the young man depart, he wondered about the best place to put this chess piece to advance the game, without the piece becoming captured.

David returned to his hotel where he checked over the purchase list. It didn't take a genius to understand that, similar to mining and just about anything related to business he could think of, the farming of algae can be intertwined with international conspiracies.

He couldn't help but reflect on his assignment. There were too many holes in it, too many questions. Despite his education, he had endured a rough background having been raised in a mining family, learning that family comes first and foremost, traveling to new schools and countries every couple of years; all the while, seeing, or hearing about men dying in the industry, and personally having gotten into the occasional brawl. He remembered his father's words: *If you get into a fight, do your best to finish it.*

David not only learned how to finish a fight, he also tended to start them. Terminology varied from one country to another. "Anger management issues" was the term most frequently used in the States. He wasn't triggered by petty occurrences, or parental problems, or what might be defined as 'unspecified clinical reaction environmental syndrome'. Nor was it jokes against his country of birth or ethnicity. He'd been in enough locker rooms to share racial and cultural jabs. What pushed his buttons were traitors and acts of sedition and ill words against his profession. Nobody got away with pretending to be his friend and then screwed him over. From his perspective, turning the other cheek was for men who were afraid to stand their ground.

Growing up in mining communities in a half-dozen countries, he was all in. He supported miners, took a stand against child labor, and embraced all miners as an extended family. The fights he started and finished were at get-togethers, parties some girlfriend would invite him to where somebody might belittle his mining background or when celebrations in bars became problematic.

David knew that Al-Yamani was aware of his character flaws. He also suspected they were one of the reasons why he had been chosen for this job.

Chapter 6

David's plane entered Ulaanbaatar airspace in the early afternoon. Looking out the window, he could barely see any structures through the gray haze.

Retrieving his medium-size suitcase and backpack from the overhead, he departed the plane in a very cold gloom, went through customs without a problem, having shown papers that quickly let him pass through, and he quickly found a waiting taxi.

Not at all concerned about the journey, David dozed lightly in the cab until the driver announced their arrival at his Five Star Hotel. He set aside its external Two Star appearance. Whatever the place turned out to be, he'd stayed at worse. This included living at a wide variety of locations including mining camps in New Zealand, Australia, Arizona, Alaska, Germany, Morocco, and Spain, following his father's jobs.

He checked the bed for small critters and inspected the room, which resembled a primitive attempt at Westernization. Before unpacking, he eliminated various crawling things as he saw them, then went through a number of exercises to stretch his long frame. He followed this with a short nap that turned out to be longer than he wanted.

He awoke hungry and changed into what he had brought for clothing, already having experienced its inadequacy. He didn't feel like eating in the hotel restaurant and speed-walked to a Korean restaurant immediately next door to the hotel that handily adjoined an Internet Café. He ordered takeout, took it to the relatively warm café, and settled in behind a computer in the half-empty room.

Prepared to ask for assistance, David was pleasantly surprised to find the keyboard with English lettering. He went to work, taking occasional bites from his boxed dinner.

Short moments later, a taller Mongolian woman took a seat next to him, removed her hooded jacket to reveal a heavy sweatshirt with the words, "Hang Ten" emblazoned on the front in red lettering. The picture of a large blue wave and a lone surfer stood out beneath the lettering. She began to type.

David ignored her. He'd seen stranger things in his travels. If she had walked in naked carrying a spear and a nose ring, he might be surprised, but not shocked. At the moment, he wanted to learn more about the city's smog problem and more about why Groebels had become so invested, subjects he hadn't had time to pursue in preparation for the trip. He'd seen enough damage around the world caused by both rogue and industrial mining operations to appreciate the environmental issues, but this wasn't about mining, per se; it was about options and choices. If there are no options, there can be no choices. The more he read online, the more he understood the depth of the plight the country was in and why Groebels had become involved.

"Damn," he mumbled, followed by, "This is something else. I don't believe it."

"Can I help you?" A voice came from his right.

David turned to look at the woman. Her English was perfect. He grinned, "Sorry, I'm just surprised at what I'm reading."

She leaned to her left and glanced at his screen. "Oh, that," she said, then turned away.

Intrigued, David leaned back in his chair and made the obvious comment. "You speak English."

"So do you," she retorted, giving up her own enterprise for the moment.

David laughed. "What brings you here?" he managed to ask to this forward woman.

"Life's circumstances," she replied, curtly, without great cheer. "And you?"

"Same," he replied, a little more pleasantly.

"Tit for tat," she said, wondering if it might

be possible to find a man with whom she might converse in her own language, albeit he did have an accent. Was it British or Australian? Around here, she didn't see beards like his too often.

"New Zealand," David said, reading her mind.

She laughed. It was a good laugh. "What really brings you here, uh . . . "

"David."

"I'm Anna. Business or pleasure?"

"Business. And you?"

"Same. I teach English, or I should say American. It's what they want," Anna offered. Then she took a flier and asked, "How long are you here for?"

He answered, "A day or two, then I have to go down to lower Gobi."

"The lower Gobi? How interesting," she proclaimed. She imagined the hot summers in the Mojave Desert in Southern California, a four hour drive from Malibu to Furnace Creek or El Centro. The last time she had been to the agricultural center of El Centro, she had run out of gas during flying insect season in the summer and had to remain locked in the car without air conditioning until the auto club arrived.

"It's not like I'm going to live there or invite my friends and family for the weekend," he replied. "It's business for a short while, maybe weeks, maybe months. Anyway, why don't you tell me about your teaching?"

Anna was about to explain, when both noticed heads turning in their direction, apparently interrupting their own work.

David said, more softly, "Say listen, Anna, let me print out what I have in these articles and if you're okay with it, we'll find a place where we can get some coffee or a drink. After we chat, I'll release you from bondage and you can go home, or wherever. At least it's company for both of us and I can practice my American."

After Anna finished laughing, it didn't take her long to make up her mind. Nara had gone to her family's ger for a couple of days, due to a family emergency. Like a weight had been taken from her, Anna decided to go all in, at least for the chat and hot coffee part. The rest would take care of itself.

"You're on," she said, "but in all honesty, we both need some seriously warm clothing. It's going to be well below zero tonight."

"I've pretty much come to that conclusion," David confessed, with absolute honesty. He took one last bite from his food container, tossed the rest into a trash receptacle and followed Anna out the door. She led him in and out of a few stores in an effort to find what she was looking for without having to cross the busy thoroughfare.

A half hour later, with each outfitted in a fur-lined comfortable Mongolian Deel, she led David to one of several nearby bars. The hour was early. She selected one, allowing him to choose a table. He preferred one in a corner, away from the chatter of the mainstream patronage that would later fill the place, if they stayed long enough to see it happen.

Asian music came from an unseen source. A man sang a mournful song in Mongolian. To David, it sounded like a cross between American Indian and Irish, with a bowed instrument playing double-string in the background accompanied by a flute that could have been made from bamboo. The background sounds soon picked up into a captivating fast beat rhythm.

Looking around, David felt a sense of familiarity. Aside from the music and the language, he could have been in a bar anywhere the world; humans relaxing in a friendly atmosphere for food and drink. "What's your preference?" he asked, preparing to walk to the bar counter, not wanting to wait for a server.

"You choose," Anna answered. "Anything except rancid mare's milk with butter and salt."

David walked up to the barman. Within moments, he returned with an unopened expensive bottle of Russian Crown Prince Vodka and two shot glasses. If a poker table had been present, he would have been hard-pressed to decide which was more to his liking. He reached inside his habit and pulled out two bottles of beer. He set them on the table and opened the bottles, using a bottle opener on a small key-chain.

"You're a Boy Scout, I see; always prepared," she quipped.

"Never leave home without it," he returned. He saw Anna start to grin and asked her what was so funny. She had removed her outer clothing and sweatshirt to expose a long-sleeve cotton blouse, not so thick that it couldn't hide her full figure. Blue jeans adorned her lower half.

"The song," she replied. "From what I can gather, a father is delighted. His son is going to receive one horse, five sheep, and a camel from the bride's family for the dowry, but he's lamenting that he has no use for the camel and wants to trade it for another horse. Apparently, a true Mongolian would rather be without a woman than without a horse. I'm told there are more love songs about horses than about the female gender.

"The Mongolian horse is special. It can travel long distances, it's friendly, loyal, and serves as a great food source for these people, both in terms of meat and milk."

"Thanks for the educational material. I can see why the father is concerned," David stated, "Although the word 'nag' might pertain to either the wife or the horse," he gibed, leaning back to avoid Anna's faked punch.

"Tell me about your parents, where you grew up, that sort of thing," he requested, returning to the moment.

"You first," she said, expecting a tale out

of the ordinary. Beginning to unwind, David shrugged. He tasted the vodka from the shot glass, allowing the taste capture him, then he downed the remainder. He followed with a sip of beer. Leaning back in the chair, he revealed, "We're a mobile mining family. My father is a good man. He likes poker, beer, and blowing things up. He's about my height and a few pounds more of muscle. He got his face partly crushed by a rock fall. Unlike me, he likes a scraggly full beard. My mother is good at calculations from working bars for years and never lost a fight. She would slap me if I ever said 'yeah' instead of 'yes, ma'am'. That's the condensed version. Your turn."

Anna nodded in acknowledgment, took a shot followed by a drink from the bottle and said, "My parents are Chinese, as are their parents, in case you hadn't noticed. My father is big-shot defense contractor and a sort of Buddhist. My mother is an English teacher and a sort of Christian. They let me decide what I wanted to do with my religion, so I decided to leave it alone. They both forced me to speak two languages the best I could. My father insisted that there are two things a person must learn to be successful, language and math. School was easy for me and somehow life brought me here."

"We have exacting parents in common," David summarized.

"More like parents with expectations. Your

turn again. Tell me one single thing you remember most about growing up," she requested, taking another shot and sip. *Anna, not too fast too soon,* she cautioned.

"Oh, boy. I'd have to say it was when we lived in Southern Arizona where my dad worked at a big copper mine. I was out riding my bike and when I came up to our house, I saw a roadrunner bird on top of the peak. I must have scared it, because it flew off. No, it didn't fly, it formed an absolutely perfect gray delta shape with its wings and glided some distance with its long neck in front and the feet trailing until it landed in some scrub and disappeared. I never forgot that perfect shape."

"I've seen pictures of roadrunners, although I don't know if I've ever seen a picture of that," she said. "For me, it was when I was on the beach with a couple of girlfriends on a late afternoon in Southern California. We were waiting for the sun to set. Nobody else was around. Then things got strange. Thousands of seagulls took off at once and the waves stop crashing. The ocean became still as glass. Then the water pulled way back. You could see the sand where the ocean used to be. I might be crazy, but I'm not stupid. I yelled for my friends to run. We grabbed everything in a flash and ran up the hill to a big stairway that led to my car on top of the cliff. Just then the tidal wave came in. It crashed down right where we were laying and raced up the sand where it hit the cliff face taking out the stairs with water flying a hundred feet in the air. We got totally soaked. I managed to get my keys into my shaking hands to start the car and we got out before the next series came in."

David grinned, slowly nodding up and down. "Okay, you want those kinds of stories," he said slowly, thoughtfully, stretching out each word. He took another shot and a long pull of beer, then offered, "Here's one for you. This one happened during a blizzard in Madrid. I was out with the guys. We were pretty toasted. We got lost and nobody could see squat when we heard an explosion and a fireball . . ."

Three hours later, with the vodka bottle well-dented and three beer bottles in front of each of them, the pair decided to call it a night, until David asked, "What are you doing tomorrow? Want to get to get together again? Same time same station?"

Anna weighed the options. Sleeping in or getting up early, either way she wouldn't be running on all cylinders. "I'll do my best to be there. If I'm not, then it's your fault."

"No worries," David replied. "It has been fun."

In a short time, Anna went from being crestfallen to being delighted. "Yes, it has been great fun. Thank you," was all she could stupidly manage, her speech definitely slurred.

David quickly departed for the hotel less

than a minute's walk away. Anna opted to begin the trek to her apartment. The cold would do her good. Drunks were everywhere. This time, she happily counted herself as one of them. After months, she felt her old self again. She glowed with the totality of the experience—a night out with a nice man, no, not nice—hot, a man's man. She had run out of stories, not so this David. Depending on how much he wanted to reveal, she could listen to him all night.

Eventually, they parted. Escaping a few aggressive moves by an assortment of men who had their own best interests in mind, she returned to her room throwing off her garments. Flopping onto her bed, Anna but her hands behind her head, wallowing in the feeling of the past few hours.

She and David had talked without pause the entire time. At one point he called her courageous for what she was doing; yet they had absolutely nothing in common; he, with his high adventures in mines, his travels, using explosives, his varied college degrees and his connections; she with nothing but a single story to match his. Despite this, she had the ability to pay rapt attention and to ask seriously relevant questions, many of which caused him to pause before giving a reply.

I will never forget this night, she thought, followed by another, *Be careful, you could be in over your head,* before passing out.

After David got comfortably in bed, he un-rolled the papers he had requested the Internet Café clerk to retrieve from the printer and began to read, quickly summarizing the contents of the pages.

Ulan Bator was described as a city in a val-ley inhabited by 1.5 million and, climatically, subject to a thermal inversion effect, that is, warm air over cold air, where temperature in-creases with altitude. Hundreds of thousands of cars contributed to the smog problem. Half of the population is nomadic. These nomads live in gers, most without electricity and most be-low the poverty level, whatever that meant. The country is trying to become civilized, but doesn't quite know how to go about it. Some 80% of the pollution comes from the ger district, which has three sections: one circles the city, another is in the city center, and one permeates the areas be-tween the two. That arrangement is defined as bad city planning.

Each year, 200,000 gers in the city burn 600,000 tons of coal. Sometimes they burn wood, other times cow chips, and if all else fails, they burn garbage. The government is now sell-ing a cleaner coal few can afford.

David leafed through the pages relating to the health issues, finally turning off the light. Be-fore he slept, he contemplated the seriousness of his role in it all and more fully appreciated why

Al-Yamani had tapped him to make this project work. All the while, thoughts of Anna intruded, until he fell asleep.

In his experience, an excess of vodka had the advantage of not causing a hangover the next day, it only made a person run slow until he could get another pick-me-up later in the day. He ate two eggs and toast spread with marmalade in the hotel restaurant washed down with generous portions of high-octane Middle-Eastern coffee. After breakfast, he returned to his room and dressed appropriately, then walked out to climb into an idling taxi parked directly in front of the hotel on the paved surface roadway. The cold morning air bit at him, in contrast to the blast furnace air during the summer months where he had spent several years of his young life.

David got in the passenger seat and handed the driver a slip of paper with an address on it. The driver wore a New York Yankees baseball cap. He looked to be of middle age with the wisp of a beard. The man raised his eyebrows when he read the paper, repeating the words "National Defense University, 1630 Main Baatar Highway."

Taking a close, appraising look at his passenger, he pulled into the traffic, barely missing a man and a few frightened, confused goats huddled together, all trying to make it across the street in the morning rush-hour traffic.

"You read English," David remarked, when

the driver paused blowing his horn at anything within sight.

"Yes. I teach myself. Also I have good teacher Anna in school at night," replied the driver.

David wondered if he had heard right. "Did you say 'Anna'? What does she look like?"

"She is American. That is good for teaching English. She looks like us, not like you."

Small world, David had to smile. "Tell her David said 'hello', he requested. The driver appeared amiable enough, so he asked, "Do you make good money driving a taxi?" He wanted to learn as much as he could about the people and the culture, as was his wont through his many travels.

"Some money, not good money. My family lives in ger outside city. We move here from steppe for me to work. Not my car."

Over the next twenty minutes, the men engaged in banter until the pavement gave way to hard-packed gravel. A short while later, the cab pulled in front a building complex set-back from the road and buffered by a parking lot at its front. The initials MNDU were etched in stone at the entrance of a central three-storied edifice also constructed of stone.

The lot held scores of vehicles, which included Russian and Chinese made cars, with additional representations from Volvo, Mercedes, Toyota, Hyundai, Cadillac, and various diesel pickups.

He noticed the straight upright telephone poles leading to the complex, unlike others in the city proper, many of which leaned slightly off true, as though loosened at the base and blown by directionless winds. The ones here carried lines not found on the other poles he had seen.

The driver's eyes bulged when David handed him a considerable number of U.S. dollars for his efforts. The man must have had the sudden urge to return the fortune, until David quickly said, "Thank you and buy what you need for your family."

At that, David turned and walked up the steps to meet the man who had been forewarned he would be coming. From what he'd been told, students from the Mongolian National Defense University, or MNDU could attend the Military University of the Russian Defense Ministry, the United States War College, and the Turkish Military Academy, which meant there was no lack of brain power or fighting skills. On the down side, the country's armament consisted mostly of aging soviet tanks, armored cars and artillery. Their air defense forces have few operational aircraft with a focus on radar and navigational services along with rapid deployment in times of crises.

Despite these drawbacks, the fighters trained here knew a few things about ground warfare in frigid conditions. Centuries of international and internecine warfare arguably began when one of their own, some 800 years before, overran 25 million square miles of Asia and North Africa, something much of the world still remembered.

Chapter 7

An armed guard greeted David when he entered the building, handing him a box for the placement of his garments. Displaying credentials, he removed the fur-lined hooded robe he wore, but left on the heavy boots suitable for climbing Mount Everest. This was not out of place. Now down to his jeans and woolen shirt, he walked through the airport-type scanner. At the same time the box went on a conveyor to receive its own scan. Once that had been accomplished, another guard took the box and placed it next to several others lined up along the wall. He gave David a claim number motioning for him to continue toward a carpeted reception area.

Approaching a pale skin European-looking older woman at a reception desk, David asked for Robert Farmer's office. "Just a moment, sir," she replied, in British English. She picked up a phone, made a call, and then said, "Mr. Farmer will be right down. Please have a seat." She motioned to several chairs nearby.

Dr. Robert Farmer headed the Drone Technology Division of MNDU. He wore Wrangler jeans and a red Western press-button shirt rolled up at the sleeves. A 6'0", he looked to be some two inches shorter than David when he casually ambled down the stairs, his smile broadening, once he saw his visitor. Farmer stuck out his hand. "At last I get to meet David Alday. Khaled warned me you would be arriving. You can call me Bob."

David shook a solid, moderately calloused hand that had no nervous moisture. Farmer looked to be fit at a healthy sixty plus years of age with penetrating blue eyes. He wore no glasses. Clean shaven, he had a full head of brown hair parted down one side. He looked like he could fit in a laboratory except for a weathered face that bespoke years of outdoor work, possibly military in nature; if so, probably of officer ranking.

"Pleasure to meet you, Bob. Shall we get on with it?" David prompted, anxious to see his new big boy toy.

"Absolutely. Follow me. Is that Aussie I hear?"

"Kiwi," David replied, "Although, I have lost a lot of the accent over time and travels, from what I'm told."

Farmer led David down two flights of stairs into a lighted tunnel perhaps 50 yards in length to arrive at a second flight of stairs, this time upward. At the top, Farmer pushed open a steel door, motioning for David to enter.

The 20,000 square foot room was a machine shop and mechanic's dream with drill presses, power saws, polishers, large upright tool boxes and accouterments to service a number of creative enterprises. Numerous men worked on various devices, as though they were part of a James Bond thriller. No women were present. Thick frosted windows surrounded the interior at the upper level to admit light and to minimize the drain on the power grid.

Farmer led his guest across the room to the far side where a number of drones on various tables were laid out in various stages of completion. "Yours is in the next room where we have an outdoor roll-up exit door." Farmer said, proudly.

Before them, on a pedestal, in the adjoining work room, like a resting bird, sat a light blue drone, some seven feet in length with a wing span of the same length. Its wings were broad, the tail slanted downward. The nose looked like that of a dolphin with a large hump at the forehead position.

Farmer explained. "This is both fixed-wing and gas powered. It's not great at hovering, but it can stay aloft for about as long as you want it to. For your purposes, it will be versatile enough. This one is a VTOL with two props in the front that can rotate downward to give it vertical take-off and landing ability. The optics are German and the electronics are from Motorola in South Korea. The skin is meshed with wires to keep it warm from power generated by the batteries, of which there are two rechargeable Lithium-ions. Plus, it's gas powered, all of which add up to a lot of weight, so you won't be winning any speed contests. You can run on batteries or gas or both. It handles differently than the counter-balanced quadra-copters you used to fly . . ."

"I've done surveillance with fixed winged units too," David inserted.

"Right. I stand corrected. I suspect you'll need those skills too. Notice the entire top of the body and the unusual shape of the broad wings. They glisten because they're photo-reactive. In a word, this thing is a flying solar panel and since there is almost always sunlight in Mongolia, this baby can fly forever, that is, once it's outside this city where it can get the necessary sunlight, either that or you're running on gas. Also, you've got two panoramic cameras in the front for forward and downward viewing. Be careful with it. This one cost about 200 grand. There's a lot of new tech here we're trying. You'll get first honors; actually second after me."

Farmer picked up a device that looked like a laptop with a deeper base. He opened the top, bringing it to life. He explained, "This lever controls which camera you want on—you can split the screen thusly—to give you two pictures at once. You've got a 50x magnification on each. Here is where you can set the infrared wavelength you're looking for and here is where you can choose the shade of green or blue or red or whatever, lock it in, and you'll get an accurate match. Notice the underside of this bird is the color of the sky. It won't be seen from underneath when it's in the air, and the motor is outfitted with noise suppressors.

"You can also set the GPS coordinates. For example, if you know the degrees, minutes, and seconds of anyplace you want, it will fly there. If you were say, 200 miles from here and you dialed in 47° 54' 11.0364" N and 106° 54' 20.6784" E, it would fly directly to this location.

"One last thing. See these four arms folded underneath? They're the same kind that companies use to drop off packages or to pick up samples from distant agricultural areas to return for analysis. Those grabbers are commonly used in the agricultural industry. We thought they might come in handy for you to get a sample from the middle of a pond where workers can't get to."

Farmer went on. "This country can drop in temperature more than 60°F in minutes. You can be at 40°F below in the desert or 120° F degrees above, when you think you're in southern Russia. A couple of years ago I was down in Gobi when I thought a 1000' tall tidal wave was moving down from the north. It was, but it was a dust storm pushed by a cold front moving at 50 miles per hour. The sharp interface between the two is the deadliest part, but what's deader than what's already dead, right?"

"Damn, what did you do?" David inquired, intrigued by the tale.

"Hid," Farmer summarized, succinctly.

"That usually works," David agreed, thinking it might be a good story to tell Anna, should they meet again. "Okay if we give this creature a try?" he asked, using Al-Yamani's word.

"Go for it. Take it outside."

"Will the transmitter work with the door closed?"

"Yes, it responds to the same frequencies used in Walkie Talkies. It penetrates structural materials including metal."

At that, Farmer pushed a button on the wall to activate the outer door like a garage door opener. A blast of super-cold air entered the room. David waited several seconds for the turbulence of mixed air to settle down, then lifted the drone by remote, quickly flying it outside, and waited until Farmer closed the door again, which engaged automatic room heaters.

David began to fly, both men watching on the color monitor. A gray pall suffused the picture as though they were swimming in a murky lake, until the large bird reached a half mile in height. The sky above became light blue without a cloud in sight, but the darkness below stretched the length and breadth of the city and beyond.

No buildings could be seen in their entirety, unlike promotional pictures he had seen in travel magazines.

David worked the controls, the cameras, and the sensors for the better part of an hour, getting a feel for the keyboard, both in clear air, and within the dark pall of the city. The quiet atmosphere of the day obviated checking the stability of the plane during inclement weather, but the infrared provided the images he sought, as did the cameras. The battery-charge display remained stable. He was able to see an infinite number of stable heat signatures surrounding the city like a donut—the outer ger district— differentiated from countless other energy sources within that circle, some moving not stable, which he ascribed to vehicular motion along with all the other gers.

Satisfied with his practice run, David returned the drone through the open door to gently perch it on its resting place, both men standing far back in case of a mishap.

"What say we have a spot of tea, old chap," Farmer said, in an obviously phony British accent. "We have an excellent little cafeteria. We have to feed 115 students today and every day."

"Spot on, Mate," David replied, in a return jest, suddenly remembering he had a date in a few hours. His mind shifted to his careless and enjoyable evening the night before. He believed he might be suffering from what his father termed SLD, or severe lack of debauchery. He followed this thought by wondering whether Anna Chan would show up, or if it was another one and done. With his luck, he probably scared her away. He saw her for what she was and, without a doubt, she saw him for what he was. Per usual, he had opened his big mouth and had told her too much about himself on a first date—always his death knell.

Chapter 8

Both met on time at the Internet Café. Anna came in several minutes after David. It was difficult to tell one patron for another because of their garb, except that David had been waiting in the seat he had occupied the night before and wore a full beard, a dead giveaway. A power outage had occurred later in the day and the single heat-generating stand-alone air blower struggled to catch up in a room the size of a single car garage. Body heat may have contributed more warmth than the heater.

At her entrance, David gave Anna a cheery smile and said, "Let's get out of here, babe. Are you hungry?"

Babe? "Yes, and I know a good place I want to visit. I'm tired of mutton. There's a terrific restaurant in the Edelweiss Art Hotel. It's highly rated."

"You're kidding. That's where I'm staying," David exclaimed, surprised at the coincidence. He couldn't keep himself from blurting, "Hey, at

$68 a night in a five star, I might have to borrow some money from you."

She laughed, tension easing, hoping for the best. "Lead on," she commanded.

Twenty minutes later the couple dined in a quasi-Western restaurant. A Mongolian stringed instrument group played some distance away. This time the conversation revolved around David's assignment to assist in the growth of algae. For the moment, he decided to say nothing about the drone, although he did repeat Farmer's story to her delight, ascribing the origin of the story to a business associate.

For a moment, he played conspiracy theorist. What if Anna were a spy tracking his movements to the MNDU and to wherever he went afterward? He quickly dismissed the thought. No spy is going to drink as much as she did in fear of saying the wrong thing.

Comfortable in their surrounds, the couple found a lounge area where they relaxed over the same drinks they had partaken in the night before. To her delight, for their main dish, David ordered a 10 pound 33 inch black-speckled Taimen, a fish in the salmon family, larger than those found in European rivers and lakes. It came from one of the 4000 pristine Mongolian rivers, where anglers from many nations frequently caught their fill, some to eat there, others to pack on ice to take home.

The couple relaxed and spoke, sharing lives,

eating at leisure. Today must last forever. To-morrow may never come. Anna's educational background and her quick mind allowed her to intelligently engage David in his description of techniques he would use in his new employ. Neither wanted to leave.

Nara would return tomorrow, or was it today, and if Anna was going to have a fling, she might as well do it now. About to remark that maybe they could finish their conversation at her place, or his, for that matter, he suggested, without a hit of shyness, "Anna, I'm probably going to be leaving UB in a day or so after I take care some business, so why don't we go to my room and bring our drinks with us."

There it was. The offer. Doing her best not to jump up and kiss him, she pondered the request, trying not to rip his clothes off on the spot, then demurely accepted. Still, she was rocked by a revelation. Very soon, this delightful man would be out of her life to become a special memory to fade with the passage of time like the sound of a train quickly moving out of earshot.

Suffused with the glow of an unpretentious tender night of love making and slow explora-tion of the other's body, the couple showered and dressed for a late breakfast. Finding a table and placing their order, David said, "I'd really like to see you again, Anna, but I don't know how or when that can happen."

"What city will you be nearest down in Gobi?" she asked.

He told her and she said, "Just a second. She walked over to the clerk, asked a question, and followed his pointing finger to a rack against one wall filled with brochures. She rejected, *See the Majesty of Ulan Bator by Bus*, and *Inexpensive Camel Rides for the Tourist*, selecting instead anything that had to do with maps, cities, and distances. Bringing them back to the table she opened the map of the country and David pointed to where he would be stationed.

Anna lamented, "That computes to some 800 kilometers from here, or about 500 miles. That's like 5000 miles anywhere else, considering there are few, if any, stops in-between."

She unfolded another map filled with rows of bus schedules to find that the ride would take at least 12 hours, in part because it had to stop at points for food and bathroom breaks for the passengers.

"Then you or I will have to do the return trip too. It's untenable," she admitted, woefully.

"You could fly," he suggested, "but you said you get a subsistence allowance from TAB. It may not be affordable."

"That's not the problem," she said. "I have my own money, but when I signed up, I agreed to live on what they paid me. It's sort of like a Peace Corps thing with them; you know, live like a native to understand the native, although,

I will admit to cheating now and then."

David gave a funny look and said, "Cheating is a relative term. There's nothing wrong with it, as long as you don't get caught by people who are not as successful at it as you are. Besides, cheating is an integral part of any system where humans are involved. People become successful by thinking outside the box. They're not constrained by the concept of cheating. Look, you're not a Peace Corps Volunteer and your job is to teach, not intermesh with them so much."

"Tell that to TAB," she said, getting a small glimpse into his view of life. She felt sick. Why was this happening? Life didn't have to be cruel all the time, did it? They had connected. Admittedly, the odd circumstances of their meeting and their stations in life were magnified by their disparate circumstances, which also served to magnify their feelings, but so what. She had never felt this way about anyone, whether a long term relationship or a one night stand. David was special and she believed him when he had told her the same thing. If she was being used— for what she didn't know—then so be it. As of this moment, she was willing to flow with the river, over the falls or not.

David placed his hand over hers and said, "Tell you what. I don't have a problem with money either. One of us will make arrangements to see the other. How's that?"

Anna leaned over and kissed him on the lips.

She whispered, cautiously, "We'll see how it works out, as long as we try to stay in touch all the time. Okay?"

Anna suddenly backed away, remembering something. "Oh, tomorrow is a work day. Nara, my bodyguard, third arm, partner, watch dog, assigned hostess, whatever, will be back this afternoon, but if you don't mind her joining us for dinner, we can at least visit for a short while. Sorry."

"No worries. Same time, same place?" he concluded, looking forward to the meeting with anticipation, whatever its guise.

Chapter 9

After Anna returned to her apartment, she reviewed the brochures she had brought with her. She checked out the arrival and departure times of flights between Ulan Bator and Arvaykheer, followed by another to Dalanzadged, followed by a car ride to Sanglyn Delay, which might take a full day, the same length of travel time as if she were taking a bus, everything considered. It would be well worth the effort, if she could stay with him as long as possible.

The connection between them could not be denied, although she strongly cautioned herself to move slowly. He didn't seem to be the type who would demean her. Anyway, what was another heartbreak? Talk about hit and run. This could be a real soul breaker, on foreign soil, no less, a great addition to her resume. She would love to open the discussion with him over dinner, but she didn't need Nara involved in her love life. She wasn't home in Malibu anymore, and she didn't know how the social networking game worked here. She decided to let Nara play the guessing games and she would work it out with David, if and when they communicated at a later date.

She was about to put away the scheduling brochure when a sentence in italics at the end of the pamphlet caught her attention. *All times of arrivals and departures may vary greatly, depending on climatic conditions.* Anna reflected on the statement. She had to laugh when she translated plain English into politico-correct-speech. What they were trying to say was that, if the pilot can't see the fucking runway through the smog or the sandstorms, why bother landing or taking off. Therefore, it's okay to take a little extra time to build up courage before arriving or departing, pilots and passengers included.

Nara walked in, pulling Anna from her ruminations. With hugs and healthful greetings, Nara set down her backpack and took off her heavy garments.

"Tell me, Nara, how is your mother?" Anna did have legitimate concerns for the welfare of her new friend's family.

"She's well. She was bitten by what you call a pit viper, the same type we find in our residential sections of the city here."

"Jeez, that's awful." Anna replied, scratching herself. *Great, pit vipers now.*

"They got her to the hospital where she got antivenin. They keep a lot of that. How did you do alone?" Nara inquired.

"Oh, I had a nice, quiet time while you were gone. I visited different parts of the city. Wait, I almost forgot. I did meet a nice man who invited me . . . us to dinner tonight," Anna told her easily, trying to disguise her hormone-driven thrill at the thought.

"Okay, that will be fun. Wait, I almost forgot," Nara said, handing Anna a small 7" x 11" manila envelope. "The clerk said this came for you."

Anna turned down her mouth in a show of curiosity. She took out a number of pages, all of which had the TAB logo in the upper left corner. Pulling out a letter she read:

Dear Anna: We have received nothing but glowing words about how quickly you are learning the language, including sign, your facility to teach, and the successes of your students.

Therefore, we are pleased to announce your immediate transfer to Darkhan. You will find travel and residential arrangements enclosed.

Sincerely and warmest wishes,
Sandra Carlson

Without a word, Anna dropped the letter and began sifting through the brochures. She found the one she wanted and began to read. Seeing the stricken look her friend's face Nara picked up the letter she had dropped. In a minute, Nara put her hand over her mouth and exclaimed, "Oh, my."

Anna saw Darkhan on the map. It lay 150 miles to the north of Ulan Bator and had a population of perhaps 3% of their city. It was also much farther from David and close to the Russian-Siberian border. She might have to spend the next 22 months there, while in the midst of winter. Surprisingly, Darkhan bragged the second largest city in Mongolia with 40% of the population living in gers. *Whoop tee do and Blah, blah. Who cares?* Anna thought.

She needed a hug. She needed to let loose and to cry on the shoulder of a strong man, but she had to give way to Nara, who voiced her own concerns. "Anna, that means we will have to say goodbye. You will be going alone and living alone. My family is here and I am paid to be only with you here. I will not get paid now, but it is more than money. I will miss you so much."

At that, both women began to sob.

Chapter 10

The never-ending situation at the airport did not escape David's attention. He went to Plan B. He called Robert Farmer to explain his problem.

Farmer said, "Good timing, David. I have to bring down a plane-load of supplies on my monthly run and you can ride along. We'll leave from the air force base out of town. You don't think these guys here fly out of the commercial airport, do you? There's a nice old two-prop never-say-die Douglas Aircraft DC-2 we can take. I liked to fly those in my old bush pilot days. I'll make sure to leave room for the drone, but we'll be packed close to our 3600 pound weight limit. If I had my druthers, I'd like to have a DC-3 with twice the capacity the way things are going down there. It sounds like it'll be just the two of us, that is, unless you want take a passenger, hah hah," Farmer chided.

Two days later Farmer donned a pair of head-sets and gave a set to each of his passengers. The cargo bay was filled with crates and barrels.

The plane lumbered down the left runway and slowly rose, heading south. Anna sat behind David, giving him a light shoulder massage, as though they had known each other since forever, instead of a few days.

She had slipped him a note during their dinner with Nara two evenings previously explaining her quandary. When he found a way to excuse himself in order to read it, he learned that note also told of Nara's mother's recent escape from the snake bite. Grinning, he offered a simple solution. Give her, say $200 in small bills to explain to your classes that a snake bit you and you'd be out for a few days. That would be equal to three month's pay, a windfall for her and her family.

A half hour out, Farmer said, "Dinosaur hunting is big here. The Mongolian Academy of Sciences and the Institute for the Study of Mongolian Dinosaurs oversee the tourist attraction. Off to the right about 150 miles is a community called Bulgan, noteworthy for the Flaming Cliffs, a paleontologist's dream of formations that look like castles with spires and turrets, all turning red in the evening sunlight. They tell us some 20,000 years ago, inhabitants of the area used dinosaur bones and egg remains for tools and decoration. There's another big area for egg and bone hunting down in southeastern Gobi. It's a heck of an underground business.

Some discoverers protect their finds with armed guards like they were protecting gold mines.

"If you do get to Bulgan, you'll want to go when they hold the annual winter festival where they have camel races and play camel polo. It's quite the colorful event. You'll see up to 6000 camels during the winter festival.

"We get more than a half-million tourists each year, many who come to look for them, along with a lot of fishermen and general sight-seers, mostly from China and Russia, of course, but also from South Korea, and Japan."

"You sound like a travel agent," David remarked.

"You would be, too, if you saw the country as much as I have," Farmer replied.

For the next hour, the vast plains of the off-green ground cover extended out to infinity. Trees and shrubs were utterly absent. Snow topped distant mountains. Occasional gers planted next to a stream and numerous smaller lakes announced their location displayed by their blue-whiteness against the color of the background, along with black smoke coming from their chimneys. Occasional clusters of goats, sheep, yaks, camels, and sometimes horses, were under the watchful eye of their owner, identified from the air by their gait or herding pattern.

"It's gorgeous," Anna exclaimed, her face plastered to the side window. "What is that, a hundred square miles of wild flowers on earth as flat as a pancake? Is that a herd of camels over there?"

Without looking Farmer said, "Yes, those are Bactrians. They have two fatty humps to serve as energy and insulation against the cold climate, as opposed to single-humped camels where they store water in a true desert."

Anna confessed, "To think I've been looking at buildings, people, and traffic for two months. I feel like I've been in a dark closet and instantly transported into a bountiful wonderland."

Farmer smiled in agreement. "This is just the beginning. Stick around long enough and you'll see camel races and the longest horse race in the world with competitors coming from abroad to race through more than a dozen micro-climates including sand dunes, grassland, thorny bushes, swamps, rain, and mud, heat, and whatever nature stores up to welcome the riders. In fact, a young British girl won the race a few years ago.

"I love it here. I'm making plans to move here permanently, which, to me, means the small town we will soon arrive it."

Anna mused, "It sounds like it might be fun to spend some time touring the country."

Farmer said, "Touring is great fun, no matter where you go, as long as the government lets you. Here, there's no problem. I wouldn't try it in Russia, or a few other countries I can think of."

Anna contemplated his words and decided to

ask what was on her mind. "Can I ask a personal question? You seem like a free spirit. If you're married, what does your wife think about your moving?" Growing up in a city of millions, she had never conceived of isolating oneself from the perks of civilization, although once she made the statement, she saw the hypocrisy in it.

"Was. She didn't make it," Farmer answered, solemnly.

Anna took his response in stride, until moments later she remarked, "What's that black patch down there to the right? There are machines around it."

Farmer looked to where she pointed and said, "That's the Table Top coal strip mine. It's a new joint venture between China and Mongolia. From what I hear, it's likely to be the biggest one in the country—Anthracite no less. That's your area, David."

David answered, "Surface mining for coal costs only a fraction of deep mining for the reason that takes less men and less materials. All they do is to remove the overburden, which could be 50-200 feet of soil, dump it to the side, and scoop out the coal. The backstory is that those lakes and streams around the area are poisoned from the heavy metals in the coal dust and it's probably why you don't see anybody living anywhere near the place."

"You mean the two countries share 50/50 in the profits?" Anna asked.

"Not really. When China goes in, you can count on them taking a larger slice of the pie. It this case it might be more like 70/30."

"That hardly seems fair?" Anna said.

"Fair is an interesting word worthy of a lengthy discussion," David inserted.

David went into lecture mode, "Anthracite is the best grade of coal with the least pollutants. It burns hotter and longer than other coals. At 98% carbon, it doesn't release any gases of concern. Up to this point, most of it was found in your country in northeastern Pennsylvania."

Farmer laughed, "David, I grew up out there, right where you are talking about. In this instance, we mine it, while China buys it for pennies on the dollar. It's too expensive to do the operation ourselves and to keep the coal for our own use. At least, that's what the government says."

"That's fucked up" Anna said, without thinking. *I have to quit reverting to my old SoCal life and watch my mouth here,* she thought.

Farmer stopped laughing long enough to become serious. "The environmental problems here are profound. Extreme weather conditions have increased 7-fold over the past three decades, which means more dust and ice storms on the one hand, more droughts on the other. What forests we have are quickly disappearing through fires and illegal cutting leading to flooding and loss of top soil and native species. Industrialization is attacking the land from another aspect through coal-burning factories, while rampant mining activities destroy both mountains and flat lands, as you can see.

"If you've read anything about the Great Depression, you might have read that food growth was inhibited by the presence of high winds and disturbed land. In large part, that's what happening here. It gets worse each year. Add sand to the mix from the dunes to taint the stew.

"Mongolia has strict mining laws. Namely, you to put it back the way you found it. The good news is that when a company is finished with the coal seam, they will replace the soil. The problem is that now it is scooped up and replaced upside down with the rich top soil on the bottom. Nothing will grow there except for scrub plants. The eco-system of the land is destroyed."

David concluded, "That process goes on all over the earth. There's no stopping it."

"Ouch," Anna said, cautiously. "Right here in the middle of the scenic wonder of wild flowers."

"Unfortunately, it is what it is. Mongolia has the largest coal deposits on earth. We also have everything else, gold, silver, cobalt. Mining is crazy here. We have joint ventures with a half-dozen countries. It's a big stink. The government is confused. They know what they need to clean up and modernize their larger cities, but they need the cash flow to do it, so they're selling their soul to get there, which is contrary to the well-being of a nomadic society. It's damned if you do and damned if you don't."

"Beauty and the beast," Anna lamented.

An hour later the terrain changed from green grass to winding rivers running through a forest of spruce followed by hundreds of square miles of light brown sand. They had officially entered another micro-climate zone of the larger Gobi.

After another hour, a ring of brown barren hills appeared in front of them. As they got closer, structures within the ring made their appearance.

Farmer said, "There she is. We call her Naidvar."

Anna announced, "That means 'hope' in Mongolian."

"Correct. Notice the ring. It tops at around two thousand feet. Geologists think the ring is an impact crater formed from a meteorite, sort of like the one in northern Arizona in the States and in a lot of other places. It filled in over time, but it's perfect for us. They think the rock came in on a slight angle from our direction, not straight down. That's why there's a teardrop shape of the valley with the wider part to the south. Look to the southeast. See that dip in the mountain? We were able to cut an access road from the valley to the rail line five miles to the east so we can service it both from the air and the ground. The road leads south to Bayannur, China, where we do our processing. Our product gets trucked in."

Anna asked, "What is that golden color in the center of the crater?"

Farmer answered, "Those are golden poppies in the middle of the brittlegrass. You can see it's an elongated oval and follows the shape of the valley. It starts in the middle of the crater where the flowers spread over two miles in width and tapers somewhat toward the southern mountains. The ground there is slightly depressed. We get maybe three inches of rain a year, which settles in the depression enough to give us a richer soil, hence the poppies. To me, it's a beauty mark."

David said, "You wouldn't have a backhoe down there would you?"

"Sure, we have a shed with all that equipment, including a front end loader, backhoe combo. Why?"

"Oh, I might like to do a little digging at the base of the mountain, if I get the chance, that's all," David threw in.

Farmer began to fly a circuit around the hills pointing out various structures. "David, those are your ten ponds, five rows of two each, each pair enclosed in a building with a Plexiglas–paneled roof to let in sunlight. We can grow year-round. When a pond is mature, we screen off the algae, drain it, weigh it, and put it into aluminum containers. No need to refrigerate here. Flatbed trucks come up from Bayannur, China, about 100 miles south, to pick up the load. If not, we can hitch a ride on the Trans-Siberian Railroad that runs through there all the way to be Beijing."

"Nice runway off to the east; huge, in fact," David commented.

"We needed to build something like that for larger cargo planes to bring in materials," Farmer said. "That building nearest the airstrip is our warehouse, which is tied to Administration, which is tied to the commissary, which is tied to the residence hall, which is tied to the Biolab and the hospital. Everybody gets paid monthly. We also have a bank, commissary, library, gym, small shopping center, and, if you'll notice, we have a cell phone tower. It's not perfect, but it's a damn sight better than not having one, I can tell you that from personal experience."

At that very moment, a strong cross wind combined with an updraft to jerk the plane sharply to the right while Farmer fought the controls, ignoring Anna's scream. David held on, have experienced worse during wartime. A Piper Cub or smaller Cessna might not have survived.

Ignoring his white-faced female passenger, Farmer continued with his monologue, "Your residence will be in the lower left portion of the building, or southeast corner, away from foot traffic and about 50 feet from the corridor that leads east to the commissary. After processing, the oil is returned by railroad to UB where it ends up in storage. Admin handles all the details. All that processing and shipping adds a good 30% to our overhead."

"That sounds about right," David commented. "I'm seriously impressed. Tell me, How do you get your energy? I don't see any coal fires, but I do see a lot of cables."

Farmer laughed. "Geothermal, my friend. See that tall structure to the east near the hill? We get steam 24/7/365 to power our turbines. The structure next to it is our water pump. When that meteor hit way back when, it blew out the top layer of basalt on the crust. The crater filled in and compacted over time.

"Several years ago, while mapping the country, a U.S. Geological Survey satellite noted a five-mile diameter red dot, more like a teardrop shape, when they were partnered with our government. The red was a heat signature. Mongolia sent down some people to investigate and discovered that the ground is heated because the layer of insulation is gone. They knew the water table was down about 500' or less, and figured if they could go down further, they might hit the mantle. Bingo. Water plus heat equals steam. Ergo, we've got heat and water, all you could want. Right now, the air temperature is below zero, but all of our indoor areas are maintained at shirt-sleeve weather. The ground never freezes here so we use minimal energy and can grow all we want. We're five degrees higher latitude than

Chicago, but you'd never know it down there."

"That's crazy, man," David declared, adding, "You keep saying 'we'. Are you part of this?"

Farmer grinned. "I helped build the runway. In another life, I was in charge of airport management, which covers a lot of different disciplines. I helped with the layout here. Notice all the buildings are connected by a covered tunnel, including the five buildings over the ponds. Nobody has to be outside if they don't want to. Each room has its own TV and hot shower. In fact, that building over there to the west of the ponds has floor space of 20,000 square feet. That's our greenhouse. You name it, we got it."

Anna said, shaking her head in awe. "My parents had one. I used to play in it. I love greenhouses."

"There's your new playground," David mused, then regretted the words, knowing she would be leaving for Darkhan soon and leaving behind something she loved, maybe more than one thing.

Circling the mountains, Farmer continued, "We've only used a fraction of the available space. We have a lot of room to grow. Each building can be added onto, including the Biolab."

"It's like a self-contained cruise ship. Who runs the indoor lab operation?" Anna asked, having recovered enough to keep her voice on an even keel.

"That would be a man by the name of Batu Gansukh and another man named Temujin. Batu is a little fellow. Got his degree in science from the Ulan Bator University and wanted to go to the States for more education. The University of Texas had the program he wanted and he was accepted. He stayed long enough to get his Master's degree. Anyway, a little man from Mongolia didn't quite fit in with the cowboy culture there, so he left. Months before he came back, though, he met a Chinese girl who was just graduating. They hit it off, got married and both are working here."

"Interesting. What does she do here?" Anna inquired.

"She teaches English," Farmer replied. Then, "Hang on. We're about to land."

In a few moments, the plane taxied next to an open hangar and stopped. The three dressed for the cold and the men unloaded the drone to place it out of the way. David held the keyboard against his chest. A number of men arrived with flat carts to unload the crates and wheel them away. Anna wasn't aware that the drone had been on board and inquired about its use. After David explained, she asked, "How are you going to survey the ponds when they're in different buildings? Oh, you fly in one end and use the connecting tunnels. Got it."

Farmer overheard her words and said, "If you think that's neat, wait until night when the stars come out. Guaranteed, you've never seen anything like it."

The administration building was replete with several occupied offices, each with a computer and a man or woman present. "This is where we do a lot of our data correlation," Farmer explained. "The people here tell me they strongly suspect we're being monitored, maybe hacked."

"By whom?" Anna asked.

"Probably by the Chinese. We haven't run across too much Russian activity lately. For the guys down south, it's easier and a lot less expensive to steal technology than it is to start from scratch on your own. It's something they're good at."

"Let somebody else do the grunt work, then take it from them," David summarized, then he added, "Wait a second. It's no secret that almost everybody is growing algae. So what's to steal?"

Looking around, Farmer came to an abrupt halt outside of earshot of anyone else. When Anna stopped to take a closer look at one of the computers, he leaned in to David. Lowering his voice he said, "Because we can double, maybe triple the growth the rate over anybody else, guaranteed."

As they walked, David felt the germ of an idea form, but when he tried to concentrate on it, like a dream, it evaporated.

Farmer led the pair through the walkway

leading to the Biolab, the heart and soul of the operation. Doors on either side of the hallway were marked with a number and a name such as Machine Shop, Glass Blowing, R&D, Chemistry, Microbiology, and Janitor's Closet. He stopped at one marked Production and pushed open the door to reveal a vast room filled with machinery.

On two sides of an aisle, independent machines serviced independent vats. White-coated technicians occasionally pulled samples, immediately checked the acidity level, and brought the sample to another man who ran the samples through a spectrometer to determine the level of oil in the liquid. At the far end of the huge room stood three walk-in freezers with a forklift parked to one side. Large centrifuges were aligned against one wall with a hose and floor drain connected to each.

Another white-coated man kept a close eye on the operation, saw them, and approached. At an even five-feet in height, the man couldn't have weighed more than 100 pounds. He might make a better living as a jockey than a man trying to ride a bucking bronc in a rodeo. He wore jeans, a blue polo shirt with the imprint of a brown camel over the left shoulder, and brown sandals—a man of the earth and sky.

After greetings, introductions, and wishes for good health, Batu led them down the aisle and explained, "Each of these vats has 200 liters in its growth medium. That's about 50 gallons each. We have twenty of them and can produce a crop every two weeks in each compared with every two months outdoors. We add the liquid with a lot of nitrogen, phosphorous, and potassium, then add our seed culture and take occasional samples from the port you see on the side. We bubble carbon dioxide through it and mix it with an internal paddle. When it's ready, we centrifuge the mass and ship it off to international partners for their extractions.

"Numerous species of algae are grown around the world and each produces its own set of oils. Our oils will go to a distillery to make biodiesel, butane, and even jet fuel."

Anna absorbed everything she heard and saw. The sound of the humming machinery, the heady odor of algal growth, and the slight smell of machine oil put her into another mental state. Why had she given up chemistry? She was good at it. For the tenth time she remembered that she had gone to a campus rally about social injustices and decided to change majors. It had cost her an extra two years and what had that gotten her? Did a free trip to a lab in Mongolia count?

"We do have a problem, though," Batu continued. "We're losing a lot of product. Somehow the amount of oil we're getting doesn't match with our predictions. We're harvesting too late."

Anna had sudden thought and asked, "How do determine when it's ready to harvest?"

"We do continuous monitoring and when the amount of oil peaks out, then we shut it down right then," Batu answered.

"I might suggest a couple of things to do something differently," Anna offered, delicately, not wanting to overstep social bounds, which might broach on an insult. She had only just arrived and already she was getting into trouble.

"I'm listening," Batu said, openly.

Go for it, Anna. You'll be leaving soon, anyway, she told herself. "Check the pH and not the oil. The acidity level will shift to alkaline right before the algae start to go into the death phase and release some of their oil. You want it to maximize inside the cells before leakage. To my way of thinking, unlike humans, there's a difference between end of life and beginning of death, as far as harvesting is concerned.

"The second thing is, you can confirm this by sonicating the cells in your sample to rupture them and release what's inside rather than measuring what's the medium."

Batu looked around at each of the others, contemplating. Everyone there understood one fact about expertise. Sometimes, it takes a different person's perspective to solve a problem. He said, "We will follow your suggestions. If either works, you're hired."

Farmer looked at David and shrugged slightly, as if to silently announce, "Hey, she's yours, not mine."

Anna said, "I wish it were true. Don't think I personally wouldn't love to work here, but I'm under contract. If I break my lease, the landlord will hold me liable for rents due. In my case, TAB invested thousands in me and they will want a full return on their investment, if I leave early. So it's Darkhan for me for the next couple of years."

Anna wondered why she had said this. She had all the money in the world. Why was she suddenly concerned about repaying a debt of a paltry few thousand, unless she was using that as an excuse? *Anna, it's about making a commitment to yourself and for the sake of our parents,* she quickly concluded.

"Darkhan. Nice," Batu announced.

Anna felt sick. It was as though she had been shown a free all-you-can-eat buffet of her favorite foods, but had been ordered not to eat anything. Looking is free, but no touchy. A sense of panic overcame her and she looked around to find what she wanted, a water cooler in the corner. She casually ambled over to it and pulled a large paper cup from the dispenser. She filled the cup and drank most of it, refilling it and returning to the group. She hadn't realized how dehydrated she had become. In a health-related course during her TAB training, she had been told how extreme cold with low humidity can suck the water from a person as much as can a dry desert. Somehow, the cold itself didn't seem so bad, until you got frostbite.

When she returned to the group, Batu put his palms together in front of him, bowed his head slightly, and said, "My humble apologies to all three of you. I am forgetting my duties as a host to an honored guest in my home."

"No apologies necessary, Batu. This is not really your home, this is your workplace. If we come to your home, you can honor us then," Anna replied in Mongolian.

Batu's eyes widened. He clearly appreciated her way of allowing him to save face. They were now friends.

Anna asked, "Why did you say 'nice' when I said 'Darkhan'?"

Batu replied, "Aside from being colder than Ulan Bator, sometimes it is quite manageable. Everybody wants to go there to study. It has a lot of Soviet influence with Cyrillic script everywhere. It has 10 higher educational institutions and another 40 public schools. Also, the air is a lot cleaner than where you are. The literacy is close to 100 percent. Hopefully, you'll be tied in with some good people, but a job is a job. Right? Do you know where you'll be working? I'm jealous."

Anna's emotions had never flip-flopped so much in so short a period of time. From being enraptured, to deflation, to hope, to a feeling of impending loneliness, to excitement about her teaching, and at the same time, missing a man she wanted to be with, but couldn't. She pulled out the TAB envelope from a pouch she had slung over her neck that substituted for a purse, handing it over to Batu. "That's the letter and where I'll be staying. To be honest, I never read the part about where I will be working. I've been a little of disturbed about the whole thing."

Batu took the contents from the envelope. The other two men easily looked over the small man's shoulders. In a moment, he cried, "Mongolian University of Science and Technology, are you kidding me? Only the best go there. If you need somebody to carry your bags, I'm your man."

At that, everyone broke out in laughter, with Anna laughing the hardest and loudest. She needed the release. Like a bird stupidly flying into a window and, from the ground, shaking the cobwebs out of its head, looking around to see if any other birds had seen it, she too looked around to notice other workers stop their activities to watch the commotion.

"What are you going to be teaching?" Farmer asked.

"English," she replied. "You don't know anybody up there who speaks Mandarin, do you?" she gibed.

"No, but I do here. It's my wife," Batu offered, stunned by this woman in front of him who had just provided great ideas about fixing their production problem who is also being transferred to the top college in the country.

Farmer leaned toward David and said quietly, "Looks like you got yourself a winner there, Mate."

"Easy come, easy go," David replied, moving his head back and forth sadly in disappointment. Then he said, "Bob, why don't you take Anna and show her around while I speak with Batu and this Temujin for a few minutes.

Farmer led Anna by the arm and began to show her the operation in another part of the building, getting the hint that David needed to talk technical details with the others without her being present.

Batu motioned for David to follow him to a desk where another man sat wearing occidental clothing with a yellow button-down shirt. Batu whispered to David, "He likes yellow because it's the color of intelligence."

David whispered back, "I'll have to try that sometime. See if it helps."

Batu said, "Temujin, meet David Alday, our new commander in chief hand-picked by the boss."

The taller and senior Mongolian turned to face the pair and grinned broadly. He looked to be well into his sixties, with short salt and pepper hair that matched his short mustache. He stood to shake hands with their guest, whereupon David got right to the point and immediately asked the relevant question.

"Gene splicing," Temujin responded, with a low voice.

Batu went on to explain. "When I was first hired to head the harvesting operation, Mr. Al-Yamani asked me if there was anybody I wanted to bring along with me. I knew that one of my old professors, by the name of Temujin, who had endorsed me for graduate school in the States, had retired and was looking for something to do. We trusted each other, which counted for a lot, and I invited him down here to work on the project.

"I did have a little misgiving in that he was a geneticist and, as you can suspect, every professor believes the universe revolves around their area of expertise. Still, he was ingenious and active in the lab with his students, so I asked him to join us.

"It didn't take a genius to know what he was thinking when he saw the cultures and understood the issues at hand. That was when he went to work."

Temujin grabbed the baton. "I took the defective DNA codes in a strain of cancer cells that caused the cells to rapidly reproduce and spliced them into a culture of our species, grew up a batch, and in a short time we had our seed inoculum. I should add that because of the rapid growth, traditional supplements had to be modified in the growth medium, otherwise it won't work. That's another one of our secrets."

Batu inserted, "If anybody appreciates what we're doing, it's this man. He grew up in a ger, his family had lived in them for generations, happy to burn wood and cow chips and free from the overreach of the big city. Circumstances forced them to move into the ger district where coal was abundant. Water wasn't. Those living in the outer ring still have to dig their own wells or get water from a kiosk, and those are scarce. He attended schools in UB and finally went to Darkhan for higher education. He will tell you that if they'd had abundant biofuel during his early years, he would probably still be living out on the plains. Life worked out for him, but not so for most of our people."

Farmer spent some time with Anna offering her to tour a lab of her choice. She expressed an interest in microbiology. Inside, she found what she thought might be a complete laboratory with an autoclave, marble counters, glassware galore, microscopes, and items she had never been exposed to.

Farmer introduced her to one of the white-coated scientists. Anticipating her question and holding up a covered Petri dish with a few off-white and some red colonies growing on the surface, he said, "We check random vats to ensure there is no significant amount of bacterial contamination."

"Why are some of those colonies red?" Anna asked.

"Some species of bacteria adapt to the ultra-violet radiation we use to grow the algae, just like those growing in evaporative coolers used in a lot of countries where they adapt to the heat."

Anna processed the information. It might come in handy someday.

She walked over to another technician who was pouring a flask of cooling agar into other Petri plates. He explained, "We add a solution from one of the vats into the agar, stir it on a magnetic stirrer to randomize the mixture, then pour it into the plates. When the agar cools enough, the bacteria will begin to grow. When they do, we count and identify them."

He went to an incubator and pulled out another Petri plate, handing it to her. See the colonies on the surface and also inside the agar?"

Anna took the plate and examined it closely. She saw globs and disk shapes within the matrix. Handing it back to the scientist, she asked, "Why are the colonies different shapes?"

"This is pretty technical," the scientist answered, looking at Farmer, who gave a nod of approval to go on.

The scientist explained, "Whenever a gel cools, unseen micro-fissures form, like cracks in a rock. When bacteria grow inside the split they are more flat and circular, sometimes they bulge on one side—depending on the amount of pressure on each side. When there is even pressure on all sides, the colonies grow to form a spherical shape. That's the short version."

Anna thought deeply after listening to the scientist's explanation. The smallest life forms were subjected to the laws of physics which played just as much a part of their growth cycle as the presence of nutrients and competition. She saw this similar to the smallest airborne mold spores that, despite the presence of gravity, never settled to the ground, held aloft by micro-eddies of air currents—also actions beyond their control. What were the laws of physics that controlled human destiny; her own, in fact? Which laws were in play to bounce her around like a dust mote, never to find a place to settle, or to compress her between opposing forces?

Chapter 11

It felt fantastic to be wearing short sleeves and have all the hot shower water she wanted. After lunch in her apartment, Anna opened the door at David's knock, threw on a heavy jacket, put on a hat, and joined him and Farmer in their walk to a relatively warm storage facility where the drone had been moved for protection. Inside the structure stood a number of pieces of heavy equipment for earth moving and dredging, along with a mechanical pond-screening device.

The two men checked out the integrity of the drone, ensuring it hadn't incurred any damage during the flight and the occasional turbulence that had bounced them around for short periods. There was no reason for damage to happen to the tied-down device, but the flying machine could not be replaced anytime soon if it crashed because they failed to find a flaw in its structure.

David had seen the terrain on three sides outside the crater. He didn't know what lay to the south. To him, it was curious that only 3%

of the world's 4th largest desert, the Gobi, was comprised of sand, and so far he had seen little of that.

He directed the craft to an elevation of 2500' to clear the southern ring, thanks to no federally mandated altitude limit that is supposed to keep the drones in the U.S. below 400'. Once on the other side, the landscape began to change to a layer of granite and basalt with deep ravines washed by rainwater carried down hundreds of miles from the east where furious storms washed mountain sediment onto the land. Mesas and buttes were scattered far into the distance proclaiming a rich green history that once flourished eons before, giving rise, in today's world, to groves of spruce and conifers and fertile grasses for grazing.

The southern portion of the crater mountain itself was strangely smooth, worn down from ages of dust storms that had scoured its surface, like a stream pebble beaten into roundness, although the other three sides remained forested.

Anna began to chuckle to such an extent that the men pulled their eyes from the monitor to stare at her.

"What?" David inquired.

"Just a stupid flagrant thought," Anna said.

"Want to share?" David asked.

"I was wondering what my friends were doing about now. One might be selling panty hose in a mall, another might be tossing down a few too many, another might be getting a tan on the beach, and here is Anna with a couple of hot men who are flying a drone in the goddamn Gobi Desert close to the border of China waiting for the next Siberian cold front to move down from the north. Go figure."

"Reality does rear its ugly head," Farmer commented, having a good laugh at Anna's reality check.

David asked, "We're about five miles out, Bob. Do want me to bring her in?"

"No, keep going. You're invisible from the ground."

"I don't think the lizards will care much," David quipped.

"It's not the lizards I'm thinking about. Turn on your infrared and magnify. This one operates like a laser used to measure the temperature of a wall, or the operation of a heater, from across the room, except that you're a lot farther out. Keep going."

"What are we looking for?" David asked.

"You'll know it when you see it."

There they were. Red dots, some moving, some stationary; a ravine, a river, and trucks.

"Get lower," Farmer requested.

David did as requested.

"Those are trucks going to and leaving in a north-south direction to and from the ravine, which is running east and west. That means China," commented Farmer.

David dropped lower to 1000' and zoomed closer. "They're mining," he said.

"Can you tell what they're mining?" Farmer asked, eyes glued to the monitor.

"Gold," David replied. "I don't believe it."

"Why not? And why do you say gold? I know Mongolia has gold and just about everything else," Farmer commented.

"See those big lines? Those are hoses hooked to diesel operating pumps sucking water from the river feeding it into the ravine. There are men with nozzles at the other end, playing the hoses against one wall of the ravine. See how even the sides of the ravine are, almost like somebody drew them with a ruler? Now look at that big 50' gouge in the side where they're playing the hoses. Plus, they've got screens.

"Normally, you'll run core samples down several thousand feet and when you pull them out and read them, you can see what you're looking for. Then you take a lot more cores near and distant from that area to find out which way the ore body is headed. Unless it's silver, you drop a shaft, then make a cage with a motorized lift, blast into the walls of the shaft at the levels you want, and start your mine tunnels and drifts.

"Here, they're sluicing near the surface. Depending on the richness of the ore body, it takes between 2 and 100 tons of dry rock to yield an ounce of gold, that is, after it goes through the crusher, smelter, and refinery. Triple that number with wet weight. Here, there must be so much gold that they're actually catching it on the screens. The front end loaders down there are also hauling the wet muck up that path they made and dumping it into the trucks."

Farmer reflected, "They were just setting up last month when I brought in some equipment. It looks like they're heavily invested. There must be twenty or thirty men down there."

"Won't they get flooded out if it rains?" Anna asked.

"Flash floods here are rare. Today, that area gets maybe two inches a year and that's spread out over 12 months," Farmer answered. "Besides, I think they have other things on their minds."

"What are you going to do?" Anna inquired.

For a reply, Farmer said, "David, lock those coordinates in the memory and bring her home. I'm going to make a phone call."

David had a general idea of how this worked, but for Anna's sake, he asked, "Are you going to call the base?"

"Yes. Then my guy over there is going to call somebody in the Ministry of Defense, and somebody there will call a contact within the Armed Forces General Staff who will call somebody down in China. He will say that he is going to send down a gunship tomorrow morning just to check on this rumor of illegal mining and it might be a nice gesture if China pulled out its people by the time we got there, but to leave all the placer mining equipment, thank you very much. Then the guy in China would act surprised that his people would do such a dastardly act—he actually may not know about it—and he'll take care of it. By the time we get there, they'll be gone."

"That's great," Anna chirped.

Farmer shook his head. "Yes and no. This is but one of countless similar operations going on all over the country. Mongolia will now take over the sluicing operation, silently thanking China for finding the hot pocket. We can always use the gold. Next time you fly over, you'll see Mongolian trucks hauling the ore."

"That's fucked up," Anna blurted, for the second time, like a parrot practicing a new word, then slapped a hand over her mouth. David took a hard look at her. He was beginning to wonder if he did not know this woman as well as he thought and whether she might prove to be an embarrassment to him, and ultimately, to Al-Yamani.

That evening David and Anna ate dinner with Batu and his wife, Gerel, at their invitation. Although David towered a full 14 inches above their hosts, they didn't hold it against him. The meal consisted of a salad, followed by mutton stew with carrots, onions and beef dumplings. Both politely declined the traditional Mongolian delicacy of rancid mare's milk fermented to a concentration of 2% alcohol with a little curd and salt added to give it depth.

Anna stole the show. She spoke with Batu's wife, Gerel, both unleashing their Mandarin. They conversed about teaching English and Gerel talked about how she had ended up here, which set off Anna. Like a coin dropped in a jukebox, she began to play her song of complaints to such an extent that she had to catch herself, suddenly feeling embarrassed. She began to backtrack, inserting comments about how much she enjoyed the interests of her students and the kind attention she received from everyone at the university and yes, how much she was learning about life here. Still, a sense of shame remained with her. She to make up for it—how, she had no idea—because the word would get out that David had landed a lemon, a complaining bitch, a bad apple in a barrel.

Understanding nothing of the women's conversation, David contributed little. With the exception of Anna, he would see the others on an almost daily basis. He wasn't going anywhere until he had fulfilled his assignment, although he felt quite certain he hadn't been told everything.

At last, unable to hold her tongue about the subject, Anna asked Batu about the secret to their rapid growth compared with those of so many other growers, which would increase still more if her hypothesis proved correct.

The question caught Batu by surprise. He

looked over at David, who gave a quick shake of his head.

Anna caught the interchange and realized she had overstepped her bounds once again, to her great chagrin. So far, she trusted David. It was all too clear that nobody trusted her. David had not said a word to her about this secret and therefore, didn't want Batu to say anything either.

Initially, Batu had received assurances from Farmer that David was trusted at the highest level. After all, AL-Yamani had appointed him to head the program. Whether David had good judgment in bringing this Chinese looking American along with him, who had a good cover story, was up to serious question. Gerel had done a good job of feeling her out and would provide her opinion once the couple had left. To talk openly about intimate secrets of the operation was out of the question.

David interjected immediately, changing the topic, "Batu, I have an idea. Do you think your people can come up with something non-genetic that can kill the algae, or stop them from multiplying?"

"I don't know, but I can ask?" Batu said, not understanding where David was going with the question.

After the couple left, Batu asked, "Well?"

"She's angry and frustrated and can't wait to

get out of Mongolia," Gerel replied.

Batu smiled, "Like you were, my dear, when you first came."

"True, but mine was based on culture shock that I overcame. Hers is more deep seated," Gerel said.

"How so?"

"She's too inbred with the richness of her previously life to fully appreciate poverty at this level—I don't mean in Naidvar, but in Mongolia in general. It doesn't sound like she's even close to letting it go, although she does appear to have a real attraction for David. Oh, her story seems plausible and real enough. I'm only wondering if she was approached somewhere along the way, say, after she got accepted to TAB. Maybe this Sandra Carlson had a special orientation talk with her, you know, to steer her in a certain direction.

"I'll tell you something else. Anna's Mandarin is top level. If I had to use a word to describe it, I'd say it is elegant—top quality, highly educated. She speaks almost poetically in that language. Her Mongolian is leaning toward that direction too. Her parents taught her well. There are layers of her that are still covered. This woman may be confused at the moment. Although she appears to be naive, she is very intelligent. Once she spreads her wings, she could fly in any direction, a disturbing thought."

"I agree. She may be slow to react to the reality of life, but I noticed her quickness to grasp concepts and solve problems in the lab," Batu said. He went on to describe the suggestions she had made to increase production.

Batu did have a bad habit of evaluating a person without knowing them better. In this case, he felt uncomfortable about casting aspersions on Anna because of the relationship she had with David. Still, there was no other way to ask the question. "Do you think she ran into David accidentally on purpose?"

"Anything is possible."

"She is leaving tomorrow, you know," Batu threw in.

"Yes, soon to join the faculty at the most prestigious university in the country. I wonder how that came about. Listen, Batu," Gerel lowered her voice out of habit when she had something critical to say, "the Chinese are a patient people. If they have a hand in this, you can be certain she'll be back."

David dressed for breakfast while Anna showered. The night had been glorious, slow and meaningful in a way that only goodbyes can accentuate. Anna carried the heavy weight one feels when a mistake has been made and tried to make up for it in tenderness, hoping he wouldn't be able to separate her true feeling from her guilt.

David's life had been far from idyllic thus far,

but he had no regrets. He had traveled the world with his younger brother and his parents, as his father went from one assignment to another. Both his parents sat on him hard. They made him learn the mining industry, from laying track, to shoveling coal, to going to blasting school and taking mining classes in the evening after his college classes had ended for the day. He remembered a few early years riding bikes with his brother, Julian, and the time when their home had been burned to the ground when his father was the target. With those memories came the side benefit of learning how to fight and trying to rise to the top of the educational pile, always moving from school-to-school, always the foreigner.

Now, here he was in another foreign land, this time at a loss as to the language, on a daunting and crucial assignment confounded by his possibly falling in love for the first time. Or was it falling in like because they were two people who believe they momentarily needed one another?

An hour later, David stood on the runway watching Anna wave at the window of the plane. Farmer began to accelerate. In a couple of hours she would be making plans to move to Darkhan, even farther north.

At the same instant, both wondered whether they would keep their vows to stay in touch by email and phone, or would their feelings for one another fade with the passage of time.

Chapter 12

After days of absence, Anna returned to her teaching duties in UB, explaining to all her students she had been bitten by a poisonous snake and was making a full recovery. It was a small snake—as if that made a difference—and that in her home country, there were a lot of diseases—although she couldn't name more than one or two—therefore, her immune system was strong. She ensured that a lot of what she said was lost in the translation. These people weren't stupid.

Saying her goodbyes to Nara, she caught the midnight train to Darkhan (why did their trains always have to leave in the middle of the night?) from an unheated train station.

The train cars were warm enough for the direct trip. Unable to sleep on the wooden benches among another dozen riders in her car, she reflected on her present circumstances. She minutely examined what David saw in this plain woman, who had grown up privileged, one who had never traveled abroad before this fling.

What she saw in him was a man who vibrated with electricity, whose hands were calloused, but tender, a man with strong shoulder muscles, who had gone without a real childhood, who came from a family of miners and either studied or had worked his entire life. According to him, either alone, or teaming with his father, his mother could get into knock-down fights with the best of them, but he refused to go into details. She ran the family. When she said 'jump', you said 'Yes ma'am' and did it right then. Anna ached with jealousy.

He couldn't possibly see anything in her, a simple woman who rode a bike with the girls in the gym, watching soap operas on the bike's TV. She was kidding herself. Forget the loving emails she had traded with him over the past three days. The dust had settled. The past was over. She thought, *Get real, Anna. Wake up. Write it off as a reckless jaunt. Start a new life in Darkhan and, in the end, try to come away with some good memories.*

Some 500 miles away, David Alday wondered the same thing. How could a women, who grew up in a stable, peaceful environment, stay with a man who must seem to be a migrant worker? Whenever she wanted, she could get in a car to leisurely travel whenever she wanted, to cavort on a beach, a woman who had easily slid through school. How could she fall for a rough man or identify with him in any way? Maybe it is better they call if off.

Anna arrived at Darkhan at shortly after 3:00 am. A few enterprising and desperate taxi drivers awaited the train's arrival. Anna managed to grab the second in a line of three, a jovial man who drove too fast, anxious to get home. Surprisingly, a staff member had been elected to greet Anna upon her arrival, having read her previous communiques.

By 4:15 am, warm and comfortable in the modest women's dorm room, Anna slept in until 7:00 am when the wake-up bells aroused her. Time for breakfast.

The next months almost flew by. Anna was not assigned a driver or a "friend" to accompany her on her experiences with the inexpensive public transportation. Still pervasive, but to a much lesser extent, the citizens of Darkhan lacked the smell of diesel exhaust, coal dust, or cigarette smoke on their clothing and bodies when compared with those of Ulam Bator. Almost as a mockery, though, black billows of diesel exhaust announced the movement of the buses.

On a good note, she was treated almost like royalty. In a male dominated society, she was still the ideal of her Mongolian friends and academic associates in that she looked Mongolian, and could speak American English fluently without an accent. When she wasn't teaching, she visited the homes of professors, who forced her to dig into her memory store, to prompt her to stretch her mind.

Anna did her best to stay in contact with David. At first, it became almost like a dating game similar to the ones she used to play when she had signed up for dating apps back home. She would tell herself, "I'll check the app once a day to see what's going on," then, "Okay, maybe twice a day, or whenever I can get free," to "Damn, I got a hit. I'd better check it every chance I get."

David was thankful that both of them were tied in to a solid Internet network; his under the auspices of the Ministry of Defense and hers with the Ministry of Education. Their messages began to get hot. So much so that the lovers decided to back off in case they might get caught, until Anna began finding other Mongolian emails (in the typical Cyrillic Russian script) to make theirs look like children kissing each other on the cheek. If worse came to worst, they could revert to pig-Latin. Even Russian or Chinese cryptographers wouldn't be able to decipher it.

Three weeks after the Chinese had been requested to leave their illicit gold-mining activity, and only a little more than two weeks after Anna had left for Darkhan, David received a secure email from Farmer saying that the government desperately needed his drone-flying skills to root out similar activities in other areas of the country.

David considered the complexities of this request. First, he worked for Al-Yamani, not the Mongolian government, and therefore, would need permission from his boss; second, he already had a critical assignment, which the government well understood;

David found this a curious request because the government was known to engage in large-scale open and clandestine coal mining operations with the Chinese, Russians, Romanians, Americans, Canadians, and Australians.

Having no fear of adventure and knowing that fighting takes many guises, David's sense of loyalty overrode other requests. Thinking this the end of it, he declined the offer to resume his routine of monitoring the ponds and syncing their maturity with his data, along with learning the intricacies of the overall operation. All this, while Batu and Temujin found that both of Anna's suggestions were absolutely spot on and the yield increased beyond expectations. They needed her back on-site.

Chapter 13

In early April, the temperature in Darkhan had warmed to a balmy 27° F, but 300 miles to the west, it had dropped to -20° F and in the Naidvar crater, it was unseasonably warm at 42° F.

A week-long national holiday was in the offing, which meant nine days, weekends included. The on-and-off-again lovers gained enthusiasm, as the date approached for Anna to take the train back down to UB and to join Farmer. He felt confident she didn't know he questioned her authenticity. She had not been vetted and Al-Yamani had better things to do than to research the background of one of his employee's girlfriends.

Farmer concentrated on his upcoming task: that is, to make his monthly run to bring supplies to the lab which included two additional freezers and dozens of jugs and bags of concentrated growth nutrients. These would be diluted and added to the vats and ponds, along with proper shipping containers in case the trucks did

not bring back the ones they had taken previously. The increased yield had filled the freezers at
the facility and more space was required while
awaiting a number of staked flat-bed trucks to
come up from China to pick up the goods. The
pickup was off schedule, not an unusual circumstance, except that the increased yield meant an
unusually large amount of crop awaited pickup.
Farmer followed David's directive:

**"Bring down a number of shipping containers and we'll
move what we have in the freezers to the outdoors. Batu says
they'll be fine."**

The huge indoor biofuel production research
facility rivaled any in the world. Save maintenance staff, the miniature city held experts with
degrees in chemistry, metallurgy, physics, electronics, and related hard sciences. One of their
goals was to create a device that could be inserted into the existing ger stoves that would
contain the fuel to flame through porous holes
or to heat a solid ceramic container without the
production of smoke.

Plans were made in preparation for Anna's
arrival, so that when she did appear, Gerel greeted her as though she were a long lost cousin.
The women jabbered continuously in Mandarin
about anything and everything while walking
through the various building facilities. Their
object was to flush out any other Mandarin
speakers as possible infiltrators. Gerel's private

objective was to learn more about this mysterious woman. Her prediction regarding Anna's return proved to be correct, causing her to be even more suspect.

David had the thought that, because production records were routinely sent by computer to Al-Yamani, they might slip in a false name of a secret growth compound. If used, it would actually kill any life in the vat or inhibit its growth in some way. Considering their fear that communiques were being hacked, this would provide the hackers with misleading information and might kill their attempt to copy and even hack.

Anna spent her nights in the small town with David, their bond growing stronger each day. Their activities were no secret, nor did anybody care. When not in the biofuel building, Anna spent hours in the greenhouse, where warmth and humidity returned her to her childhood years where she would play in her mother's greenhouse. At night she would lie out in a lawn chair and gaze at the galaxy edge-on in the crystal clear skies graced with an occasional shooting star. This view presented more stars than she had ever seen at once. This was still the northern hemisphere, so she recognized a lot of the constellations, although not necessarily by name.

Despite the efforts of herself and Gerel, no other Mandarin or Cantonese speakers came forth and they wrote off the entire matter as misinformation. Meanwhile, Gerel put her suspicions of Anna on hold. Everything appeared peaceful and wondrous.

Until a vial containing one of the genetically modified seed cultures went missing.

Chapter 14

It took several hours to load the plane with scores of empty containers that once held minerals and trace elements brought down on the previous trip, while Anna, tearfully, said her goodbyes. The prepared herself to feel alone once again in her anticipation of returning to her teaching duties. She had frolicked for more than a week, finally unwinding, only to get rewound again. What was it the great Khan had said? "Remember, you have no true companion but your shadow." *Some companion.*

Anna sat in the co-pilot's seat. For the first hour, neither she nor Farmer spoke on the flight north. At last, Farmer began the small talk, steering the conversation until he delicately inserted, without a hint of jest, "You know, Anna, just to let you know, some people believe you might be a spy."

"What?" she said. Her head whipped around to stare holes through the pilot, whom she had accepted as a trusted friend. She already had the niggling perception she wasn't trusted. Now, Farmer had spoken the words out loud.

"Just saying," he answered "You might think about it."

Jerking her chain, he shifted gears and offered, "I called ahead and found something that might help you. A new train schedule had been implemented during our absence and a 4:00 pm departure time has been added. You should make it to the station in time."

The couple spoke no more on the trip home. Her mind reeling with Farmer's declaration, Anna left with a courteous smile, caught a taxi from the base to the train station, purchased her ticket, and found a seat. There was no way she could doze. The activities and adventures of the past days flitting from one to another, from deep passion, to star shine, to labs and the giant structures over the ponds and the greenhouse with solar panels, drones, jabbering with Gerel, and spies.

Some 30 minutes out of Darkhan, the train began to rock slightly, then more severely the closer it came to its destination. When she arrived shortly after 7:00 pm, the entire city was in darkness. She dressed warmly before leaving the train and the moment she stepped out, a bitterly cold howling wind slammed her, along with a sleeting rain coming in sideways that added physical insult to her mental injury. From what she could see, everything was covered with ice, including the power lines, what few of them there were. The digital thermometer at the station read -35° C. She made a quick mental calculation and came up with -24° F. She didn't want to know what it was with the wind chill.

With only occasional nearby candles visible at the station, at least the city had found a bus driver willing to make some extra money to service the customers departing the train at this new, more convenient hour of travel. Anna shouldered her back pack, got onto an over-crowded bus, and soon encountered a drunk who poked her behind and grabbed her breast. She elbowed him hard. He stopped. She didn't wonder why there were so many drunks, but she did wonder why she never saw anybody handicapped; no wheelchairs, no canes, no walkers. Is everybody completely ambulatory in this country, or are they hidden because some of societal custom? She guessed the truth.

At least forewarned what to expect, she stepped off the bus to hail a taxi among others fighting to be seen in the darkness. She pulled a small flashlight from her pouch and shined it at the only headlights on the road, those belonging to the bravest of cab drivers. One saw it and her. It made a U-turn in the middle of the street, narrowly hitting hurrying jay-walkers, hoods up, heads down, not looking. Another cloaked and hooded man, also from the bus, made a valiant effort to grab the pack she had slung over one shoulder. She slapped him hard across the face, but he persisted. She slapped him a second time on the side of the head and kicked him in the shin just as the cab arrived. She was not overly excited about the attack. Farmer had put her into a foul mood. She knew it wasn't his fault. He was only the messenger. Even so, no rationalization could allay the pain she felt. She piled into the cab and relaxed on the way to the dorm. All in a day's survival. *Hell, girl, except for the weather, it could be L.A. or even a bad date.*

Expecting an acceptable temperature of Darkhan when she had researched it only days before, she realized she shouldn't be surprised at the turnaround. Hurrying up the steps to the dorm, she was surprised by the ice on the floor, on the stairs, and on the landings. Apparently a number of water pipes had burst. She was to find out later that the janitor responsible had been taken ill at the time of the storm. It might be the Institute of Science and Technology, but it was still operated by fallible humans.

She carefully climbed the stairs lit by numerous candles along the stairway, managing to reach the second floor without serious incident.

Anna threw down her overstuffed pack on the floor—long since deciding it was easier to deal with one piece of luggage than two—and flopped onto a cold bed. Not surprisingly, the heater was out. She had no doubt the school commissary was closed. She hadn't eaten since breakfast and, like an entire city full of people, had no idea when the power grid would be restored. *Wish I was in a nice warm ger right now. Civilization sucks,* she thought, and for the first time in a long while, she began to cry, even more so when she discovered that the predator on the bus had stolen her cell phone.

At the same time, events were quietly chaotic in Naidvar. As per standard practice, Temujin maintained a base stock of the original genetically modified culture in the refrigerator as insurance against something going wrong in the vats. An unforeseen power outage, contamination by bacteria or viruses, a bad preparation of media; any could ruin one or all of the mixtures. This would require rigid cleaning, a weeks-long process, but in the end, they could be restocked from the base culture.

Typically, Temujin refreshed the cultures by periodically transplanting them into new test tubes. Now, one of the six screw cap vials was missing. No one had misplaced it, Temujin insisted, in fact, no one was permitted in the refrigerator unless they had clearance to do so and he personally hadn't touched any of the tubes for at least two weeks.

David took charge of the investigation and met with the two scientists. Who had access to the lab and the cultures? Everybody. There were no locked doors anywhere. There had never been a need for locks.

David huddled with the two others next to one of the new freezers Farmer had brought down, while technicians went about their daily routines in the white noise of machines humming and the odor of algal growth.

David said, "I don't get it. Where do you take what you stole? You don't grab a cab or walk away from here. We are essentially locked down. I'm open to ideas."

Batu offered, "It might sound crazy, but maybe someone will fly in a drone and the bad guy has a way to load it on. Then the drone takes off."

"We need to post a watch in that case," Temujin stated, deeply concerned. He had encountered thievery of equipment in his career. Nobody steals a culture.

"There's no sense stealing it and keeping it here," David mumbled. Then he asked, Temujin, how long will that culture stay alive out of the refrigerator and who had the clearance to go into the fridge?"

Temujin shrugged, "I can give you the names of the people who had the clearance; in fact, I can point them out to you here. That doesn't change the fact that anybody can come in at any time during the night.

"The answer to the other question is, 'fairly long'. Once the culture warms, the cells will begin to reproduce. They are not bacteria that reproduce every 20 minutes like *E. coli.* Ours grow a lot slower. Their reproductive rate would normally double in number every five days. In our modified strain, it's one third of that, say 36 to 40 hours. If left warm, like in a pocket next to the body, the culture would overgrow in a week or two. It would begin to die quickly after that. If kept cold, it could still be viable and workable almost indefinitely."

"Therefore, the thief would have ample time to get the tube out of Naidvar," Batu summarized.

David said, "There are no incoming flights are there?"

"Nothing scheduled," Batu said. "And it would not be feasible to search everybody and everything. It's a screw-cap test tube, for Khan's sake. We'd never find it."

Batu and Temujin looked at each other, both nodding in agreement. Impasse. "What now?" Batu asked.

"Let's think about it and see if we can come up with any ideas, no matter how crazy. Let me know," David said, totally perplexed, turning toward the machines, slowing watching the operation, pondering.

The thought occurred to him sometime between 2:30 and 3:00 the next morning. Nobody was scheduled to arrive at Naidvar, and nobody was scheduled to leave. However, a flight did leave less than a day earlier. He'd make it a point to call Farmer in the morning to check the plane. On second thought, that made no sense, either. If somebody had hidden the vial on the plane, they would have to go to the military base to retrieve it. Good luck with that, unless, like in some spy movie, somebody posed as an official or a mechanic or whatever and wanted access to the aircraft. No way, not under Farmer's watchful eye.

David tried to get back to sleep, but he was pissed. Some unknown entity had pushed one of hot buttons. If he had the opportunity, he would do great physical harm to the person or persons responsible. He despised traitors more than murderers.

While he fumed in anger, something associated with his first idea popped into his head. Farmer might be out of the picture, but Anna wasn't. Perhaps she was carrying it inadvertently. He'd better contact her in the morning, as well. This thought was followed by another darker one. *What if she had taken it?*

Calling Farmer didn't help. According the woman at the front desk at the National Defense University, an hour after Farmer had returned, he had taken a taxi into the city to attend the Asian Wrestling Championships. He probably wouldn't take his laptop or his cell phone, no doubt trying to separate business from pleasure.

When he mentioned his thought to Batu, the scientist blushed and confessed, "David, to be honest, Gerel and I were wondering if she is who she is pretending to be."

Once alone, David, painfully, forced himself to go through the list of *what ifs* as pertains to the women with whom he had fallen in love. When asked, she wouldn't say she had the vial, if she didn't. If she possessed the vial, would she admit to it? If she admitted to it, how would he prove that she would destroy it if he asked her to do it? An element of trust on his part might interject itself. The cold businessman in him preferred hard facts.

Chapter 15

David had heard about wrestling being *The* sport in Mongolia. Similar to soccer, it had international appeal, although the national horse race and camel races came in there somewhere for popular interest. At least he would be able to watch the matches on TV. If he had known, he would have liked to attend. But he didn't know and trapped down in Naidvar, he had no way to get there.

Trapped was a good word. He had never been in a situation where he couldn't escape if he wanted to. He might have to pay the price if he did leave, but at least he had a choice. Not so now. Perhaps he and his colleagues might be advised to remain in place for one reason or another, but not trapped. It gave him the unique feeling of not being the master of his own fate. Instead, fate had become his master.

Next, he tried to contact Anna, but got no reply to any communique he sent via any medium. Her cell phone went to voice mail, the Internet was dead, and the phone lines were down. On-line, he located the weather station. It presented details of the storm that had barreled into Dark-han from Siberia downward into UB. He had no way to contact her. He missed her; he missed the freedom to move around, to drive, to fly, any-thing. He lamented that it could always be a lot worse. He could be in a gulag, or living in Iran or North Korea.

Intellect and rationalization only went so far. With a sinking feeling, David Alday knew he was currently out of commission. The game would go on without him.

Anna hadn't noticed the flier beneath her door when she returned the night before. She had slept in her clothing with her gloves on and only her face felt chilled. Using one of the candles that are always provided for such emergencies, she retrieved the notice that must have been put there sometime before the power outage, when-ever that was.

SCHOOL RECESS
Asian Wresting Championships
April 19-24
UlaanBaatar
Buyant Ukhaa Sports Palace

**Note: Buses will be leaving the school on April 18 at 8:00 am sharp. Students wishing to attend should be prepared to stay for the duration. Please pack accordingly. Your stay will be at the Ulaanbaatar National College. Buses will be provided on a regular schedule to come and go from the college to the sports palace.

The message was repeated in Mongolian written in Cyrillic script, which had nothing to do with the Russian language. Many languages share a common heritage. Not so with these two. They were completely different. One simply adopted the script of the other, along with its own script, along with that of English.

Anna thought, *Great. That's today in* . . . she checked the watch in her pocket . . . *about an hour. The entire country will shut down again for the biggest sporting event of the year.*

It made no sense to stay here. Actually, it made no sense to go there, either. She never had an interest in sports. As such, she didn't know a thing about wrestling, except for how to spell the word, but she sure as hell would rather go to a familiar smog ridden city than to stay here and freeze her ass off. She couldn't even talk to David about it. At least there in the city, she had friends and knew of several ways to contact him.

She might as well take the clothing she had with her. Nobody would know the difference, except that it might not smell at all.

Chapter 16

A total of 250 competitors from 19 nations competed in the Asian championships. Thousands sat in the bleachers to watch the five day event held in five rings simultaneously. Anna sat with her students, not understanding the sport—much too physical to her liking—but happy to be in a new environment of cheering and enthusiastic people from so many countries. The vast majority of spectators were men. Students on either side explained the sport to her and told her who to cheer on. Anna had no fallback plan, no second place. Love it or leave it. She decided to get into the moment and joined her associates in their cheering, occasionally asking why they thought our guy got cheated.

Even at that, like any tournament overwatched, Anna soon had reached her limit. She fervently hoped for the blizzard to pass. To her great dismay, it had followed them down into UB, shutting down her hopes of contacting David. She wondered if he had been trying to contact her, or had given up the effort.

By the end of the five day period of the tournament, the weather had cleared when the buses arrived to take them back north, although it remained unseasonably cold. At least the buses were more comfortable than the train. In the end, Mongolia had won a single gold in a senior division while Iran would take the overall competition. (She couldn't understand why Iran was considered Asian instead of Middle Eastern, but concluded the answer to be one of life's mysteries.)

Finally at home and preparing to enter the dorm of the college with the others, she caught sight of what looked like small gray-brown lumps at the side of the main building curled up in a nest in the snow. Curiosity made her trek several yards to see what they were and soon noticed five dog pups, four of which were dead from the cold and one barely alive. She had never owned a pet, nor had any inclination to do so. Tenderly, she picked up the pup and put it beneath her robe, unnoticed by anyone. It couldn't have weighed more than a pound. Examining the poor thing, she noted the throat, chest, belly, and inside the legs to be pure white, the forehead grizzled with short black and gray hairs, as was the back.

From what she had learned about the Mongolian culture, dogs are considered family members and are given a name. They are buried as if they were family. Animal rights groups have found homes for thousands of them. She certainly had no intention of making this discovery a part of her life, but she sure as heck could try to bring it back to health before finding a good home for it, however one did that in this land. Discovering it to be a male, she gave it the name of Tugi, meaning *silly,* but implied *impulsive*, a strange name that had nothing to do with anything, except perhaps to describe herself. Still, she liked the sound of the word. For a short while, she would have a companion, another to hold and love on a continual basis, something she desperately needed; one who might not have suspicions of her intentions, one who took her at face value.

The power had come back on, but not the Internet. She had given up trying to call David because she couldn't remember his cell number even if she borrowed someone's phone. *Thanks to civilization, the human mind is losing its ability to remember*. As the days wore on, she brought Tugi a bowl of mare's milk and a bowl of mutton stew with noodles and pieces of goat meat. Whenever she opened the door upon returning from teaching or luncheon, Tugi would wag his tale and begin to yip, licking her endlessly. She spent some time playing tug with him and after three weeks of watching him gain strength and weight, she took him out for a short walk.

Apparently, she wasn't the only one who walked their dog in the endless field of grass behind the institute. Once outdoors in the vast prairie land, she found peace, the hard training of her teachers taking hold, in that she perceived the blue sky representing peace, the green of the grass representing prosperity, the soil representing mother earth.

Anna brought her focus to the present to find one of her students walking a large black and furry Bakhar, a huge dog popular among natives for herding. It must have weighed 130 pounds. Fearlessly, little Tugi ran up to it and yipped his tiny voice to the amusement of the larger animal. Both owners laughed briefly before Anna rescued her newly adopted playmate.

"Teyrïn cono," said the young man.

"What? Tugi is a wolf?" Anna declared. She had not given a thought as to its breed.

"Teym" (yes), came the answer. "When it grows up it will kill and eat anything with four legs, even two legs. It is a spirit animal and a hunted animal. Wolves don't bark, they whine and yip and howl."

Anna had a difficult time understanding all her student said. She would have to look up some of those words. However, her sense was that it might not be a good idea to keep a wolf as a pet. The man made sense. Generations of breeding, beginning with wolves in eastern Asia, and probably Siberia, many thousands of years before, led to various breeds of dogs. Over time and planet-wide cultivation, these animals had been tailored physically and mentally to deal with man's needs; therefore, she now cultured and nurtured a primal un-cultured wild animal. When barking evolved was anybody's guess. This neither scared nor concerned her. Only the welfare of her new companion was foremost in her mind, forcing herself to admit that this lost creature filled a terrible void in her soul.

Sometime later, after both animals got some exercise, Anna returned indoors to prepare for her signing class. One of the first phrases she learned was how to ask forgiveness for her ig-norance. All her students, young and old, em-braced her honest comment, even though her failures with both the language and the signs were self-evident. She could count on many of them to graciously assist her, greatly enhancing her rate of learning.

Seeing Anna enter the rear door with a pup-py on a leash, a clerk approached and told her the Internet had been restored and she could use the house computer to check her email, if she so desired.

When she saw that David had blown up her email looking for her, she immediately respond-ed. After they exchanged everlasting loving vows, he explained the situation with the miss-ing vial and sent:

Have you gone through absolutely everything in your pack?

She replied: **Not really. I haven't had a chance.**

Please do it and call me back, he directed.

She went back to her room to remove every single clothing item, one at a time, and shook it out to find nothing. She checked the side pouches. Nothing there. She told him so.

Are you absolutely certain? This is critical for a lot of reasons, he sent.

Anna flushed. She thought, *Of course it's critical, David. Everyone thinks I took it, which explains Farmer's statement. Which means Batu, Gerel, and Temujin also think I'm a spy. If it isn't here, they'll think I'm lying anyway. Great, Anna. What next?*

Flustered, she walked up the stairs again; this time in no great hurry. A small cosmetic bag lay at the bottom of her pack. She had been so engrossed in searching her clothing and various zippered compartments and pouches that she hadn't paid attention to it. She couldn't remember the last time she opened it. Unzipping the bag, she poured out the contents and there she saw the vial amidst the tubes and small jars of cosmetics. .

Taking it downstairs, she reported her find to David who replied,

Fantastic. Is there any writing on it?

"Yes, says TJ-13-1A.

"**Perfect. Temujin says to put it next to the heater for a** few hours. That will cause the cells to rupture and the DNA to become dysfunctional. Then leave it out with your cosmetics and stay away from the room as long as possible for the next couple of days. You might be attacked if you take it with you. We want them to have the vial. It will be useless. I love you. D.A.

She wondered whether she would still be on the hook. In her mind, David was suspicious, even though he claimed to love her. One thing she could be certain of: Suspicious minds are devious. Once the bond of trust is broken, there is no relationship.

Chapter 17

That same afternoon, Anna sat on her bed reading the letter from TAB.

Dear Anna, we have received an offer to pay off your entire debt to us should you decide to resign. We are not at liberty to reveal the source of the offer. We can only say that if you decide to leave us, please give us two weeks advance notice, although, in all honesty, it will be difficult to find a replacement. If you do decide to leave, you will be sorely missed and have been one of our best teachers. Our door is always open to you.
Please inform me of your decision.
Warmest,
Sandra Carlson

Anna was shell-shocked. What the heck? It had to be David. Following the advice of her mother, she hadn't said a word to him, or anybody else, about the money she had inherited, tempting as it might be, lest the bloodhounds attack. Why would he do that without consulting me first? How absolutely base. From the dark recesses of her mind, she began to see her lover from a new perspective, quickly pulling herself out of a line of thought she refused to cross.

She scratched Tugi's ears while he lay in her lap. He had grown considerably, and she openly took him with her to classes to the great interest of her students. In fact, class attendance had increased ever since she began the practice.

On the one hand, she had committed herself to serving out her term with TAB. After that, she would decide what to do with her life, and most likely, leave Mongolia. Maybe a lot of people didn't want here. On the other hand, the offer was incredibly generous. On the third hand, how dare he interfere with her life? At least she could have been consulted. Furthermore, what did Carlson mean by "Inform me of your decision?" Did that mean she had the option to stay without any strings attached and she could leave any time she desired? Apparently so. At the moment, in the light of the walls coming down around her, being obstinate sounded like the best option. If they wanted to chase her out, then they'd have to try harder.

She took a deep breath to avoid sounding angry or confused when she return- emailed David about somebody paying off her debt and or saying she felt like an outcast, and no, love doesn't conquer all. After some time, she received a reply:

Dearest Anna, I would never do something like that without asking you first. Yes, I want you with me and hopefully, you want to be here, too. But on my honor, I had nothing to do with making that payment. We can figure out who did it, that is, if you want to give it a try, although I'm not sure it really matters. We can talk about it as much as you want. I will support your decision whatever it is. I know you are considering going back home, but if it helps, I have a job position for you here in chemistry. I need somebody I can trust to help me. Love you, D.A.

Anna leaned back in her chair and contemplated. The dog sensed her turmoil and whined. She stroked him gently, thinking. He was getting heavy and weighed well over thirty pounds by this time. "Tugi, get off. You're getting too big for this," she said, and gently pushed him from her. Reluctantly, he left to lay by her side.

David's response hit her hard, especially the part about trusting her. She didn't want to go back home until this played out more. She didn't want to be The Man's girlfriend, or whatever she might be considered. She wanted to be part of something. At least now, she had options.

She'd been at this whole teaching business for eight months, training included. She still had another year and a half. If she joined David, then what? Suppose he had to leave? Was she paranoid in thinking he might be setting her up? She decided to sleep on it.

Except that she couldn't sleep. She ran

through each possible scenario, trying to garner the feelings that went along with it, from loneliness, to frustration and boredom, to instant gratification, to lab or horticulture work, and even teaching English with Gerel, another one who distrusted her. She faced one of those crossroads in life that seldom come along. If you don't know which decision to make, then make no decision at all. There was no urgency. Give it a couple of weeks or longer, if necessary.

At least, that was her plan.

With the stock cultures under lock and key, David sent an email to Al-Yamani, with the assistance of Temujin:

Dear Sir, I believe you said this is a secure line. You asked me to explain the method we use to obtain our fast growth. We utilize a hard to obtain micro-alga *Botryococcus braunii*. We found it to be easily contaminated by viruses which slow its growth potential. By adding the hormone serotonin to the mix, the rate of algal growth exceeds our expectations. We are still working out the mechanism(s) for this puzzling occurrence, but are confident that we can continue with our successes.

Sincerely,
Badaar Temujin,
Chief Scientist
Naidvar

Once the letter was sent, David and Temujin high fived. David glowered, "Let the Chinese hack that. In a few minutes they will be cele-brating and will spend millions on a boondog-gle, no doubt experimenting with endless con-centrations of the hormone trying to figure out what they are missing and how the hell we got so much of it to use."

Temujin grinned, "It was your idea to give them the name of a completely different species. Let them scrounge around for it."

"And it was yours to throw in some crazy addition of a mammalian hormone that might put the algae to sleep, if it had human charac-teristics," David concluded, hoping to end the matter.

A moment later David returned to reality. He needed Anna's mind. The woman was only now realizing her potential.

By long-time prearrangement, a return email read:

Dear Mr. Temujin, thank you for that valuable informa-tion. We will immediately put all of our resources into the project we spoke about, which is the enormous growth of algal investments. We are making plans to be the top produc-ers in a short period of time.

Signed,
Khaled Al-Yamani
CEO
Groebels Mining, Inc.

A separate email addressed to David arrived only minutes later:

David, I need you to go out to Mandalgov. We're partnering with the government on opening up the biggest silver mine in the country. Unskilled labor is killing us. They're collapsing the tunnels instead of expanding them. I need you to fix the problem. Dr. Farmer will be bringing supplies on his regular schedule on the 15th, which means that he can drop you off at Mandalgov on his return. The job site is located some 50 miles north of you.

Keep in touch, Khaled

Temujin read the short missive and said, "David, Mandalgov is exactly the opposite of us. You had to have passed over it on the way here. After lush rivers and forests, you run into mountains and undergrowth without the forests, except for the occasional cluster of trees. There are so many wolves there the government authorized the sheep herders to carry firearms, something you might consider. The miners can be unruly, too, and the herders are a different kind to tough breed. You're going to need to be an American Cowboy on this one. The terrain and climate are too harsh for agriculture and the vegetation is too scant for herds to survive."

David contemplated the scientist's statement. He answered, "Khaled says the site is some distance from the town. Maybe the terrain will be different."

"I hope so. Good luck," Temujin responded sourly, upset that his friend and their site manager would depart for some time.

Not two minutes later, while David pondered the assignment, another email arrived. This time it was from Anna.

Sweetheart, I decided to give my two week notice to TAB! Today, I am contacting Bob for a ride down to join you. I want you to meet Tugi. I can't wait. Love, Anna

Chapter 18

David threw his hand to his forehead when he read Anna's missive.

"A horse is better than a woman," Temujin contributed.

"Thanks for that. I feel more relieved now," David moaned.

"I don't know why. Is it a Western thing to feel good when there is confusion? Or is it bad news? Sometimes I don't understand Westerners. I hear Americans are the worst," the scientist replied.

"First, I'm not a Westerner, Temujin. I'm a Kiwi. Secondly, it's a form of humor . . . oh I don't know anything anymore," David groaned. He needed to talk over the situation with friends. Social norms be damned, he invited himself over for dinner with Batu and Gerel and talked Temujin into coming with him. Working through this quandary required some serious brain power.

In their small, but comfortable apartment, with pictures of family members adorning their brightly painted walls, the four sat before their meals and gave Thanks for the offering. One minute into the meal Gerel jump-started the conversation, "David, let's be fair. Give her an alternative. Maybe she can open her own school in Ulan Bator."

She's already committed," Batu said.

"Committed to leaving TAB, not to leaving teaching. She could open up her own school, cater to the wealthy and keep instructing those who want to pay, even no charge in some cases. It's called free enterprise."

"Or she could go back home," Temujin threw in.

"I don't think she'd do that. She's too strong a person and she's come too far," David replied, not at all confident about his words.

"She wants to come here for you, not for the city. She already told you that in her email," Temujin said.

"But Mandalgov isn't Naidvar. She will be going to a mining camp," Batu said.

"David, you need to tell her everything," Gerel threw in.

The attendant politely knocked at Anna's door the next morning and said that, as requested, he would inform her if an email came for her. It had.

Curious as to why it had taken David so long to reply to her enthusiastic letter of the previous evening, she soon returned to her room to read the lengthy email printout.

She tried to put herself in his position. Lying awake, she surmised he had spent a lot of time composing every sentence. The letter was a mixture of longing and political correctness, of cautions, without the sound of condescension. It was filled with truth and strength.

"What are we going to do, Tugi? she asked herself, rhetorically. Her heart knew the right answer.

The dog's ears perked at his name. She spoke to him quietly, explaining their plight, convincing herself that she was ready to go to the next level with her lover. What the hey? She wasn't a prisoner. She could pull the plug on everything and go back to start a new life back home. She didn't need this shit.

"Does he think his little surfer girl is afraid of getting frightened by taking firearms training or living in a ger in a mining encampment? It's you I'm worried about, Tugi. You might be big for your age, but my little house dog is in a country full of pack wolves, right?"

After she spoke those words, Anna knew they applied to both of them.

Tugi jumped onto the bed and licked Anna's face in response.

Tugi shook in fear the entire flight down to Naidvar. At 42 pounds in weight, he wasn't so small anymore. Anna's right hand ached after shooting some 500 rounds from a 9 mm semi-automatic pistol Farmer had trained her to use, field strip, and clean. The indoor range at the base required the use of headsets, which he awarded her, along with the weapon itself, a holster, and some boxes of ammunition. He had similar gifts for David, along with a Winchester 30.06 rifle. *A new sheriff is coming to town,* Anna mused. David's best gift to her was that he claimed to still love her, once the vial had disappeared from her room on the second day, after she had followed David's instructions.

When the plane lifted off, Farmer said, "I'm going to take you over to where you'll be staying on the south of the nearest mountains about an hour out."

Once he crossed over, correcting for updrafts, he dropped in altitude and circled. Pointing to Anna's side, he said, "There, on the side of the mountain, about half-way up is the operation."

Anna saw a train with a good twenty open ore cars parked at the bottom of the hill where a conveyor belt was depositing ore muck into one of the cars, doubtless awaiting the next trip to the smelter at the outskirts of the big city up north. A road led to a large flattened area where a large diesel generator operated the equipment used in the mountain side, and for the small community of gers at the base of the hill and outward.

Different from the terrain nearest Mandalgov

some miles away, the hillside was lush with vegetation, forested with spruce, except for a denuded oval-shaped area encompassing the road to the mine and the landing outside its portal. Some distance away, flocks of sheep were being herded. *These miners doubled as herdsmen and farmers, or was it the other way around?* she wondered. Several of the gers sported sheep pens where, she'd been told, night watchmen would be posted with rifles.

An hour later, when the plane touched down and taxied to a stop in front of the hangar, Anna released a grateful Tugi to run his heart out around the entire inside of the compound with no other pets to challenger him, while she and David embraced. The cloudless, breezeless air temperature was a balmy 70° F. The usual collection of workers began to unload full containers from the plane, which were replaced with empties.

Anna felt deliciously free. At the same time, she questioned whether commitment mattered when somebody takes away your freedom to teach in trade for their own interpretation of your freedom. She hadn't realized how deeply she had invested herself into the teaching program, but she had, and now it was gone. The sense of duty and investment she had gained had been new to her, only to find them replaced by a sense of guilt and a trace of resentment; against whom she couldn't say. Maybe someday she would find out and have words with him or them.

For the moment, it was time to make the evolutionary jump to her next commitment spelled David Alday, and see if that, too, came crashing down.

Anna spent the next few hours in the greenhouse, touching, smelling, nibbling strawberries, joining workers in their labors. At first fearful of Tugi who accompanied her, Anna explained to the others about his growing up around humans and there were few he growled at and none he had eaten lately. She returned to the Biolab late afternoon to give her belated hellos to Batu and Temujin, who, at least on the surface, were delighted to see she had made the right decision to join their family. Maybe if David trusted her, they all might.

Three days later, she said her goodbyes again when Farmer flew them to the mining area outside of Mandalgov (Mandalay) early the next afternoon. In the absence of a runway, he used the hard-packed road itself that cut through to Ulaanbaatar. He first checked for the absence of vehicles, herds, and ore trains, the tracks of the latter running parallel to the roadway.

David and Anna unloaded their meager supplies to be met by a man in a Ford 150 pickup, who introduced himself as Sandoval, the project foreman, a Spaniard hired by Groebels to oversee the project. He was a large, rough, and unshaven, but clearly intelligent and probably more open with them than with the native workers. He may be have been forewarned that, like he, David would be amiable, but demanding. Also, David might be young, but his experience covered a lot of subject areas, some of which might be unsavory to the uninitiated.

Seeing her dog, Sandoval said, "Best keep a close eye on that one around here." The side arms David and Anna wore and the quality of the rifle David carried had not escaped his attention.

The landscape glowed with a peaceful beauty. The hills and plains were covered with trees and undergrowth, which abutted rolling sand dunes and small streams, thanks to an annual rainfall of some four inches in this area, aided by small underground watercourses that found their way to the surface. Anna had never considered the mating of streams and sand dunes, but then, she had not considered a lot of things before this. The township itself, twelve miles east of the mining operation, had a population of some 12,000, which frequently saw the influx of the miners and their money accompanied by the outflow of liquor; not a strange relationship.

Sandoval drove them down a washboard road a couple of miles leading from the highway, such as it was, toward the outlying gers where his guests would be housed. In a moment,

David said, in Spanish, "What part of Spain are you from?"

Sandoval's face lit up like his long lost family member had come to visit. Within seconds David explained that while attending mining college at the University of Madrid, he had also assisted with their blasting program. Then Sandoval explained that his education and mining experiences were all in the Barcelona area.

David asked, "Really. Did you ever eat at the Roig Robi?"

Sandoval laughed, "Once, when somebody else paid for it. I couldn't even afford the tip back then."

"Same with me," David said. "You must be good if Groebels hired you."

Sandoval replied, grimly, "As any coach will tell you, good is only as good as winning the game you're playing. So far, here, we're in a losing fight."

He stopped the vehicle in front of the most outlying of the gers. The passengers got out, bringing their few belongings into their new residence. The warmth from the coal-burning stove felt good. The furnishings had been completely set up. David noticed the hole surrounding the chimney exit been closed, not enough to touch the metal pipe itself, but enough to keep the heavy cold air from settling down into the residence. Anna had earlier explained to him that old-school nomads kept that opening wider in order determine the time by tracking the position of the sun as it cast light upon the floor. After telling him, she had wondered out loud about how much we had lost. He knew what she meant and left it alone.

Seconds later, he directed, "Honey, I'm going to check out the mine. You get things organized here. You can let Tugi out, but keep him on a long leash. Don't let him go out alone in this new place. The native wolves can run 30 miles a day, so sneaking around a few gers a mile or two from their hideouts to eat a morsel like him is pup's play for them."

He set the rifle next to the door and got into Sandoval's car. At this point, he felt a little more comfortable about Anna's use of firearms. They'd found time to have another serious practice session with handguns and the rifle before leaving Naidvar. Anna had a sore shoulder to prove it.

Short minutes later Sandoval stopped at the landing outside the mine entrance after passing through their own version of the ger district. One of the gers had a 12' Airstream mobile home parked next to it. Dozens of the round homes spread out on both sides of the road. To get there they had to cross the tracks to circumvent the parked train, a daily chore for virtually everyone who had to walk the hill to and from the job site.

Two reinforced buildings, one of them under lock and key, were situated on the newly created portal to the mine. The first held standard light work equipment such as axes, jacks, shovels, copper mesh, spikes, water pumps and compressors, and lengths of spare hoses for both. The other held cases of dynamite, blasting caps, and detonation cord.

Once out of the car, the men donned hard hats with their attached lanterns and battery packs that were in the bed of the truck, ensured each was operating, walked into the portal, and climbed into a battery-powered buggy on wheels.

It immediately became evident to David that this silver mine was similar to others he had been in, his father had told him about, or he had studied. Once geologists analyzed their core samples, they determined the most suitable location to create a portal, or mine entrance. In these mines, no shaft was necessary and no rails were used. Using heavy machinery, a 10' x 14' entrance is created, large enough for a truck to enter and drive downward at a 7° slope for miles, if necessary. The ceiling is covered with copper mesh held in place by 5' long lag bolts to prevent rock falls. Horizontal side tunnels are created off this main haulage level at 90° angles, sometimes hundreds of yards apart, going either left or right to follow the silver veins. When a large patch of silver is spotted, the area surrounding it is spray painted for later blasting.

By the time they had reached the last of 10

drifts, the workmanship had definitely declined. The blasting was irregular and the front end loader had not taken away the ore muck. The ceiling threatened to collapse.

Sandoval explained, "I've got standard three-man crews working each drift and they're all good men. In the morning it will be straightened out, but come later in the afternoon, it will be a mess again. We're losing time and product. I've got one guy who is cutting air compressor hoses, another guy isn't dropping the shovel on the loader when he's finished. We're so far behind, I could lose my job."

David carefully inspected the walls of one drift. He saw the expected integration of the silver together with quartz and ruby crystal formations, with the occasional presence of gold.

The men walked to the rear of the drift to where it veered off into tunnel "A" where a poor blasting job had not made it easy for a front-end loader to enter. David walked to the rear of the tunnel and traced the lines of silver occasionally intersected by line of pinkish cobalt. Turning to Sandoval, he asked, "Who're your primary blasters?"

"Native guys. They have the degrees and the experience. A lot of them worked jobs in-country. They came highly recommended. Why?" Sandoval asked.

David knew the miners loved their job and stayed with it. They might grouse about wanting a promotion or a pay raise, but they didn't quit so they could hire on as truck drivers or grade school teachers.

David answered, "First, in the last drift I was in, somebody might be blasting in the wrong place. The ore body leads downward some 10 degrees, not straight ahead. "Who's your translator for the rest of the crew?"

"Me," Sandoval replied.

David laughed, "I'm impressed. If it was Arabic or Spanish I might be able to help you. Here, I'm a fish out of water."

Sandoval laughed in return. "I'm married to a local. I met her in Spain, believe it or not. That helps a lot."

"Do you have files on these guys?" David inquired. It wasn't the blasting he was concerned with as much as the overall quality of the workmanship. It appeared to be degrading the more the day wore on. But he had to start somewhere.

"They're in my office, come on," Sandoval offered. The men climbed into the buggy. Sandoval drove back up to the portal where they exited, climbed into his car, and three minutes later, he pulled in front of the Airstream.

"This is your office?" David exclaimed.

"One and the same," Sandoval replied. "I couldn't pass up the deal. Oh, and you're both invited for dinner."

Without further explanation, he led David inside and invited him to take a seat. David did and pulled his Walkie from his belt to call Anna. "How's it going? I'll be back in a few minutes."

"We're fine. I took Tugi out for a long walk around the grounds. He got to sniff at the other dogs, got into fight or two, and seems happier for it," she replied.

"The mood I'm in, I could use the same. Fighting must make the heart grow stronger," David quipped.

"Huh?"

"Never mind. Oh, don't worry about dinner. "We're invited out. Bye."

Sandoval pulled two manila folders from the top drawer of a file cabinet and handed them to David, who had taken a seat in a small recliner. The trailer could have come right off a sales lot, it was so well maintained. A good floor heater offered ample warmth for the small space.

Sandoval saw his guest take in his immediate surroundings and remarked, "Gets a little dusty and shaky when these big storms come down on us."

David turned the pages of one file, read, and picked up the second, "On the surface, both men look good, great certificates, fluent in English, solid background and recommendations. In any case, I'd like to talk with them." David handed back the files and Sandoval replaced them.

A small bookcase stood next to the file cabinet. Like a magnet, David's eyes were pulled toward it. "Do you mind?" he asked.

"No, they're my wife's. She's the brains, I'm the grunt. Have a look," Sandoval offered.

Reading the book spines, he noted, *Henry David Thoreau, Walt Whitman, Astronomy and the Mongolian Sky, The Complete Works of Ernest Hemingway, The Great Philosophers. Archaeology for the Ages, Edible Plants of Mongolia, The Life and History of Genghis Khan, Biography of Napoleon, Chinese cooking, Russian Cooking, Cervantes* . . .

"Damn," David remarked.

"I know, frightening isn't it, but somehow we got along for 32 years with three grown children," Sandoval confessed. "Anyway, I've got to close up shop, so I'll let you get back home. Later for dinner, all right?"

"See you then. I don't mind walking back, either," David replied, and began the trek back to his ger, anxious to share his thoughts about the mine, hoping the two women would find common ground. He had his own issues to work out.

After the cold half-mile hike, the ger felt too warm. He doffed the cap and coat he wore. As he did so, he stared at Anna. She had taken the opportunity to disrobe completely, washing herself with one the towels their hosts had provided, while standing next to a wash basin.

Ignoring his entrance, she blissfully moved a little to stand in front of the stove with her underwear in hand. Staring at her figure, he saw her back toward the stove, luxuriating in the radiant heat. Finally sated, she bent over to put on her panties, stupidly frying her right butt cheek on the side of the stove. She yelped with pain, drawing Tugi's immediate attention, ready to defend his mistress, while she applied the wet washcloth to the damage. David began laughing. She quickly turned to see him for the first time and his increasing laughter set her in motion. After she quit laughing in turn, she finally sobered, and with tears in her eyes, admitted, "Damn, that hurts."

Chapter 19

Mongolians typically eat one full meal a day in the evening. During the day they drink milk, or tea, with flour products and some cakes, but do not engage in a three-meal-a-day practice. This dinner turned into talk-a-thon feast when it soon became obvious the men had no role in the conversation between the Anna and Sandoval's wife, Shorni, so after dinner had concluded, with the two women totally ignoring them, Sandoval motioned with his head for David to follow him.

Once outside, Sandoval led him to the trailer only a few feet away, climbed the step, opened the door, turned on the light, and invited David to take a seat. Sandoval went to the small refrigerator, pulled out a box of Cuban cigars, and a bottle of vodka. He looked over at David, raising his eyebrows, and his guest gave an unqualified nod flavored with a wide grin. Sandoval obtained two glasses, inspected them in the light, and poured several fingers of liquor in each. He handed a glass to David, along with a cigar.

Each man found a comfortable seat and faced one another. Sandoval opened by saying, "Mining scuttlebutt has it your family was mixed up in the mountain getting blown up back in the States; that and other things. Care to comment?"

"About the blow up or the other things?" David asked.

"You can start with the blow up." Sandoval suggested, with a slight wave of the hand holding the lit cigar.

David explained, "That wasn't me. I was twelve when it happened. My dad and Uncle Draco—well, we just call him that because he's like family—they were the ones who caught the guys when they tried it a second time. Actually they only caught one. The other died when he fell through a raise 60' down to the level below. In the first instance, they were working a job that had so many tunnels and cross-drifts the inner mountain looked like an ant farm. Some bad guys came in and used a boatload of explosives to collapse the entire mountain."

"How about you, any adventures?" David asked, not offering too much too soon.

Sandoval smirked, sarcastically, "In the international mining industry? Never. Except when I decided to ask Shorni to be my wife and had to get into a big fight to show her my love." He pointed to a scar down his left jawline.

"I guess you won the fight," David hypothesized, grinning.

"As the saying goes, you should see the other two guys," Sandoval said.

The men shared stories, until a knock on the door interrupted them. Shorni appeared. She walked a few steps to the bookshelf, pulled out the astronomy book, and left without saying a word.

Against every instinct to stare, David dismissed her presence, but to him, she was absolutely the most beautiful woman he had ever seen. He couldn't describe why the set of her facial features and complexion stuck him, but they did in some deeply profound way. She was one of those genetically freakish people who had some inner inquisitive spark that made everything a wonder to them, who had some universal beauty that could appeal to any person of any culture, a self-taught woman who knew what she was about. She was so comfortable with herself and her life that you wanted to be around her, hopefully to osmotically absorb some of her inner quality.

In order to reinforce that sense, Anna came in and beckoned both of them to come outside for an astronomy lesson. The glory of 400 billion stars awaited counting in the moonless sky.

Shorni proved to have an encyclopedic knowledge of myths and legends regarding astrological signs, the rotation and wobble of the earth, and, in her eyes, how they had affected the development of the civilized world. She explained the obvious to her guests. "Back a thousand and two thousand years ago, nobody had television, or much to do after dark. They lived by the motion of the planets among the stars, which they tied to occurrences in real life. Time, people and myths combined to form organized religions. The dark forces were always with us."

It could have been anywhere, but it wasn't. It was the crystal clear skies of Mongolia and the tutorship of a woman with a small flashlight covered with a red lens who pointed out constellations and facts and rumors pertaining to each. Suitably impressed, like a person who seeks a savant, Anna absorbed the information and wondered if planetary alignments had shaped her own destiny.

At that moment Anna felt less than the tiniest creature. She wondered how a human could feel superior to anything with that lighted globe hanging over them. If that didn't bring out humility, nothing would. She felt no different than an ant arguing with another about which carried the bigger piece of leaf.

Shorni went on, finally being able to share her knowledge with somebody other than her husband. She explained about the Big Bang and how it stared everything, about warps in space-time, gravitation, and galactic formations. Anna asked endless questions until Shorni said, "I've got deep space pictures taken by the Hubble and the James Webb space telescopes if you want to see them."

David was more captivated by Anna's interest in what she was being told than he was by his own considerable interest.

Shorni led the group inside, sat at the computer and dialed up what she wanted. An image popped up on the screen of countless galaxies small and large of varying shapes and sizes.

Anna gasped. Her hand flew to her mouth. "My God, they're the same. It's all the same," she uttered, staring ahead as though in a trance, the wheels in her head churning, computing.

"What," David managed to say.

"It's what Shorni said and what I saw in microbiology. We're looking at an exact duplicate picture of a bacterial culture plate. We stirred the bacteria in the lab the best we could, but they still did that they wanted, just like the Big Bang. There was no randomness there either. The Dark matter is the gel with fissures caused by gravitation and other forces, such as even and uneven cooling. These result in galactic alignments to give us clusters and superclusters, and chains. There are invisible small galaxies we can see with special light frequencies just like we can with cultures. We need to study cultures more to understand the universe. Give me a chance and I'll prove to you there is so much more. My head is spinning with ideas."

At last, when the four returned to the ger

next door, always under the protection of Tugi, Shorni pulled out an ancient, well-worn, hand-me-down set of Mahjong tiles and proceeded to teach the game to her guests.

Chapter 20

In the morning, David accompanied the two blasters, watching them go through the paces. They had met, conversed, exchanged information, and to David, he and the lead man could teach each other a few things.

Over the next several days, he and Sandoval ensured that the ore muck from the drifts had been moved to the haulage level and that the blasting to open up a new section at the rear of a drift was also without question. In David's view, he would have drilled the holes in the rock for tamping in dynamite sticks in a slightly different position to ensure a cleaner cut, but basically the work met with his approval.

During those days, Anna, Tugi, and Shorni took long walks. Anna wore her sidearm and took the rifle, keeping a wary eye on her dog that wandered into and out of an occasional copse of spruce and elm that had escaped from the hillside like errant children.

Much of the area was covered with gray

sparrow's saltwort, gray sagebrush, wild onion, and low grasses, such as needle grass and bridle grass, drought tolerant species quite suitable for grazing. Vast acreages of wild poppy ranging in color from orange to blood-red ran amok to contrast with the blue sky, both of which challenged the cone receptors in the retina and the hormone levels of any human appreciative of such wonders.

At once, a ferocious animal fight caught the attention of the women. They ran to where they last saw Tugi enter another thick copse to find him in a fight with a marmot, a large rodent weighing 8-12 pounds, considered a delicacy. Anna brought her rifle to bear, but Shorni stayed her. "Tugi must learn to fight," she said. "Wait and be quiet."

To her, the bushy-tailed brown mammal looked like a cross between a small bear and a beaver when it sat on its haunches. Its burrows were demarked by a pile of dirt around the entrance. The hole could be up to five feet deep and over eighty feet in length. She soon learned that the social animals readily communicate with different sounds, depending on the predator, by using a different chirp or whistle for each. In this manner, the social animals communicated with one another and with their young.

A short moment later, while the women remained silent in the darkness of the cove, Shorni pointed. First one, then three, then five wolves appeared, fully grown versions of Tugi. Again Shorni caused Anna to pause. Tugi had won the fight and began to eat its hard won prize. She motioned for Anna to step out of the woods with her, and upon seeing the women, the wolves sauntered away. Tugi remained focused on his work.

This walk became a daily pattern for the three of them. On days when Tugi killed a second time, they would bring the marmot home for their dinner. Soon, he would provide for a number of families. He became a favored guest under the watchful eyes of everyone in their small encampment.

Anna quickly became adept at skinning and preparing marmots and mutton, while she also learned the secrets of cooking a variety of dishes on the 12" surface of the ger heater.

Each day, Anna and David found time to work with Tugi training him to their voice commands. The dog learned quickly. In that country, there was no other way to learn. Soon he would grow to weigh 100 pounds, large for a wolf.

Over the next three months Anna assisted in the cooking for the two families under the watchful eye of her teacher.

Sandoval hired more blasters and more men. Two shifts were now in operation. Following David's recommendation, production of silver, gold, cobalt, manganese, and zinc increased significantly.

David cut back from his self-imposed work schedule of 4-6 hours a day to nothing. Production soon decreased. On a suspicion, he looked behind occasional rocks to find liquor bottles stashed. He confiscated them and instituted a search of the men when they arrived for work, confiscating more bottles, a practice that solved the production problem. In the absence of strict supervision, the men had been drinking in the later part of their work day, which always resulted in poor work and pranksterism.

At one point, David and Sandoval were deep into a mountain with a six other men when the power went off. This included the water pumps to remove mountain water that almost always accompanies mining activities. Power went off for lighting, fresh air influx, and stale air exit. Only battery-operated headlamps operated.

"Bad sandstorm," Sandoval remarked. "We'll have to wait it out." He called the men working the tunnel to gather in one of the drifts off the main haulage level. He had most of them turn off their headlamps to conserve the lighting. It could be several hours before the storm passed and the generator could be repaired.

"Don't worry about the ladies," Sandoval remarked. "They're a lot more comfortable than we are. Those gers are weather proof and, believe me, whatever is out there, she's seen worse. Got your deck with you?"

David pulled out an always handy deck of

cards from his back pocket and proceeded to show the game of poker to the uniniated. A few minutes later, one of the miners declared, "Hey, boss, look what I just found hidden."

At that, everyone snickered, the bottle was passed around. It had to last eight men six hours, until it was safe to emerge from their shelter in the dark of the night.

The following evening, Anna sat outside with Tugi next to her, getting his ears scratched. David slowly approached and handed Tugi a treat. "Sandoval got a call a while ago. They want us back in Naidvar," he said softly.

"I knew that would happen," she replied, with a touch of melancholy. She had tried to wrap the majesty of the world around her like a cloak, something she could take along. She had learned so much. "When?" she asked.

"Day after tomorrow. Bob's coming down to pick us up," he said.

"Maybe we can come back here on a regular basis. It's not too far to drive," she suggested.

"I'd like that."

"Anything, just not Ulan Bator," she gave a shudder.

"If I get assigned there, I'd quit Groebels," he declared.

"You'd do that for me?" she queried, looking into his eyes.

"For all three of us. We're family," he said, putting an arm around her.

Chapter 21

David needed to get back to Al-Yamani. The connection between Groebels headquarters in Cologne, Germany, and their location, in Mongolia, was weak, but workable, given one's patience.

David tried to understand when he asked, "Khaled, what's so important in Naidvar that you need us there?"

"I need you both. Batu says their pond yields are down 8% since you stopped monitoring."

"That's a lot," David said.

"Since your absence, they've added two more ponds. Things are busy."

Al-Yamani change directions. "David, do you have any idea of Anna's IQ?"

"The thought never crossed my mind. I have a feeling she's pretty smart," David responded, not certain where the man was going with this.

"Well, I do and I don't want to frighten you. Let's say it is significantly above average. It sure scares the hell of me. We may have a lot of good people in our employ, but I suspect she sees things differently than the rest of us. Hopefully, she won't crash and burn along the way."

"What does that mean?" David thought hard to come up with anything that would point to what Al-Yamani was describing. All he could come up with was an occasional good idea she might have.

"It means I can't imagine what the world looks like through her eyes. She's a data processing machine. Her talents are tied to analytical thinking and mathematics. I'd hate to play her in chess, or bet against her in a casino. If she sees a color, she probably sees it in a hundred different hues. Ten to one she doesn't even know it. Once she does and gets a handle on it, look out. We've been tracking her and we could use her input in several areas."

When David explained the conversation to Anna, she said, "I don't know what any of that means other than maybe me being a good teacher. I see myself going along doing a job. How do I know what I look like to other people? I'm no different than anybody else. There are a lot of things I'd like to do and a lot of things I wish I hadn't done. You're the engineer-business guy with the drone. I have a degree in social sciences. For me, I'll be happy to work anywhere I can help. I need love and attention and to feel like I belong to something important, like a lot of other people.

"While we're on the topic of me, I might as well tell you about an idea I have. If you install the same frequency sensors inside each of the pond houses to give automatic readouts to a central location without having to spend time flying, it would be more accurate because you would have continuous readings. Start with one pond and see how the data correlate with the drone readings. Then go from there. I might be able to put it together for you."

David had already seen what Al-Yamani had talked about regarding her perception and ability to process problems to find a solution. Not wanting to put any brakes on her development, he said, "Damn, girl, let's give it a try."

Or maybe you could personally look at their hues and tell me, he thought, somehow falling deeper in love with her.

By this time, Farmer did find a DC-3 from somewhere with a much larger cargo capacity than the older DC-2. It was strange to see the big twin-engine touch down on the highway two miles out from the campsite. Only the background sound of the big diesel generator broke the silence of an otherwise deathly quiet of the small mining community, save the cries of the occasional falcon and plover, or the howl of a wolf, or their collective yips when they cornered a rabbit.

An hour after lift-off, the four landed in

Naidvar with room to spare on the large runway. No sooner had a quaking dog and three humans departed at the hangar when Batu approached still wearing his white lab coat.

"My greetings. Miss Anna, I am telling you that we only now received a call to inform you of the death of your father and the lines are available for you to use."

Anna stood frozen in place for a moment, a large wolf on her right, David on her left, Farmer behind the three. In a daze, she let Batu lead her to the administration building. There was no reason to hurry. The others let her make the necessary calls while they supervised the unloading of the plane.

Several minutes later, Anna appeared. Tugi ran over to her wagging his tale. She bent down to nuzzle him while the others waited. "I have to go home. I don't know for how long," she said, tearfully. Her emotions roiled once again. Her father was dead, she had to go back to the place where she grew up, and she would have to leave both beauty and the beast.

"Do you have the money?" David inquired, without digging deeper.

"Yes, but I'll have to figure out how transfer funds and make the flights," she responded.

"Why don't you let me do that for you? Don't worry about the money," David offered. "Here's a better idea. Why don't you sign an employment agreement with Groebels? We can arrange it so that you get free travel."

"Free travel to wherever *they* want to send me, right?" Anna answered.

"Correct, which means going home as quickly as possible. It also means you'll be in solid here. You did say you wanted to feel like you belonged," David inserted, cautiously.

Anna liked being free to move, even if it was with the man she loved, without being obligated to Groebels. Despite her wealth, there was nothing wrong with drawing a paycheck and saving what she could, but her gut feeling told her that taking the plunge to become part of the outfit is not a decision to be made during a time of crisis. She took the middle ground and said, "Honey, I'll let you make the flight arrangements and I'll pay you back. I just need to get home."

She felt terrible in that she hadn't maintained regular contact with her parents, to keep them up on the latest developments in her life, to share her feelings with them. It would have pleased them to get a call or a letter from her on a regular basis. Had it been such an effort to contact them, with all the nuances of international communications, or had that been an excuse? Hell, she'd made contact with a couple of her college friends more often than she'd communicated with her parents. No, she had failed him and her mother. Poor Daddy. Worse, once she returned, she faced the possibility of making the hardest decision of all: whether to return to Mongolia, or to stay at home.

Flip flop. Flop flip. So went Anna's emotions. You don't bring Tugi home and expect a wolf to be a lap dog. You don't expect an adventurous man like David to stay at home to watch Sunday Night Football for entertainment. It came down to what she wanted balanced versus what she needed. This wasn't like shopping in a supermarket. At least there one could look at the cart and return what you didn't need before checkout. Here, uncontrollable life-changing events filled her cart with no returns.

She had promised to call Naidvar when she arrived home safely; once, after the funeral, and again, when she was ready to return. The last was open to question.

Driving the coastline seemed surreal after such a relatively short absence. Entering into her own 4100 square foot home left her breathless. To the new Anna, the home smacked of insanity. Why would three people live in so much space, let alone a single person? Where was the warmth of a ger, the heady smells of human closeness, the family chatter, the reduction of material goods to the almost absolute basic necessities one required to survive? She had a flagrant, almost comedic thought, that if one out of ten Americans is officially described as a hoarder, and human nature being what it is, what would a hoarder's ger look like?

When she spoke with her best friends, they ooed and awed at her descriptions of what she had seen and done, speaking Mongolian to them, even while they whispered among themselves that she had flown into the cuckoo's nest.

Only her mother stood by to hear her out, to give her solace and council during her own time of grief, when she cried, "Anna, your father left you a lot of money. Early on, he had a vision. He invested heavily into oil and technology. You'll soon be receiving money well into the tens of millions. I don't even know how much. He didn't believe in telling a single soul how much he was worth, not even his spouse, because to him, you never knew when things might go south.

"He always knew you would be successful. He did wish you would have called more, we both did, but we had so much faith in you, we knew you would make us proud and you did."

So she and her mother drank wine together and laughed and cried all night. Anna told her all about Tugi and every detail of what had happened. She showed her the scar on her butt cheek where she had burned herself and she thought her mother would never stop coughing from laughing so hard.

Anna and her mother visited their banker and their family's trust attorney, both of whom were in San Diego. The most interesting meeting came when their attorney delicately advised Anna, "Ms. Chen, your father had a considerable interest in various international . . . uh, concerns that have brought in a lot of money and will continue to do so. We anticipate a return of a million a year from that one particular investment. Would you like us to continue pursuing those concerns?"

Anna looked at her mother, who simply smiled. Turning back to the attorney, she asked, "Were they illegal investments?" The attorney merely smiled and sheepishly answered, "Illegal is a funny word. We don't anticipate a problem to occur."

With those words she understood. There is a short gap between obtaining government contracts for the development of missiles and investment into the black market business of arms sales.

"Then, by all means, continue as you have all along," Anna answered, not wanting to know more at the moment.

After making a short stop home in Malibu, Anna drove mom up the coast several hours to Monterey to show her where she had trained a million years ago. The two played on the sand by the surf, something Anna missed terribly. But it was time to get back to her life, because it was not here. It wasn't becoming a checker at a supermarket and it wasn't getting another college degree in . . . what?

She swore she would keep in touch with her mother and prepared to return to a landlocked country that knew only strife and a robust people, more than half of whom were dying from the very air they breathed. She was part of it. At least for the present, she belonged.

Of all the mind-bending things she had learned from Shorni, two great lessons stood out. You can make of yourself in life whatever you want to be. And, the more you accomplish, the easier it becomes to accomplish more.

PART II

Chapter 1

From the air, Anna saw Naidvar in a different light, as a child brought into a new toy store and given free rein to play in its expanse.

As for Tugi, he had not been completely satisfied sleeping with the shawl Anna had left him. He preferred the actual human to her mere scent. That became evident the moment the plane taxied to the hangar and the huge animal almost knocked her off her feet. She endured his slobbering kisses and did her best to keep her lips safe from his saliva, saving them for David, who was kept busy holding back the animal.

The trio returned to their residence where she deposited her bags. She had brought a few extra possessions from home, about which she incurred no problem from Mongolian security, once she displayed the credentials David and Al-Yamani had provided her as an employee of Groebels. She felt insecure in understanding what role she might play as an employee, leaving the decision to those who would guide her.

Now back on familiar turf, Anna spent her time in the library reading chemistry and micro-biology, while learning from Batu and Temujin. She believed her new role would lean more toward returning to her roots in the sciences, as opposed to social networking. That said, with nearly 16 square miles of usable land within the crater and only a small percentage of it taken by structures, she managed to find time each day running and playing with Tugi in the vacant areas, when she wasn't consulting with scientists about the intracacies of microbial life.

Anna came in one evening overjoyed, bubbling with excitement. She declared, "I know how to do it. Temujin told me how."

David found himself adjusting more frequently to Anna's idiosyncrasies as she lapsed into her own universe at times. "I'm listening," knowing she would have told him anyway had he not said a word.

Anna went on, excitedly, "When I explained about how I would like to see bacteria between the colonies, he said that's easy to demonstrate. They do it all the time in basic micro classes. They splice a gene from a jellyfish that codes for fluorescence into E. coli. Then the bacteria glow red when they grow and multiply on the agar surface or within its matrix. It seems as though all I would have to do is to apply the right frequency of UV light to the culture to have a better chance of seeing fainter colonies."

David smiled and said delicately, "Honey, astronomers already have a dozen tools to do that. All they need is more sensitive instruments and voila, a whole new universe will open up to us."

"My point exactly," she said. "Once again, the smallest matches the largest. It's one more way to prove my comparison. I'm going to make discoveries about the universe by studying cultures."

So far, the idea about sensors within two of the structures correlated well with readings obtained from the drone. They had been installed to monitor the most mature ponds and if they worked out, all the buildings would be wired into a central system. David saw this as shift in jobs for him, because, despite his reluctance to do so, he had no doubt he would be flying the device outside the compound on a regular basis. Farmer had explained that the USGS satellites were needed in a lot of other areas to perform more vital tasks, such as earthquake monitoring and ice melt. Therefore, it behooved them to come up with their own data regarding illegal mining operations.

A restless Tugi needed to kill something. Anna asked David if she could take a break from analyzing data from the vats. She wanted to take the Dodge 4-door 4-wheel-drive pickup from the garage to exit the crater and go some distance farther than she had in the past. Gerel would go with her. She grabbed a Walkie, along with the Winchester and her sidearm, a box of ammo for each weapon, and drove through the only exit from the crater on the east side south of the ponds.

She returned more than two hours later, with the bed of the truck loaded with several marmots and rabbits, a few of which had been shot. Tugi had brought down a gazelle, after tracking a large herd for several miles, with Anna following at some distance, fearful of becoming trapped in the icy slush of the steppe. It had been a frightening, yet exhilarating, adventure for her to keep the truck from stalling with little chance of rescue miles east of the crater. It had also been an awakening, while the two women watched Tugi through binoculars instinctively stalk the herd to eventually make a choice and go in for the kill.

After the take-down, she drove forward to retrieve what she could of the maimed carcass. Gerel advised her on taking necessary precautions while trying to pry a kill away from her pet without herself getting attacked by him. The women compromised by permitting Tugi to work on a front leg while they cut off a hind quarter, showing it to him, tossing it to the side and letting him do what he would with it while Anna slit open the remains to remove the entrails, as David had taught her. She backed the truck up to the remaining carcass, lowered the tailgate, and with considerable effort, the women managed to heft the heavy remains into the rear of the vehicle. Although the truck was equipped with a front winch, they saw no way to use it to their advantage. After patiently waiting several minutes for her pet to finish his meal, Gerel advised her to return, permitting Tugi to complete his personal project without disturbance.

Parking in front of the commissary, the women waited for kitchen staff to remove the animals. Gerel claimed one marmot for herself. The others would be used for a large batch of stew in the kitchen. A good half-hour later, Tugi appeared at the compound, all the happier, snout covered with blood he continued to lick off.

This daily outing became their routine, until late one afternoon, Anna received a call from David asking them to come in early. He awaited her when she pulled in. He put his arm around Anna when she exited the car and said, "Two things, honey. Your idea for the sensors worked well. We've ordered enough for the other buildings."

"That's why you called us?" she asked, curious at his request. Gerel looked puzzled, as well. Thus far, they had only bagged two marmots and a wild goat.

"No, a couple of emails came in for you."

"Oh, are they from mom?"

"No, you'd better read them," he suggested. The three walked over to a computer in the main office, where a woman attendant gave way to Anna, who took her seat.

From: Minister of the Interior
Department of Education
To: AnnaChan@Naidvar.com
Dear Ms. Chan:
It is my pleasure to inform you that you have been selected to receive the Teacher of the Year award by the Institute of Science and Technology for your teaching of English.
Understand that it is highly unusual for a foreign national,
especially one not on staff, to receive this award. (I am also
informed that part of this award should go to your Tugi, who
helped garner interest in your classes.)
As per custom, you will be celebrated on national television, along with other educational awards to be presented
at the same ceremony. You and Tugi are both invited. Please
prepare a short acceptance speech. (Here he gave a date and
place for the ceremony.) We will be sending down transportation to receive you two days prior to this date.

Anna looked up a David, wide-eyed up, who just grinned. "Congratulations. If it's all right, I'll go with you, but basically, I'm staying out of it. This is all you," he said.

Gerel chirped, "What a wonderful surprise. You deserve it. I can't wait to tell Batu."

Anna held onto Tugi's head in her lap while she read further:

It has come to my attention that your contributions to
the growth of our Naidvar project cannot be overemphasized.

Thanks to your efforts, we now have enough biofuel, and, along with a new ceramic delivery system, to warrant a trial run in one of our ger districts. We invite you to head this project.

Please acknowledge receipt of this email.

Sincerely,

Anandyn Tomobaatar (Tomo)

Secretary of the Interior

Governor and Mayor

Ulaanbaatar

Anna slumped back in her chair slowly shaking her head. What just happened? Tears came to her eyes. It was all very nice. She didn't feel like she deserved this. She didn't know herself what she was about, being thrust into a national spotlight, as though she had won a lottery by accident when all she was doing was going through her daily routines.

This Tomo guy is a heavyweight. Even his last name meant Iron Hero. The river was carrying her along swiftly. Now she had to go back to Ulan Bator, a place she hated with a passion, but she had to tell them she loved it with a straight face. What a mess.

Serving dinner, Gerel said, "This is all Anna's cooking. She picked the vegetables, cut up and seasoned the marmot along with pieces of gazelle, and prepared the noodles. You have her to thank."

The TV was on mute with regional wrestling matches on display. After a few bites, Gerel picked up the computer printout of Anna's email, read it, and passed it over to her husband. "What do you think, Batu?" she asked.

"It's a two-edged sword, I'm afraid," he replied, in all seriousness.

"She can't turn it down," David mumbled, between bites of stew.

Anna inquired, "What does that mean? That it's both good and bad? Why is it bad?"

Gerel said, "On the surface, it appears to be good, although to me, it seems to be a little . . . how do you say . . . out of left field?"

Batu said, "I grew up with Anandyn. He was a little more cunning than the rest of us. You might call me a conspiracy theorist. The way I see things, it looks to me like you are being set up to become the next national hero."

"What?" Anna exclaimed.

"Everybody has them," David said. "Why her?"

Gerel nodded, "For sports, yes, and maybe a politician or two who might be today's favorite, but Anna's fresh and original, somebody who is seen by some as a person who wants to do good without asking for personal gain."

Anna scoffed, lapsing into Mandarin, she said, "Oh, come on, Gerel, let's not get overly dramatic. I'm not so naive as to believe I'm not being used. Why, is the question."

David didn't understand a word. He did get the gist of the retort. It sounded like a complaint. Anna's tone and gestures transcended linguistic barriers. He said, "Argue what you will. What's wrong with inspiring people to follow your lead? Are you afraid you'll make a mistake or that it will blow up in your face? If so, turn it down."

Anna remained silent.

"That's it, isn't it?" he said. "The scientist in you doesn't have all the facts to make an informed decision. At the same time, others are making the decision for you. It's your neck on the line if something goes wrong."

With pursed lips, Anna reluctantly nodded her ascent.

"Simple fix," David added. "If you have to make a statement, tell them you are a small part of the project and this is only a preliminary trial. If it works, it can be expanded, if it doesn't, the families who tried it can go back to their old ways. Nobody will fault you for your honesty, if it does fail. In fact, you will be lauded for it. You'll be one of *them*. You're just as invested in this as the government. Everybody is in the clear and you keep working to find a way to finish the job."

"That could take a lifetime," Anna moaned.

"Are you on a schedule?" David concluded.

Three days later, on stage, when Anna gave her acceptance speech in English, 500 people in the audience applauded. When she gave the same speech in Mongolian, the audience erupted. The Minister of Education asked for David to bring Tugi, the real star of the show. From the rear of the audience, David brought the wolf forward with cameras panning every step. They climbed the stairs where Anna bent down with the microphone and said in Mongolian, "Tugi, say hello to everybody."

Tugi stood on his hind legs and waved both paws forward to the great astonishment of those watching in person and on television. Anna gave him a treat, knelt down, to receive both of Tugi's paws on her shoulders while she hugged him, then led him off the stage with David. The story would be told for ages and pictures of this teacher, who had trained a giant wolf to be her pet, would soon be seen on coffee mugs, trinkets and photographs. Similar to countless households and businesses in India that posted the picture of President John F. Kennedy on walls along with those of relatives, others in Mongolia would post the picture of their two new heroes. Business must go on.

Chapter 2

After completion of the photo shoots and interviews, it was not business as usual for Anna when she and David met with the minister, governor, and mayor, all three-in-one. Tugi lay at her feet.

It could have been a director's office anywhere. A simple desk, a phone, a computer, and a couple of chairs, with widows looking out at a city with a variety of building sizes and shapes. These were clustered in the center surrounded by countless smaller buildings; in this case, interspersed with gers, which, in turn, were surrounded by granite outcroppings. These were interspersed with fields of short dried grass.

After the exchange of pleasantries, Tomo turned businessman and said, "Anna, if I may call you that, our own engineers took the design for the ceramic heater your people developed and made a couple of slight modifications. We ran Btu (British thermal unit) tests inside a few gers and found the design worked as well as we

hoped it would. There would still have to be lo-
gistical issues regarding delivery and safe usage
of fuel and various consumer-related problems.
Those need not concern you.

"We have 100 gers earmarked for the first
trail run on the eastern portion of the city. We'd
like you to be the face and the voice of the program on television and radio. We would like to
use a simple blitz campaign, something about
which the public is both weary and leery. A new
approach would be welcome."

Tomo paused, giving Anna a moment to
think and to consult with David, whom he knew
was associated with Groebels, the other half of
the deal. He didn't need the project to flounder
at this point.

David wondered who the 'we' were in Tomo's
statement. He'd been in his share of business
discussions and this entire enterprise seemed to
be moving a little too fast for his comfort. Momentarily yielding to a superior force, he said,
"This all sounds very organized."

"Thank you," replied Tomo.

"Incidentally, sir, your English is impeccable.
I can barely pick up an accent," David rejoined.

"I could say the same of you," smiled the
minister, hinting at the Kiwi's accent. Jokes
among friends. "A degree from Harvard Law
School didn't hurt, I suppose," His teeth glinted.
He'd told the story before.

The man was imposing. He'd dressed his

short, bulky, frame cleanly and neatly, like a lawyer going to trial. He may have wrestled in his younger years. His features were clearly Mongolian with no trace of Western influence. His ebony black hair hung loosely about his shoulders, as opposed to the westernized trend of keeping it short. From where the couple sat, no gray hairs announced themselves, strongly suggesting he used a colorizing agent; his nails were manicured and polished. The suit he wore might have been cut in Hong Kong. The man had a lot of money and he was no fool.

David asked, "How do you see Anna's role in this?"

The minister glanced at Anna first before replying, "I see her initially visiting a ger or two with cameras present. This would be without Tugi, at least at the start. We would film her talking to the occupants, who would actually be our own people. She'd tell them about our program. Our own people would be enthusiastic and Anna would step back and let our technical crew demonstrate the new ceramic heater."

The minister grew somber. He said, "We can't fake anything about this. The press can spin it any way they want, we can't help that. We have to be above-board about everything. When this starts to get off the ground, Anna will begin to make appearances at more gers, then back off and make a few pre-recorded messages for television, which won't take more than a couple of days. Script writers and makeup people will do the rest and none of that will happen until we feel comfortable. Everything must run smoothly. Does that help?

"Oh, one more thing. Given we don't hit any snags, it would help a lot if Anna applied for Mongolian citizenship. Meanwhile, we can put you up in a hotel, although . . ." he glanced at Tugi.

This business about citizenship caught Anna by surprise. She was too shell-shocked to react. They'd talk about it later. David commiserated with her. She must feel like she's playing a board game called The Great Camel Race, where somebody is rolling your dice for you and you move the appropriate number of spaces, hoping your camel doesn't get snake bitten, step in a marmot hole, get sent back to the beginning, or worse, step on a land mine before you reach the jackpot.

Anna didn't like any of it. She was stuck between a rock and a hard place. She replied, "If it's all right with you, sir, we wouldn't mind living in a ger in the same area where we'll be running the tests. We can meet the people, while Tugi can be out in the open." She looked at David for his approval and he assented.

"I'll have one set up immediately and by the time we get you there, it will be ready to go," the minister cheerily agreed, picking up the phone.

Anna said, "Could you make sure to have

one of the new units installed in our own ger? Also, on the way there, maybe your driver can stop at the Narantuul marketplace. I want to pick up some food. In fact, why don't you plan on coming over to eat with us this evening? I'll cook and take my chances," Anna invited, flooding the minister with information. Tit for tat. A big chess move by a knight.

Moments later, the couple, plus Tugi, entered the back seat of a Mercedes provided by Tomo. On the way to the marketplace, David turned to quietly speak in Anna's ear, ensuring the driver was out of earshot. "If this succeeds, he will get the glory. Unfortunately, as the face of the program, you will serve as an out for him in case anything goes wrong. It could get ugly, despite what I may have said earlier. You don't have to do this."

Anna nodded somberly, deep in thought.

The Narantuul marketplace at the east end of the city is one of the largest is Asia, rivaling those of Istanbul and New Delhi. Occupying some 60 acres of land, it attracts a quarter-million visitors on weekends and brags some 15,000 vendors selling whatever the imagination can contrive. Numerous buses originate from many locations throughout the city to carry the non-driver to and from the attraction.

Anna wanted to purchase ten pounds of horse meat for Tugi, some quality mutton, a stock of noodles, and a variety of vegetables. Rancid mare's milk did not interest either of them. David settled for a bottle of quality liquor and several bottles of beer to offer their guest. It would be rude not to offer something to drink upon his entry. Not having a clue as to Tomo's married status, David didn't have a problem inviting him for a first-time business/social dinner, something in keeping with his own experiences.

Limitless varieties of clothing were available at the market, from the cheapest Chinese or Russian wear, or the most expensive native dress. Historically, inhabitants of the area known as Mongolia dressed in wool and animal skins, from undergarments to top clothing, including soft low-cut boots to sturdier knee-highs for riding through denser areas. The main appearance of the traditional Deel was that of a large decorative overcoat.

It had the typical long sleeves, wide flap that folded up on the chest and buttoned at the right shoulder. The Silk Road that led from China to the Mediterranean in Roman times changed the dress, as did the advent of synthetic fibers over the course of centuries. The wealthier chose to overlay their warm Deels with silk and colorful brocades. Anna considered herself to be closer to a peasant than to a person of wealth, so she chose to look for a patterned synthetic with a fur lining. Dressing as a true peasant might draw derision, considering her growing status.

Anna told him, "If we buy too traditional, these days, it's mostly worn ceremonially." She led him into an open air store with clothing racks full of colorful wear for men and women.

"What's your favorite color?" she asked.

"Turquoise, I guess," David replied.

Anna replied, "Okay, the color of sky. It also signifies loyalty. Hospital workers wear blue because it has a calming effect to the eye and helps to lower the blood pressure of patients, or so they believe, although I'm not up on any clinical studies to that effect." She poked through the racks of men's Deels pulling out one made of thick wool. She held it up to him, put it back, and found one considerably longer.

She handed it to the proprietor, a woman dressed in a pink Deel lined with sheep skin with silk inlaid with pictures of various animals down the sides outlined in blue. "I want one like yours," she told the woman.

"We won't get the pointed hats, unless you want one, dear. Just about any hat will do these days including top hats, baseball caps, or Russian fur-lined types with ear flaps. We won't get the knee high boots, either, unless you want to be riding in the hinterland. However, we will need other warm comfortable foot ware." She selected for herself a pair of calf-high leather boots that zipped up for easy on-off.

David tried several sets until he found a pair that fit, each of taking turns holding Tugi. "We'd better get going. Our driver is waiting," he said.

On this surprisingly clear crisp day, numerous men walked their dogs on leashes, although none had the appearance of Tugi. Many gave the trio a wide berth playing it safe, except for one youth in his late teens who saw a chance to steal, a common occupation in any grand bazaar. In a crowd, he cut the strap that held the cross-shoulder pouch that Anna used for a purse, and ran off with it. David yelled "Stop Thief," and took off after the man who dodged in and out of the shoppers, carelessly pushing many aside.

Anna yelled, "Go Tugi." The dog took off like a shot, quickly passed David, and bit deeply into the calf of the runner, who screamed and turned to fall on his back. When David arrived short moments later, the youth was desperately trying to hold off a huge slathering wolf by its collar as it snapped again and again, fangs dripping saliva onto his face.

"Tugi stop!" David commanded with only an instant to spare. He had to repeat the command, while yanking the trailing leash back before Tugi backed off. The youth had completely soiled himself. He scrambled to his feet and hobbled away as fast as he could, snot running from his nose, tears in his eyes, one leg trailing blood, leaving the purse on the ground. Scenting the fear and the blood, feral Tugi charged forward, nearly yanking David off his feet. It took all of David's strength to hold him by the collar. The youth never looked back, emotionally scarred for life, not looking forward to his dreams, and possibly seeking a different profession.

When Anna arrived carrying several bags, some woman said, "Isn't that the lady from TV who got the award and her pet?"

To their great surprise, numerous people around them began to applaud. Doubtless, the story of the dog chase would be embellished upon until it was turned into a legend and possibly even a fable, the way things were going for her.

While David completely enjoyed the international flavor and hustle of the marketplace in general, he knew he was seriously out of his element. He truly loved this woman, felt terrible that he had suspected her, but couldn't get the courage to ask her to marry him. To make matters worse, he felt like a tag-a-long. He had grown up with hard-core miners and earned money in school playing poker. Now, since he had met her and through no fault of his own, he found himself swirling in the maelstrom of events that were overtaking Anna, living her life as much as his own.

His heart ached for her because he completely understood how circumstances had plucked this girl from a safe haven into the unknown and unpredictable. He didn't personally fear for danger or financial ruin; it was the unknown about her that concerned him. He needed to protect his woman, but he had no idea how to go about it, because he had no control over events.

Despite his concerns, dinner with Anandyn Tomo proved to be a great source of entertainment for the couple. The men shared snippets about their lives, with neither delving too deeply. Eventually, the conversation came down to Anna and his suggestion that she obtain a Mongolian citizenship.

Tomo explained, "We're desperate. We can't move forward unless we have the human energy to do so. Our hospitals are filled; women outlive men by 8-10 years because men engage in excessive smoking and drinking. They die of liver and lung cancer, among other factors. There's cadmium, arsenic, and mercury in coal dust and in our drinking water. We're grasping at straws. Now we have a chance to try something new. This isn't our first rodeo, as the Americans like to say, but we'll take any rodeo we can earn money at." He looked at Anna and smiled. The Harvard law grad was speaking her lingo.

Tomo continued, "Anna, I made it clear we would like you to help us, if you're willing to make a small commitment. We're also prepared to increase production at Naidvar. I'll help you all I can. And David, you're the head of the project. Let's make this work. Need I say more?"

Tomo paused in his narrative, as he appeared to struggle with a thought. He took a deep breath and said what was on his mind. "One of our many great problems is that we're economically, and therefore, militarily relatively weak. Once we gain sufficient strength, our economy will springboard to the next level. Neither Russia nor China can allow that."

The couple wondered if that was a veiled reference to the stolen vial, but said nothing. If so, any one of a number of people might have told him and the theft; after all, Naidvar was Tomo's baby.

The minister continued, "The advantage to Anna's becoming a citizen is that any attack against her would be an attack against the country. She would be under our protection. Anna, you won't have to renounce your American citizenship. A lot of people have a dual citizenship."

"Let's take it a step at a time," Anna said. "We're not saying 'yes' or 'no'. There's a lot to think about."

"Good," Tomo said, and stood to leave. "Oh, do you mind if I see the new heating unit? Nobody thought I might want to see it, God forbid."

Anna opened the door of the stove and instead of glowing lumps of coal, she revealed a white ceramic container some eight inches in diameter by three inches in height, fluted around the circumference, strangely resembling a ger in its miniature dimensions.

Chapter 3

Once Anna gave her consent, it took only a couple of days to video her statements, as promised. Strangely, they had been written in advance. Not surprisingly, her citizenship had been expedited. There would be push back, skeptics, and critics who would be met with head-bucking devotees and supporters.

David called down to Batu to ensure that three shifts operated, however there was no way to safeguard against terrorism of any kind. At least the freezers were locked. Only three possessed keys: himself, Batu, and Temujin.

David had seen enough criminal activity in the mining industry to make him suspect almost everyone. Never mind that his father and Uncle Draco had absconded with what could only be described as the greatest amount of pure gold ever discovered naturally. Hundreds of pounds belonged to them and their families. In David's view, the adventure of his father and Uncle Draco was about two men stealing what belonged to the company they worked for, namely Groebels.

In Naidvar, if the program came to ruin, that could be his personal death knell, like the accused Dr. Anthony Fauci, the head of the CDC, during the great pandemic in the States. In Anna's case, the stability of the entire Mongolian government might be threatened. She was a foreigner and a citizen. David wondered who might gain the most, if any of that occurred.

The family of three spent the time leading up to the campaign by visiting the gers in their immediate area, 100 gers in a sea of a good hundred thousand white dots surrounding the city like a ring. An equal number of gers were scattered throughout the city and countless others in outlying areas would have to wait their turn for the new heating source, or continue as they were.

Throughout the country, national broadcasts featured Anna and Tugi standing in front of a ger. She said, "Hello, my name is Anna and this is Tugi. We were asked to tell you about a new program our government is beginning and many of you have been chosen to have the good fortune to help us."

This was a good line. Everyone wanted good fortune to befall them. She presented her testimonial as to the effectiveness of the new heating source in their own ger, and openly answered commonly asked questions.

"Will it cost more than their current heating

sources?" Anna read from a card in her hand.

She replied, "If it does, the government is prepared to provide subsidies to offset the cost of coal." She had been told that the cost of the program would be offset by sales to the United States and European countries who sought the freeze-dried algae for their own purposes, once the oil had been extracted. On paper, it looked good.

"What are the health hazards we face?" she read.

"None, as far as the world's best scientists can find," she replied. "It is a clean burning fuel."

Two months after the government proclaimed success in their first trial run, they announced that 1000 gers would now be converted to the new biofuel.

The family returned to Naidvar to assist in managing a growing Biolab. Planes full of materials arrived along with additional workers. Housing was increased, as was the size of the commissary and shopping center. In accelerated time, Naidvar had been converted into a massive complex, although it only occupied a tiny fraction of the usable land within the crater.

Anna spent more time than ever in the lab trying to make her contributions. She did make time to take Tugi out each afternoon, along with Gerel, for his hunting of marmots and rabbits. After dark, the two would drive out of the compound again away from any lights to look at the stars, using the astronomy book that Shorni had given Anna for a present.

The occasional distant howl of a wolf broke the silence of the darkness, until one night, Tugi began to howl in return. This surprised both women. Gerel said gently, "He was not with a pack, but calls for a mate. That is curious. Did he ever know other wolves in the area?"

Anna replied, "Not that I know of, although I would let him run where he wanted. He always returned after a short while, usually with an animal in his teeth."

Gerel said, "Be careful of the packs. He may leave you to go run with them."

Anna said, sadly, "I know. That would be his choice."

Chapter 4

David sent via Internet: **Darkhan Industrial says it will make all the heating units we need, so we're good there. Your thoughts? DA**

Al Yamani returned: **David, I leave the decisions up to you. You're in charge of the operation. Also, I need you to look at the books.**

Khaled

What was that last sentence about? Didn't he trust his own people, or the Mongolian government? Why him? He wasn't an accountant by any stretch. But an order is an order.

David rubbed his forehead, thinking, *The man has a world mining empire to operate and probably works over time to email me. In other words, let him know when the project is finally completed. Otherwise, don't bother him.*

Why the books, though? Batu had hired an accountant who had the surname of Bat-Erdene, whom he had gone through school with, along with Tomo. He totally trusted the man, although he felt Tomo might be a little too smart and slick for him. When he had asked about the accountant, Batu went off on one of little asides and told him, "He's easy to spot. He's a little bowlegged. When we grew up, I herded my sheep riding a motorcycle, he did his on the back of a horse." Batu grinned and had added, "I don't know about the great Khan himself, but rumor has it his lieutenants were bowlegged because they spent most of their lives on horseback when the Mongol hordes overran a large part of the known world."

Later that evening, his arm around Anna on the sofa and Chopin playing on the CD player she'd brought from home, she said, "It doesn't matter why he wants you to look at the books. He must know we don't do all the financial work here, only the poundage we send down to China and its projected revenue. Didn't you tell me the Department of Interior handles that? Hell, we don't even know what weight of algae we're shipping off. It's all guesswork."

Anna wasn't telling him anything he didn't already know. Knowing her, he thought she must be leading up to something.

"Which conflicts with one thing I am absolutely certain about, sweetheart, because I just found out that I'm pregnant."

There it was. Nothing complicated. The woman he loved just told him she's pregnant. David felt like quipping, "Are you sure it's yours?" but bit his tongue. Instead, he decided to man up and said, gently and lovingly, "Then I guess we'd better get married to make it official. How far along are you," he asked, allowing his joy to unfold.

"Far enough along to know I'm pregnant and not so far that I'm not horny as hell," she responded. "Get the hint?"

The chapel in Naidvar had to be multi-cultural to cover the multitude of religious necessities encompassed by three shifts of workers. These religions included primarily Buddhist, with a smaller percentage Muslim, Shamanist, and finally five percent Christian. The latter was of much higher percentage than average in Naidvar due to the number of Western workers at the colony.

Marriages had never occurred in the community until that of Anna and David. Finding someone to conduct the ceremony had to wait until they made arrangements for a priest to fly down from Ulan Bator.

The ceremony was held in the presence of Sandoval and Shorni, along with a surprisingly large number of people who were curious to attend. "You can officially engage in sexual activities, now" declared Sandoval, who clapped David on the shoulder.

Chapter 5

Tugi's ears perked, then his head came up. This was followed by an almost urgent knocking at their door. Anna and David looked at each other. Each put down the book they were reading and David opened the door. Tugi's tale wagged when he saw Batu. The scientist always had a treat for him.

Batu reached in his pocket and gave the animal what he expected. With tail still wagging, he went to a quiet place to enjoy himself in solitude. "Did you see the news?" Batu uttered at the same time.

"What news?" asked David.

"Turn on the TV," Batu directed, somewhat urgently.

"What station?"

"Any station."

Anna did so. Immediately, a split screen came up with a male newscaster on the left with Anna's picture on the right. He was speaking in Mongolian. The subtitles in English read:

A whistle-blower, who claims to have first-hand knowledge of the operation, has stated that the biofuel products being manufactured are poisonous and cautions against using them. He fears for his life and he will remain in hiding.

Our sources are trying to reach their spokesperson, Anna Chan Alday, and her husband, David Alday, who is heading the project, for comment.

Anna looked scared. David said, "Let's go find out. We'll bring Tugi. Batu, get Temujin and meet us in the lab. Everybody turn off your phones for now. Take no calls.

Anna found her life to be unmanageable for short periods. She had not been brought up in a helter-skelter life style, certainly not with anything close to the swirling whirlpools events that followed her like a magnet, sweeping her into their spin. She had strong memories of living an easy carefree life on the seacoast, lying on the beach and ogling at men. Now she found herself married with a new son in a landlocked country with her picture plastered on billboards in what few cities the country possessed, and on television; a woman who professed to love Mongolia so much that she had become a citizen; a woman who had a wolf for a pet, that slobbered over her son as much as she did; a husband whose career was in jeopardy, and, at best, an uncertain future. No, this wasn't the ultimate get-married, settle-down, live-happily-ever-after life she once envisioned.

The small group walked the aisles of 50 gallon Plexiglas vats of algae in various shades of green. The background odor of seaweed and algal blooms was unmistakable. Even at that late hour the usual assortment of technicians drew occasional samples, drained vats, or prepped others for re-inoculation. Anna and Tugi lagged behind the others looking, seeking a revelation, some vague clue.

On his leash, Tugi suddenly whined. "What is it, Tugi?" Anna said. The dog sniffed the air. Anna couldn't tell any difference from the usual smell, suggestive of the heady odor of a rank, green swimming pool, but she understood he had sensed a problem. The dog had spent enough hours in the building to become completely familiar with its odors. Something might be amiss.

She looked closely at the growth in the vats on either side of her, but couldn't see anything unusual, until she did. One of them had a slightly reddish cast with a bit of foam at the top of the slowly swirling mixture. She tilted her head from side to side to get different perspectives, trying to let the ceiling lights glint from different angles.

She noted the number at the top of the vat and called to the others. "Over here."

The three returned and she said, "Tugi picked up the smell. What do you think?" she asked, pointing to Vat 54.

Temujin inspected the vat from a distance

and from close-up. He said, "This is definitely wrong," He pulled off a sample into a flask, which he held up to the light. The others followed him to his desk, where he prepared the sample for viewing under the microscope.

Only a moment later he said, "Take a look."

She and David looked through the eyepieces, followed by Batu. What they saw was not the single-celled species they had been using, but another species. The both looked at Temujin, not understanding.

"*Karenia brevi*" the senior scientist managed to say, between clenched teeth, shaking his head and pursing his lips. "Red tide."

"You mean like the kind we see in Southern California or the Gulf Coast, and Florida sometimes?" Anna asked.

"Or off the coasts of New Zealand and Australia or off India?" David added.

"Yes, the same. It produces a neurotoxin that paralyzes the ability of fish to breathe. Other species can do the same thing. It doesn't matter. This one is here now. It's generally not harmful to humans, unless they eat shellfish poisoned by the algae. But under our conditions, I have no idea. This is absolutely frightening in many respects. We need to run immediate tests."

He called over one of his senior chemists to look up the chemical formula for the toxin, along with numerous research papers on the subject. The chemist printed out a dozen or so pages, and left to consult with two other chemists, who walked over to the vat in question. All were followed by David, Anna, Tugi, and Temujin.

The chemists compared it with the vats next to it and with those across the aisle, drew off another sample from the problematic vat, and disappeared into another room with the name CHEMISTRY painted in black on a frosted glass window set within the door.

The chemistry lab pronounced itself to be a playroom for chemists and biologists. The room sparkled with cleanliness and sanitation and enough highly advanced pieces of equipment that could please researchers in numerous fields of investigation. Under chemists' guidance, Anna had learned the operation of those machines.

The lead scientist transferred a sample to a test tube, spun it out in the small table-top centrifuge, and injected a portion of the liquid into the gas chromatograph. Short minutes later, several spikes appeared on the paper print-out. One of the scientists looked through the sheaf of papers in his hand, pointing to a duplicate of the spike. The three men took some time to review the publications in hand and came to a final conclusion.

Exiting the room the head chemist said to the waiting group, "Preliminary information suggests that the toxin is in high concentration. This means it is in a higher concentration inside the cells. The toxin is fat soluble, therefore it will be present in the oils we harvest. This is not good. We need to run more tests, but we need to kill that vat now."

Batu declared, "Call it what you want, my lab has been infiltrated." He understood bacterial and viral infections. He didn't know a thing about toxins. That was Temujin's specialty.

"How the hell . . ." David began, beginning to get doubly pissed off.

Anna said, "Wait a minute. If the bad batch gets mixed in with all the others, won't the toxin be diluted enough so it won't be harmful?"

David replied, "I seriously doubt it. However, I see two problems. First, we don't know for a fact if it will cause harm, even when diluted; and second, how do we define harm? Do you want to be the one to tell the public we permitted a toxin to get mixed in with the good fuel? Everybody will have psychosomatic symptoms. This is a public relations nightmare. The amount doesn't matter. It's either there or it isn't. Somebody will ask if we tested the other vats. We have to be prepared to answer that question."

Anna remarked, thinking of her own head on the chopping block, "Which means we could expect endless complaints and lawsuits, unless we can prove otherwise. That could be the end of the project, or at least, slow it down indefinitely."

Turning to the other three chemists, David said, "Hell, man, we have planes coming in all the time. Anybody could have brought it in. Get something to eat and prepare for an all-nighter. I'll call the chemists from the other shifts to get down here. I'm going to need some coffee and get my record book organized for this. I want printouts and data from every single test. Run random tests for heavy metals too, in case somebody asks."

Temujin went to his own desk to pull out the records. "It was inoculated one week ago," he declared.

"Who initialed it?" David asked.

Temujin looked closely at the initials, but couldn't make out the scrawl, as if it were purposely obscured.

"Hopefully, whoever did it is not here on this shift watching us. I'm wondering if there might be fingerprints around the injection port," Anna suggested, having seen workers stabilize their addition of a new stock with the right hand by holding the port open with the left.

"Good idea," David said, not surprised by her insight. "Trouble is, we're not set up for that." He mentally kicked himself for not setting up surveillance cameras.

It went unsaid that every person at the site had been fingerprinted as part of their background check, and the prints, if any, should be relatively fresh.

Anna suggested, "We have lots of gunpowder. We'll empty a few shells and gently waft the powder onto the area. It will stick to any prints. We can shoot a close-up with our cell before lifting it with clear tape, doubling our chance of success."

David did as suggested and was not surprised to find clear imprints. He emailed and faxed a sharp photo of them to the Ministry of Defense in UB, where other prints were already on file. The file was encrypted and labeled, as *National Security Priority Level 2*. Within their wheelhouse, Priority Level 1 would indicate an immediate threat to the country.

Surprisingly, a reply came back within 24 hours. By ruling out those who worked the greenhouse, the ponds, commissary, and janitorial services, the task became less complex. This would not eliminate other non-lab workers; it only meant the investigation had to begin somewhere.

During the time of the investigation, Naidvar's Internet was blowing up, as was David's cell phone. He felt an obligation to answer the calls, as project coordinator. Anna's phone had been stolen on the bus long ago, so she was free from that scourge. David spent a considerable amount of time in the late evening sending emails and returning calls to relevant agencies succinctly stating he would have more to tell them in the morning.

By mid-morning, he released the following information:

We are aware of the claim that our vats have been poisoned. This is untrue (only one vat was poisoned). We are also aware that at least one man was responsible for this false report. This same person did make an attempt to cause damage to our production capabilities, but our quality control is so rigid that we were able to quickly correct the problem. None of this activity slowed our production in that the indoor vats in which we grow the algae represent only a small fraction of our production capacity because, virtually all the biofuel comes from the outdoor ponds.

We expect to soon have the name of this criminal and anticipate his capture shortly.

Signed, David Alday, Supervisor, Naidvar Biofuel Production Facility.

Anna read it and shook her head. Something he wrote in the press release came and went as a wisp of a thought. It had to do with what he said about production ratios. She said, "You're sticking your neck out by making a futuristic guess about his capture, honey. We don't know a thing yet. Thanks for leaving my name out of it, though. Maybe we should promote Tugi to the quality control division?"

David found it within himself to laugh. "I have faith in the system, at least sometimes. In this case, whoever did it must be sweating bullets."

Later, when the prints were identified, they were found to belong to a worker whose shift ran from 10:00 pm to 6:00 am, otherwise known as the graveyard shift, the same shift they had worked to find the bad vat. He was one of the staff who had been with them for the past year. However, upon further investigation, the man had not been on shift for that week, having checked out days earlier, citing family issues in UB and had taken the next flight out.

It didn't make David feel any better when Tomo called to give his well wishes. David wondered if his condolences were buried in there somewhere. The call was basically a check. Did he require any assistance? Is everything under control? David replied by saying not to worry. The issue should be resolved shortly.

Somehow, he suspected that the minister saw through his lies.

Chapter 6

Anna was in a bad spot. Her mother had downsized, moving from Malibu a few miles south to picturesque Santa Monica, and desperately missed her daughter. She wanted to go back home, but the minister was after her for more public appearances.

David commiserated with her, completely understanding the growing demand for their product. He, too, wanted to back off, taking it a step at a time. If the program took years to come to fruition, so be it. Unfortunately, although Tomo was an elected official, he bowed to the wishes of the prime minister, who bowed to the wishes of the president. Parliamentary elections were coming up for both positions.

"Davey"— Anna liked to call him this when she needed to discuss something important— "I have to see mom and take Eric with me. Something isn't right. She needs to see her grandson. She keeps emailing me to come back. Pictures aren't enough, you know that."

Saying those words, she tried to compute the citizenship of their child. He was born in Mongolia. She was born an American citizen of Chinese decent with a Mongolian second citizenship, and her father was a New Zealander. She'd worry about it later.

"Let's do this," David offered, sympathetically, "Take off and get away. It makes you human. Take as long as you need."

"Yeah, and everybody will say I'm running away and wonder why I'm not showing my face," she stated, bluntly.

"No, they won't. You're the spokesperson. Everybody knows you're not a scientist. We made that clear from the start. Answering questions is not an option for you. Go on home. I'm hoping that, in a short time, you can get away from this project. We both can. Just stick with it a little longer. We'll live a long life after it's over."

"Thank you for your honesty," she said, and meant it, "but why do I feel like I'm trapped?"

"You are not trapped, you only think you are. You're caught up in everything. A vacation will give you a fresh perspective," he offered, weakly. She had used the same term he used to describe himself.

David dearly wished he could go with her. He was in a worse position than she. Anna was only a figure-head; he was pretty much the top dog. Nobody in their right mind would go after

Groebels or Tomo, which left him alone in the gun sights.

He understood the press. Selling air time and newspaper space was a business, no different than any other. Virtually every business operated to make a profit, even those registered as non-profits. By definition, it is the practice of making one's living by engaging in commerce. Like a politician in hot water planning a distraction, he needed the press to quickly move on to something else before it got out of control. At the same time, he needed a break. In order to do that, he needed to find a way to hold the wolves at bay, which meant he was forced to go with his gut feeling and publicly say an arrest was imminent.

Apparently, the stars were aligned—or was it the planets, he couldn't remember which—when the break came within hours of the latest press release. The National Police Agency of Mongolia, centered in Ulan Bator, reported the capture of the wanted suspect.

The man's name was the Mongolian equivalent of John Jones. His record showed him to be a degreed chemist, a man of upstanding quality, who had served in the military for three years, and was in good standing with them. He was married with three children all of whom lived in the Ulaanbaatar ger district.

Interrogation techniques used by Mongolian authorities against suspected terrorists differ somewhat from those of other nations. Within a short time after capture, he quickly announced that he was initially offered a great deal of money to poison the vat by another man who remained in Naidvar. After accepting the offer, he later declined the offer by this man to become part of any wrongdoing, whereupon this man informed him that his family would be endangered, should he refuse.

He traded protection of his family by authorities for information about the man he identified as Bat-Erdene. His statements were forwarded to David, who did not feel obliged to wait for authorities to fly down.

Word travels fast in a small community, especially when something nefarious is afoot. The suspect almost made it to the company Dodge before Tugi took a piece of meat from behind one of his knees.

Chapter 7

Anna and Eric arrived in Santa Monica to find her mother gravely ill with terminal cancer. Not wanting to overly concern her daughter, mom had said nothing about her illness; only that she wanted to see her daughter badly.

Over the next short weeks, Anna showed her mother pictures and gaily described to her every detail of her latest round of adventures, watching the stricken woman smile wide-eyed at her only child who had found "her place in life," had started a family, and who would soon come into more millions. Plus, mom now had a grandson to hold and coo over.

And so, in that manner, Anna's mother passed happily into the next life. With great pain and regret, Anna contacted a management company to put her new house up for rent and tried to return with her son to the only life she knew, only to find that she must remain seaside for another week.

When she emailed David that she was coming home, he had told her to wait. A terrible dust storm had ravaged Inner Mongolia, including Naidvar. The city had been constructed to withstand all manner of weather, but an unprecedented storm blew in from northern China for more than a day, reaching hundreds of miles northward to Ulan Bator. The only good news was that it temporarily cleared the smog from the capitol city's air, replacing it with a cloud of fine dust.

While the protected ringed city in the Gobi nearest the sand dunes survived the brunt of the gale-force wind thanks to the protective mountains, it did not survive the fallout that lasted for days. The particles carried into the upper atmosphere began to settle. They sifted into every nook and cranny of the city, befouling machinery and even the power generator itself. Everyone had been tasked with detail-cleaning everything. The ponds survived. The indoor vats were questionable, because they were working at less than full speed. This would not affect production, but it would severely affect the maturation rate of each vat, making analyses much more difficult to track. It might even introduce them to airborne contaminants.

Scheduled departures and equipment replacements had to be rescheduled until civilization could recover. Both Ulan Bator and parts in-between, including Mandalgov, near where

Sandoval and Shorni lived, were shut down, as though a pandemic had struck.

Thus, forced to postpone her flight, Anna spent her time introducing her son to the surf and sand of the beach, yet finding herself counting the days and minutes when she could return to David and the adventures of her new life. She had thought about calling her old friends, but opted against it. Based upon her last meeting with them and their shallow discussions, she saw no point in making contact. Perhaps in ten years. Perhaps she had chosen the wrong friends to begin with.

Before the funeral, following the last requests of her mother, she visited their banker and trust attorney, once again, along with a realtor, and the family's accounting firm. She poured over numbers and saw no graft, other than deductions inherently built into various unauthorized subtractions—obviously an accounting error. These were promptly corrected at her intensely stated recommendations, lest she acquire another firm and contact relevant authorities.

Fuck this shit. She had a man and a wolf to get back to.

The funeral had been simple. She possessed only a handful of aunts and uncles with whom she could relate, or were concerned with her life, expressing more interest in the money she inherited, no different than the prattle she had listened to at her father's funeral. She politely heard their sales pitches, presented under various veiled guises, while Anna politely said she would consider their proposals and would get back with them.

She flew first class on the return, but it still took 36 hours to get back to Naidvar, including the usual stop in Seoul along the way. The long trip gave her ample time to assess her situation. Eric was a prince. She had named him after her father, who had a common Chinese-American name. He slept much of the travel time and was readily entertained when he didn't require changing.

She carried with her a deck of cards to play solitaire, and two expensive sets of 152 Mahjong tiles, one to present to Gerel as a gift, and another for Shorni, should they meet again, along with Jack London's *Call of the Wild* on eBook. The game had originated in the time of Confucius, disappeared for a period of time, then re-emerged in later years. Now, some 500 million played the game, closely rivaling the number who played chess.

Anna was now a woman of wealth, which meant nothing to her in the vast scheme of things. It had absolutely no relevance to the life of her and her husband. She mused that even billionaires must worry about the loss of millions at a time. Who was watching their accountants?

She had no real complaints about her living conditions in Mongolia. Her new family lived rent free in a clean isolated city with free food and fresh air, surrounded by intellectual and well-educated people, books galore, and, with rare exceptions, crime did not exist.

She also dearly missed her Tugi. She wondered when she would come to grips with the reality that, at some point, she would have to let him go.

When Anna looked back on her life, she had so many regrets she was wont to consider life as a collection of regrets. She mentally created a plus and minus column, similar to what a forlorn person might write on a paper napkin while alone in a bar, when trying to decide whether to remain married or get divorced. In the end, the pluses far outweighed the minuses. She evaluated the meaning of the word *civilization*. Did it mean more material goods, better housing, health care and lifestyle? Did it infer more satisfaction with a particular government? It must not infer less crime, because crime existed universally, as much a part of human nature as love and hate.

Anna continued to evaluate her changed circumstances. Given that civilization meant better technology for disease control, that element only pertained to a tiny fraction of the world's population in the wealthiest countries, but could not stop a pandemic. It also brought forth audio books to reduce the personal feel of handling books and even reading itself, but did offer entertainment and, like radio, challenged the imagination in its own way. Computers instantly provided access to the knowledge base of the world, which, in her view counted for a lot, but they eliminated the ability to perform basic math functions and analytical thinking pertaining thereto, or the ability to tell time without a digital display. It introduced television and videos to eliminate human imagination, conversation, and family bonding, but entertained countless millions who needed outside stimulation; it brought forth human interaction through social media, which introduced its own problems.

Anna's plane touched down at Chinggis Khann International airport in a clear sky. Cloudless sunlight graced the city and the country as a whole. Thirty minutes later, she and Eric boarded a four seat Cessna 182 for the flight back to Naidvar. Part of her felt like a kid returning home after several weeks at a summer camp on the beach. The other part insisted she gird her loins for unexpected battles on the horizon, battles she found herself looking forward to in some perverse way.

Gazing over the landscape, her doubts fled like vaporous dreams. The past had dissipated into the foggy mist of time, the future beckoned with a big question mark. She had made the decision to return to a people who lived in unsanitary conditions, who didn't understand the germ theory of disease, who suffered from allergies and asthma, in a nation filled with pollinating grasses and black dust.

A couple of thoughts continued to make her crazy. *How could a people with such a high literacy rate have such backward thinking people?* More importantly, *Why am I even going back?* For either of those questions, she had no good answer. In her present mood, Anna decided she could do without civilization; well, most of it.

Chapter 8

Upon her arrival, Anna found that David, Batu, and another man, who was acting chief of security, were in the small Naidvar hospital where Eric had been born, trying to get information from the hapless victim of a vicious dog bite. All four knew her, but only three greeted her affectionately. One of them put his arms around her and welcomed her home while the one in the bed remained mute.

The hospital room maintained state of the art cleanliness, at least for minor surgeries, primarily because it was run and operated by occidental doctors who were provided government funding to keep the hospital in that manner. It wasn't meant for open heart surgery, but all employees of the ringed city had been screened to reduce the probability that major medical interventions would be necessary.

Heretofore, the acting chief of security dealt with family disputes, issues surrounding undue drinking episodes, and TVs that were on too loud, not suspected conspiratorial potentially international criminal activities. Upon Anna's sudden appearance in the hospital room, David recounted to her all that had happened, which brought her back to the reality of her new life. Some person or agency was trying to sabotage the program without being so obvious as to nuke the place. She took it personally, more so than her husband, who saw it for what it was; an attack against the country itself, which infuriated him beyond the realm of her grasp.

Bat-Erdene appeared to be native Mongolian—to the uninitiated, one Mongolian might look like another—well educated in accounting and sharp of wit. Unlike the captured man in UB who worked in the lab, Bat-Erdene worked in Administration as the head accountant.

Upon hearing about Tugi's attack against one of his life-long most trusted friends, Batu expressed shock. How could he be implicated in a plot to cause damage to the agency he worked for? They and Tomo had grown up together, attending wrestling matches, going to camel races, sharing rooms in college, their parents were friends. Bat-Erdene and Tomo had been the lady's men, while the diminutive Batu was the odd man out. Once Batu went to graduate school in Texas, his friends, both of whom were accounting majors, got hired by the county government and disappeared until fairly recently when Bat-Erdene contacted Batu, who ran the science division of Naidvar. Offering his services, this same friend would be on a crutch for the rest of his life to find himself accused of terrorism.

The interview went on for some time and finally, tired of it all, Anna remarked to the others, "You know, I have the perfect lie detector test. I think I'll bring in a guest. Give me a few minutes."

Anna left the room to see Gerel, who babysat a human and a dog. She returned with Tugi on a leash. The instant she brought him in the door, the patient's face turned ashen and in turn, the dog's eyes focused on him. The animal snarled, leaping against the leash, eager to finish his work.

At that moment, seeing the bedridden man and grasping what he had attempted, a new emotion came over Anna. It wasn't a momentary flash of frustration or a momentary snit, it was a feeling of full-on rage, a feeling she needed to let loose and personally finish what Tugi had started. The knowledge that she could get away with it without repercussions contributed to her desire to hurt the man further.

"All right," declared the prisoner, wide eyed, clearly in terror, drawing back on the bed from a snarling, snapping dog. "I was given a large sum of money to add the vial to the vat."

"Stand down, Tugi," Anna ordered.

The wolf reluctantly did so.

"How many vats did you have poisoned?" asked David.

"Only one," was the answer.

"Which one?"

"Number 54."

The security chief opened a manila folder in his hand and said, "You used to work for the Department of Interior for a number of years as comptroller before coming here. A few months ago, you were given the additional assignment of overseeing the safe arrival of shipments brought in for our rebuild. Is this correct?"

"Yes," answered the prisoner.

The security chief asked, "How long you spend in prison depends on what you tell us now. Do you have anybody else working here who is in on this scheme?" He was more than happy to deal with a real criminal rather than trying to play family counselor.

The prisoner looked at Tugi wondering what the dog would and could do — a killer not always on a leash.

"Who gave you the poison and gave the order?" asked the security man.

"I don't know. I was given a thousand dollars with a container of Red Alga by somebody in the department I never saw before to get the job done, when he came down on one of the flights. The vial was in an envelope. Inside were pictures of my wife and our children. I didn't want to do it myself, so I told the same thing to a worker in the Biolab. I made him do it for me."

It didn't take a genius to compute that $3400

Tugric per dollar would go a long way.

David said to the security man, "When he is released from the hospital, I want this man kept in his apartment. Bring him food. Leave his TV. Take away his phone and his computer. Search the place to ensure he has no other way to communicate. Remove all sharp objects. Fix a lock on the door so he can't get out. Nobody finds out what happened here until I say so."

Later that evening, the couple invited Batu and Gerel to dinner at their apartment with Anna doing the cooking. The hosts shared their concerns about their previous dinner with Tomo, who reinforced his commitment to help his country and the plight of its people, giving full support to their efforts.

The guests listened dutifully until Batu suggested, somewhat shyly, "Is it possible that Bat-Erdene is blowing . . . how do you say . . . smoke up your ass? I mean how do you check on anything he says?"

"You don't, I guess," Anna shrugged, reaching down to scratch Tugi's head.

Gerel said, "Suppose Bat-Erdene is telling the truth, which only suggests that Tomo did order the poisoning. Does that mean Tomo was behind the original theft of the vial?"

David said, "Somebody shipped in the red alga. It's not like we got it from our own seacoast."

Batu added, "Tomo's the one who hired me for my position."

"And?" asked Anna.

Batu shrugged. "He was totally sociable and surprisingly open, like you told me he was with you. I've always known him to be Pyccknñ Ctahdapt (Russian standard) quality, in a personality kind of way, although I will say he was a little too smooth for me."

Gerel looked at her husband and asked, "What do you actually know about his family?"

"They we're poor slobs like the rest of us," Batu stated briefly.

Anna pondered, "You know, Gerel, that's a good question and, Batu, that's a good answer. Let's see what we can find out. I used to be an Internet freak. I guess I still am. Are you game?"

"Do you mean do I want to be hunted?" replied the Mongolian, suddenly expressing concern. "Not really."

David laughed and said, "No, it means do you want to play. In other words, let's turn on the computer and Google what we can find out about him, or contact others who can find out for us."

Having been assigned by Al-Yamani to head to project, David dismissed the thought of bothering him and instead, placed a call to Robert Farmer. His voice mail said he would return the call.

David returned his attention to the others,

who were grouped around the computer and read along with them:

Anandyn Tomo, age 62, born of Mongolian parents in Ulaanbaatar, the capital city of Mongolia, received a Bachelor's Degree in Social Sciences from the University of Mongolia and a Master's Degree in International Relations from the same university followed by an acceptance to Harvard University School of Law. He returned to Mongolia and was elected to the position of Governor and Mayor of Ulaanbaatar.

"That's a fairly shallow description, don't you think?" David commented.

Gerel added, "Whoever writes these little articles is probably very busy, so don't expect a lot. This doesn't tell us anything we don't already know."

Anna shook her head vigorously. "This whole thing is wrong. It takes a good 100 grand a year to go to the Harvard School of Law, which includes tuition, room, board, and other add-ons. Where did Tomo come up with that much money for the years he attended, especially back then? In addition, a person is screened before admission to ensure they have enough to pay. I know that because one of my father's best friends at Rayburn had gone there. Also, my mother told me that my father had a secret desire for me to go there."

Batu looked as though he was ready to throw in the towel, when he said, "Suppose Tomo is the worst of the worst. I don't see there's much you can do about it? Even if he were, what could be his motive for doing such a thing?"

David replied, "One thing at a time. Right now, we don't have enough information to make any kind of decision. As for reasons, in my limited experience, the motives driving the criminal mind are pretty basic."

Chapter 9

The commissary was worthy of any in building that served a large work force almost anywhere, including second and third world countries. It offered food and drink around the clock for those working graveyard shift, serving both hot and cold drinks, along with local ethnic foods. It was basically a buffet style service in a building constructed with double-pane windows.

Although Mongolians typically ate only one large meal in the evening, that term had flexibility, considering the round-the-clock work force. For those who did not want to cook at home, limited Western-style foods were provided, because of the number of European and American workers on-site.

During a breakfast of eggs, toast, and coffee the following morning, David said, "We're in a holding pattern, honey. Since our prisoner didn't give us anything useful, for the time being, we can do something different."

"Like what?" Anna asked, wondering what her husband's imagination might have conjured up.

"First, I already made plans for myself, but I wanted to see if you'd like to join me. I spoke with Gerel to see is she'd consent to watch Eric for us in case you wanted to go with me. My idea is to take the backhoe out to the far end of the poppy field. I want to do some deep digging. Maybe we'll even scare up some field mice for Tugi to chase."

"Yuk."

David laughed at her response. "Remember those Chinese guys we caught placer mining for gold and how close it was to the surface?"

"Yes. And, let me guess, you want to find gold inside the grounds here," Anna teased.

"Not necessarily. When that meteorite hit way back when, I suspect it fractured the earth deeply enough to cause magma to come to the surface. When that happens, it can bring heavy metals with it. I want to see if we can find anything interesting. After we're done, I'll shovel the dirt back into the hole and pack it down with the topsoil on top so the flowers will grow again. I'll even give you a lesson on how to run the machine. What do you say?"

Anna pondered David's proposal for a long moment with apparent deep concern. Finally, she said, "I'll have to check my social calendar first. I know I'm supposed to go the beach, then get my hair and nails done after my massage and facial. But for you, I guess I can reschedule."

The couple finished their meal, returning their plates to be washed. David led Anna to the large storage shed the size of a three-car garage. He slid open the door. The room was warmer than the outside air. A number of fork lifts were lined up against one wall along with a Yellow Komatsu WB93R-2 diesel backhoe/loader. Next to it sat the drone.

He toured the large machine checking fluid levels and the integrity of various lines. He mounted it to open the door to the cab, explaining to Anna the safety precautions one must take even getting into the operator's seat. She joined him, carefully watching her step, while he pointed out the various foot pedals and levers that operated the boom and bucket, mirror adjusts, scoop controls, speed controller, front loader controls, gas, brakes, and stabilizers. He gave the ignition a half-turn.

He made sure the parking brake was engaged, all the control levers were set to "HOLD", and the direction control levers were set to neutral. He pressed the foot control to disengage the parking brake. Finally, he completed the turn of the ignition until the engine ran smoothly. Ensuring the bucket was in a position of low center of gravity, he buckled his seat belt and said, "Hang on."

With Tugi trotting alongside and driving cautiously, it took nearly half an hour to drive nearly five miles to the far end of the crater, with Anna hanging on for dear life. Two hours later, he had carved out a hole ten feet cubed with a ramp running down into the hole for entry and exit. Dirt was piled several feet high on three sides of the hole.

His interest piqued when he began to hit larger darker rocks, not the simple smaller boulders in the dirt that had been removed. Once he did that, he removed a single layer down another foot and got out of the machine. He called for Anna to join him. He lowered the booms to a safe position, turned off the engine and began to sift through the soil.

"What are you looking for?" she asked, standing next to him. David said nothing until moments later when he grabbed a small nugget the size of a marble somewhat grayish in color. He handed it to her.

"This," he said.

She hefted the small rock and said, "It's heavy. I know it's not gold."

"You're right," he said, picking up a larger rougher one, about the size of a baseball. "Do you still have that watch you keep in your pocket?" he asked.

Anna pulled out the strapless "Expedition" watch and handed it to David. He pushed a few buttons and came up with the compass, which he held next to the rock. The compass pivoted toward the rock. "This is iron mixed with platinum. The place is rotten with both, and most likely, a lot of other ores too. They travel together. The ore body is probably concentrated beneath the flowered portion of the crater which leads into the mountain."

David bend down and sifted through the earth again for a few moments, paused an instant, then picked up a rough green rock that looked like a tear drop about 1/2" x 2" in size. Holding it up to the light, his mouth fell open. "I don't believe it," he declared. He stared hard at Anna, then looked back at the rock. "Here, take it. Keep it safe" he said, sifting through the earth more, soon coming up with small to medium-size green rocks of different shapes and a lot of green flakes. He gently rubbed off the surface dust and blew off the rest. He pulled off his neck scarf and placed the particles into it. "Help me find more," he directed, enthusiastically, without saying more.

In an instant, Anna was by his side. Before long, the large scarf had been filled. He tied it in a knot, gave a big exhale and said, "This is ours." He felt like his father and Uncle Draco when they had hit a mother lode of gold.

"What, David. Talk to me," Anna complained.

"This is freaking moldavite, probably one of the rarest, if not the rarest gem on earth. It's a type of glass and came in on the meteorite that created this valley. It's not natural to Earth. Supposedly, it was the green stone in the Holy Grail. I only saw one before. It was found in the Czech Republic. A modern day professor discovered it on the banks of a river some 250 years ago and they think it also came in on a meteorite over there some 14 million years before. It was actually discovered a long way from the impact crater. Here, we're finding it at the crash site itself."

Wasn't he following in the footsteps of his father and Uncle Draco when they absconded with the gold? Now he's stealing the super-valuable moldavite. He wondered whether he would have taken it, if they *had* reported their gold. *Well, there's no crime if nobody ever finds out something is missing*, he thought. When he finished contemplating, he concluded that he would have to live with the guilt of not telling Al-Yamani about the mineral, only about the platinum. He would lie by omission.

He said, "Back to the platinum, I haven't personally mined it, but I'm seen videos about platinum mining. It's a classic deep mining operation. They drop a shaft down a couple of thousand feet and every sixty feet or so blast horizontal tunnels, sometimes miles long. They can crisscross to look like an ant farm when they're finished with all the drifts and their branches. If some people have their way, the mountain where we're at will be torn into sideways and from the top down. If that happens, Naidvar will be victim to the southern storms that come up from China, especially during monsoon season down there."

"What will happen to all the flowers? I mean, come on," she said, as though, he personally had the power to make the decision.

David hated to do it, but he had to steel himself, in order to give his wife the bad news, "I'll tell you what to expect. You'll see a huge hole in the ground where the flowers are. Peace and quiet will be replaced by heavy machinery that will be coming and going. The level of airborne dust would destroy the entire Biolab operation.

"Somehow, thousands of tons of dirt will have to be carted out of here for processing to get a single pound of the ore. The streams on the other side of this mountain are likely to yield alluvial particles of platinum, along with copper and silver in the sand and gravel that washed down from the mountain.

"About 80% of the world's platinum comes from South Africa with another 15% from Russia. The remaining is divvied up between Alaska, Montana, Australia, Canada, California, and a few other minor locales. Now we can add Mongolia to the list. This is a huge find that should leapfrog this country into the list of major players. The decision to do that is above my pay grade."

Anna started to say something, only to get interrupted. "It gets worse. The Biolab cannot survive with the airborne dust level from the operation. Witness what just happened with a single storm. We would be facing fine dust on everything on a daily basis. It's one or the other.

"For every ten gold mines, there is a single platinum mine. Plus, it is an incredibly complex process to separate the ore from the metals it is usually bound with. In short, this could be a huge complicated deal. With this find, it's possible that somebody could make hundreds of millions. The gems are another story. Remember, what we're all doing here is basically altruistic, platinum mining is not."

Anna shuddered when she pictured bulldozers and explosives tearing into the earth, gouging deep dark holes to pull out the ore, destroying the beauty of the golden poppies and the integrity of the entire crater. The place would devolve into another mining camp. "What do you want to do? Who are you going to tell?"

"I'm going to call the man who assigned me to take care of this place. For now, I'll shovel the dirt back into the hole. If asked, we'll say you were having a lesson in machinery operation, that's why we're here," he concluded. "No lies there."

"What are you going to tell him about the moldavite? What are you going to tell Batu and Gerel?" Anna asked, hoping he would say the right thing.

"Let me worry about that," he said.

"You don't even trust our best friends to keep quiet?" she inquired, seriously puzzled.

"It has nothing to do with trust. It has to do with saying the wrong thing at the wrong time without thinking. It's like a criminal having to tell someone about his crime, because the mind has to share critical information, like a pressure release valve. It's human nature."

Even as he said that, he wondered how he would inform Al-Yamani, who had a big stake in the operation, the man who had trusted him enough to put him in charge. He immediately came upon a solution.

He explained further, "Everybody's heard about Sutter's Mill back in California in the gold rush days of 1849. The back story is this: Sutter was a dirt poor immigrant who wanted to start a wood-working mill. He hired a man to assist him. The man discovered gold in a near-by stream tied to the Sacramento River. Both men swore to secrecy with the best intentions, but one of them opened his mouth. He was most likely drinking at the time. The following year, some 50,000 would-be miners flooded into the area followed by another quarter million. The men lost everything. Loose lips sink ships."

"Do you think your platinum discovery has anything to do with the stolen vial or the red poison?" Anna inquired. She didn't see a connection, but had to ask.

"No," he said. "I don't think anybody knows

about it, except for you and me. According to Dr. Farmer, even the geologists who first mapped the crater weren't looking for ore. They were more concerned about geothermal heat and water availability. Which reminds me; when we get back, we'd better check and see if he called. I left my phone in the room and he won't use the Internet for this communique. I had asked him to do a little digging of his own and see what he could come up with about Tomo. First, though, I need to contact Germany."

Tugi had been chasing a rabbit and, hearing also the chirping of marmots warning of danger, was reluctant to join his masters. After several minutes, when he had killed and devoured most of the rabbit, he returned to them. "Tugi, look at yourself. We have got to wash off your face," Anna declared.

Anna thought about Tugi a lot and how her destiny seemed to be tied to his. She and her family couldn't pick up and move to another country and expect him to be happy getting crated onto an airplane to land in a big city airport somewhere. And then what? He wouldn't be the same after that; probably emotionally scarred. He would be fine for a short while with Gerel and Batu, if she and David went on vacation. Did that mean she would have to spend the next many years here in Mongolia to ensure her pet's happiness? And was he really happy, or would the call of the wild be too much for him.

He needed to be let loose more often outside the compound so that he could find a pack and a find mate to run with. His genes belonged to the wild wolf going back thousands of years and wouldn't be erased by a couple of years alongside a human. Those thoughts weighed upon her.

Once in their unit, David turned on the computer. It had an English language keyboard. Others throughout the small city had Cyrillic keyboards. He had decided to do a transliteration of Arabic by telling Al-Yamani what he found, but would use the English alphabet to spell the Arabic words. It wasn't foolproof, but would lend an element of security to the missive.

After he sent the letter, David checked his phone for messages and found one from Farmer that read, "Call me."

"It's Bob," he told her. "Have a seat."

He placed the call and the connection was immediate. "What's up?" David asked.

"Very interesting. I had to get into classified military files to get the information."

Before Farmer could go any further, David asked, "Is this line secure?"

"If it's not, let them make the next move. It might flush them out," came the reply.

Farmer went on, "Tomo's parents may have been listed as Mongolian, but his father was born in China of a Chinese father and Mongolian mother. There was a lot of that going on back in the day. You have to read a lot between the lines here, but from what I can piece together, before his own parents moved to Ulan Bator, young teenage Tomo was directed by his father to become a member of the Chinese Communist Party, which he did. That didn't last more than a couple of years, but it was enough to kick start certain attitudes in the lad. Some people think he was taught the ways of the world at home by his left-leaning father, before and after they moved here; that is, profess loyalty to Mongolia, but actualize loyalty to China. And like any good traitor, he kept his nose clean, got a solid education, earned trust, and moved up the social ladder. He's still moving up. Word has it he may run for vice president, if not president, in the next election."

"How in the hell was all that written down?" David asked, reinforcing his belief that if you ask the right question to the right person, you'll get a solid response.

"Because he had an old uncle who knew the family tree that goes back many generations, all herders, and the uncle had a fervent hatred for the Chinese . . . and the Russians, for that matter. He filed a report with the military when Tomo joined up to do his duty before he went to law school. Apparently, when he was in the service, thanks to the uncle's letter, he was watched carefully, but there were no red flags, until now. The uncle has since passed away, so all we have is the letter he wrote."

What a can of worms. David told Farmer about the incident with the red alga, the chase, the capture, and the subsequent confession by Bat-Erdene that only suggested Tomo had a finger in the pie.

Farmer said, "I'm sure we can both think of reasons why Tomo would turn against his own people, but getting hard evidence against him is going to be the challenge. Just watch your backs, both of you."

David opted not to contact Al-Yamani about Tomo until he had something worth presenting, although the man had invested a huge sum into the project and should know at some point. He looked at the problem from all perspectives and decided to wait before taking a chance, not wanting to set off false alarms. So far, two threats had been stopped. He could be certain there would be more. And then do what, beef up security? Even cameras wouldn't have stopped the last attack, because the inoculation of poison into Vat 54 occurred under perfectly normal circumstances. What direction would the next surprise come from? Furthermore, Tomo was above-board and supportive in every aspect, so what was going on? He did not like the way this was headed. Two lightweight attempts had failed. Something very nasty could be in the offing.

Al-Yamani coded the return email in the same transliterated Arabic. It basically told David to leave it alone (in reference to the platinum, without saying the word)) until further notice, and to direct his efforts toward biofuel production.

So be it. Pending hard evidence, the commander-in-chief of Groebels was out of the loop regarding any subterfuge and only three people knew of David's discovery. It was no skin off David's nose either way, but he knew his wife identified with the suffering people. That meant a lot to him. So did his drive to succeed. He had never known anything less.

Chapter 10

Preparing to go out for their usual morning breakfast, Anna asked, "Sweetheart, is it all right if I take the company car and Eric to see Shorni and Sandoval? I know we all talk occasionally, but it's not the same. Besides, I still have that Mahjong set I brought back for her. Lately, they've been pestering me to visit and he's too tied down with the mine to get loose."

"Now that you mention it, I've got a case of Stolichnaya Vodka I could bring if I'm invited," he said.

That struck a nerve in Anna. She blurted, "Really, I could use a good bender. How did you get that?"

"Black market, where else."

The statement didn't surprise Anna. Once a naive social butterfly ignorant about the ways of the world, she quickly came to understand that a good 90% of world commerce was based on subterfuge and one could purchase literally anything from baby formula to weapons of mass destruction given sufficient money and the proper contacts.

Not getting the reaction he anticipated, David corrected himself and said, "I had Bob bring it down. It's in storage along with the drone. Anyway, you can't go without me."

"What's the matter? Are you afraid Tugi and I can't take care of ourselves? I'll carry my gun," she teased.

"Can Tugi change a flat tire?" he inquired.

"Well, no."

"Can you?"

"Well, no. But I can call you if I get stuck," she replied, confidently, smugly.

"And how am I supposed to get there?"

She paused in her answer, "I know, you could take a golf cart," she answered defensively, in defeat.

"Why don't you call them? We'll have a good breakfast tomorrow morning and leave, say around 10:00 am."

Given another tragedy didn't occur during their absence for a few days, the family of four got on the open road, which in this case, was not the same as US I 10 or I 90. They took the roadway cautiously, always leery of marmot holes or piles of sand that might have accumulated in low spots in the unpaved open highway, ungraced by a single truck stop, ostrich farm, motel for the wayward traveled, or gas station.

Anna found the contrast between copses

of trees intermixed with occasional streams, scrub grass, occasional buttes, wild flowers, and blue cloudless sky eerily beautiful with distant low-lying hills adding a darker brown to the mix of colors. Occasional boulders dotted the landscape like large mushrooms springing up from the earth. Many of them had been moved to the side of the road they were on to clear the way.

Anna held up two hands to form a square between index fingers and thumbs to frame the view, then pulled out a new phone she had bought and asked David to stop so that she could take a couple of pictures. "I'm tired of bare walls and I don't want religious icons taking up one wall of our living room. I want some quality pictures to hang and I've got a bunch. I know of a couple of shops in Ulan Bator and Darkhan that can print them, once we're back to either place," she declared.

"What kind of pictures?" he asked.

"Oh, scenes like this, of Eric, and Tugi with a marmot in his mouth, and you sleeping with your mouth open," she responded.

"Why wait?" David suggested, fearful of asking more. "Download what you want to Sandoval's computer, go online to find the shops, email the photos, tell them the sizes you want, and have them delivered to Bob. He can bring them down on the next flight, framed and all. Here, I'll pull off to the side of the road."

"What road?"

"Good point," he said, pulling over to the right and stopped the car a few feet behind several low boulders.

In Mongolia, driving is to the right, however cars imported from Japan, such as Honda, Toyota, and Nissan, have right side steering wheels and controls. The Dodge followed American driving habits.

Anna giggled, her hair bouncing as she did so. She had long ago decided to keep it short. It was easier to wash and dry, not to mention, more stylish.

"What's so funny?" he asked.

She said, "I know there's no such thing, but it feels as though we are at the edge of the universe. We're surrounded by rabbits, marmots, wild wolves, no telephone poles as far as the eye can see, and we're going to use Internet and cell phones to have pictures sent electronically, all to be printed in vivid color and flown down to us. "

Although Tugi traveled well, he was delighted to be set free, while Anna took her photos. Eric played with piles of sand, walking from one to the next, discovering how the grains slipped through his fingers. They neither nor expected any vehicles during their trip to the mining camp southeast of Mandalgov. There was no auto club to call and one might need to wait for several hours, or even a day, for assistance by another driver, if a mishap should occur. When Anna considered this, she felt foolish for making light of the fact that she could go it alone.

David let Tugi run free while Anna took her pictures. Several minutes later, David chanced to see a cloud of dust coming along the road north of them and coming closer. Something about the approaching vehicle engaged his attention. A quarter- mile away, he could see a large truck of some kind, definitely one of great mass. It was as out of place in the majesty of the surrounds, as an ink blob in the middle of a neatly written letter.

David yelled, "Anna, call Tugi and get way off the road. Now!" David yelled.

She did so, but the wolf was beyond earshot, or was otherwise engaged in more important ac-tivities across the road. The vehicle sped closer moving to their side of the road on a collision course with the car. On instinct, David grabbed the weapon he had placed beneath the front seat and retreated to join his wife several yards away from the roadway while she yelled for her Tugi to come.

Finally, hearing her call, Tugi, ran toward them, just as the truck was upon them. It was a large cement mixer, with a rotating drum, weigh-ing a good 30 tons, capable of crushing anything in its path. Apparently seeing the boulders in front of the truck, the driver swerved back onto the roadway, just missing Tugi, who had turned on a sudden burst of speed. Instead of delivering death, he had narrowly escaped it.

David had seen enough. Taking deliberate aim at the left rear tires of the speeding truck, he loosed the entire magazine of 13 rounds and saw the vehicle swerve slightly, suggesting he had hit one or both of the duallys.

His first obligation was to his family to ensure their safety, although his initial impulse was to pursue the vehicle had he been alone.

Anna tried to calm a shaking dog, herself stupefied. "What happened, Davey? Did that driver try to hit us?" she asked.

"That's what it looked like to me," he replied.

"But why us?" Anna beseeched.

David put his arms around her and held her tightly for a long moment. Finally, he said, "It's over. Let's go."

Slowly, cautiously, the trio re-entered the car. David started the engine, trying to compute the enormity of what had just happened. He placed a fresh magazine in the weapon and put it back between them while Anna entered an escape realm. She plugged earbuds into her CD player, while Eric claimed to be hungry.

Driving in the open spaces without radio reception gave David a lot of time to think. He ruminated about the past years of his life. Ten years ago, he and his younger brother, Julian, his father, Uncle Draco and Aunt Ally, were in the middle of long stint in Arizona, the men blasting their way through a copper mine. Then they all got transferred to Morocco to head a phosphorous operation, while working an occasional job in Spain.

His mother sat on him and Julian like a 10-ton boulder to ensure they got a solid education. Now he spoke English, Arabic, Spanish, and some Mongolian. There wasn't a lot of call for the latter. Only 3 million people spoke it. And where was Julian now? After he got a degree in geology with a specialization in locating petroleum, Julian was hired by a company back home in New Zealand.

To him, the nomadic life could have been worse. He could have been part of a military family. At least this way, he stayed localized long enough to get educated and launch into a promising career.

"I see the gers," Anna announced, breaking David out of his hypnotic trance.

The mining camp had doubled in size since their last visit. He pulled in front of his host's ger right on schedule, which basically meant a three hour block of time, either way. He expected Sandoval to be at work when Shorni came out to greet them.

The couple decided to keep their conversation light until Sandoval came home to avoid having to tell the same stories twice. David wished he could have brought one of the new ceramic heaters and a five-gallon can of fuel, but what oil they had at the lab still had to be processed in Bayannur, China, a task necessary before it could be used, and the rest was in storage somewhere in UB. Anna did give Shorni the expensive Mahjong set, supposedly carved from bone obtained from an elephant graveyard.

Shorni doted over Eric while Anna completed preparations for dinner and David took Tugi out for a run. When Sandoval arrived, David presented him with the case of vodka and Sandoval immediately poured four glasses.

At that point, the couple recounted the problems at the lab, leaving out any mention of their limited, but rewarding, mining activities, also ensuring they never spoke out loud about it at home after their find. They concluded their tales by recounting their near death experience on the way there.

"The most likely explanation is that it was a drunk driver," Shorni contributed.

Sandoval shook his head. "Even drunk drivers don't deliberately try to kill someone."

"It's starting to look like we were targeted," David admitted.

Sandoval agreed, "Could be. Everybody knows the place will fall to shit if you're not leading the troops. With you out of the picture, or word get out that somebody is after you, workers may start to bail."

Grasping the enormity of the situation, Anna said, "Who knew we were coming here? Do you think our apartment is bugged?"

David said, "Good point. I'll talk to Farmer

and see if he knows how to check for hidden microphones."

Shorni suggested, "A big truck like that shouldn't be hard to find. After all, it was traveling north to south. There isn't much below Naidvar."

"I suppose we might be able to trace the owner once it shows up," David said. He added, "Got any 9 mm rounds you can spare? I'd like to take Anna out for some shooting." He looked over at her to receive a definite nod of the head giving the strong impression of someone who wanted to shoot something.

Sandoval answered, "Sure. I'll go with you and bring a 1000 rounds. That should hold us. I have a nice little range set up. Sounds like you're practicing up for something."

"You might say that," David agreed.

"No worries, Mate. I say, enough self-defense talk for one night. I suggest we all have another round of drink," Sandoval offered. He met with no resistance.

Chapter 11

The following day Anna put Eric in a make-shift backpack, placed a cap on his head, and went out with Shorni and Tugi for their usual walk, while David went to the mine with Sandoval to inspect the growing operation.

Later in the day, the entire group met in Sandoval's trailer/office where Anna sent off the photos she had selected for printing and David contacted Farmer.

In the evening, the two women sat beneath the stars and Anna pulled out the astronomy picture book where they identified constellations and relative star magnitudes.

Finally, they all played Mahjong to close out the evening with Anna promising herself to get back to the microbiology lab for some unfinished work.

The following afternoon Sandoval informed his guests of an email that had arrived for them. It was from Farmer, who wanted them to reply.

When David typed: **Information?**

Farmer replied: **We found your truck 30 miles south of where you are now. You're not the only one with a drone. There's no place to hide out there. Driver gone, one rear tire shredded. Probably got a ride back from someone. Truck stolen the night before from a construction company in UB.**

David paused to look at the others crowded around him in the small trailer and asked, "Is there anything else we need to ask him?"

Anna adjusted Eric on her hip and said, "Ask him about fingerprints."

David typed: **Fingerprints?**

Farmer replied: **This isn't a fast moving crime TV show. It's a long shot, but we're on it. It will take some time.**

David looked around, but received no further questions to ask. So far, Farmer had not provided any helpful information. Even if he had, it would not take away the feeling that, in all likelihood, David was being targeted, and if the rest of the family died with him, so be it. Their deaths would be listed as a tragic road accident. Those things happen every day.

The same evening, the two women went out early to stargaze. Shorni pulled out a couple of lawn chairs she had stowed next to the ger and covered both the chairs and themselves with blankets. The sun was setting. Darkness fell quickly when there were no city lights to obscure the stars. Their intent this evening was to star hop with the use of binoculars in order to find the Andromeda galaxy beneath Cassiopeia. Sandoval had bootlegged packets of Swiss Miss hot chocolate powder with marshmallows from somewhere. Shorni mixed them with hot milk and poured large portions into sippy cups now situated next to the binoculars on the ground between the women.

Relaxing and looking upward, watching the darkness descend, Anna said, Hey, Shorni, what's that?" She pointed.

Shorni said, "That's interesting. We don't normally get birds of prey this late in the day."

Anna picked up the binoculars and found the object. She followed it and zoomed closer, then picked up the Walkie Talkie next to her and called, "Davey, can you come out here and look at this?"

In a moment, both he and Sandoval were at her side. David held the binoculars for a few moments, then passed them to his friend, immediately pulling out his cell phone to text Farmer.

Bob, do you have any drones over where we are at the moment?"

The answer came back: **No. Why?**

Tell you in a minute, David returned.

"What's going on?" Gerel asked.

"Listen carefully. You can hear it," David remarked.

They did as he requested.

Keeping his eye on the sky, David explained, "That's a long range single engine gas powered model. It has us under surveillance. That's why it's circling. Right now, it's conserving fuel. I'm guessing it doesn't have infrared and will run out of anything to look at pretty soon."

At that moment, the drone stopped circling and headed off southward.

"Anna, hand me your compass, please," he requested.

Anna fumbled through her heavy clothing to recover her watch. David found the compass setting and was noting the direction of the object when his cell phone rang. Farmer's name came up on the Caller ID.

David explained what he had observed and answered his questions by saying he didn't know how long it was up there or how many days they had been surveilled. He provided him the compass directives after which Farmer remarked, "I'll see if we can get radar here to pick it up. I'll let you know."

"We seem to be getting a lot of attention," Anna snorted, curtly, as though it were his fault. "Can I please have the binos?"

On their way back indoors, David grinned and said, "Say, Sandoval, do you think you could you spare a couple of sticks of dynamite, some caps, and a little det cord?"

Without asking why he wanted the explosives, his friend jested, "Sure. Take all you want. I presume you're going to do a little more target practice."

"Something like that," David replied. *You're not the only one with a drone.* Farmer's words rang through his head.

Days later and once back home in Naidvar, David paid attention to the skies the morning after their return. He saw the same drone that had been spotted over the silver mine. Wasting no time he recovered his own from storage,. He checked the fuel lines for leaks, made certain the batteries were fully charged, inspected the overall integrity of the unit, lifted off, and led the other southeast at a higher altitude than it could achieve. Unable to keep pace, the intruder turned and circled back to its home base, showing no indication of being followed.

Each day David followed and watched. From altitude, he saw it fly into a small shed the size of a single car garage. In front of the shed stood a man with a controller. On one side of the shed was a generator in operation next to a pickup truck. An electrical cord led from the generator to beneath the hood of the truck, ostensibly to provide warmth to the engine during the cold nights. About 150 feet east of those stood a ger. David had seen a second man whom he presumed was inside at the times of his observations.

David watched their simple routine. Hunting for an hour each morning and afternoon, watching the transmission feed from their drone, cooking, and not much else.

He had done it many times with his father and Uncle Draco. He preferred the use of a plunger to send an electrical charge through the detonation cord which would ignite the explosive in the cap, which, in turn, would set off the nitroglycerine, sodium nitrate, and wood pulp within the stick. In this instance, a timer hooked to a good battery served to accomplish the same thing.

When the men went out hunting on the fourth afternoon, David made his move. He flew in low, keeping the ger, shed, and truck between him and the men. Using the VTOL to land as close as he dared behind the shed, he used the grabbers beneath the drone to lower three sticks of dynamite tied together to the ground along with the timer. Farmer was right. Hovering turned out to be a challenge, taking all of his dexterity to accomplish the task. He reversed course and, flying low for some time until he was far enough out of earshot, increased power to bring the machine upward to bring it home.

Ten minutes before midnight, David returned. Remaining at altitude to avoid noise detection, he watched the midnight explosion take out the shed that contained the drone, diesel fuel for the generator inside the shed, along with ample gasoline stores for the truck and the drone. The truck exploded a moment later putting the finishing touches to the generator. Debris flew hundreds of feet into the air, some of it landing on the ger, setting it on fire.

It took some time before the men could grab what clothing they could to clomp outside and run far enough away to watch the conflagration destroy everything, many miles from help.

After David parked the drone, he attempted to crawl into bed without waking his wife, when she asked, "Where did you go?"

"I'm tired. I'll tell you at breakfast," he replied. "Plan on going back to the mine tomorrow morning."

"Already?"

"You can stay here if you want," he offered.

"No way. What time do you want to leave for the mine?" she inquired.

"Let's sleep in. We'll leave at 9:00."

In the morning, at breakfast away from their residence, he told her the story, adding, "I'm going to check on the men before we go. If they haven't frozen to death, I'd like you and Tugi to come with me. I might need a translator."

Before leaving again, David flew the drone out to the site of the accident to see the men huddled by the side of the road, which was about a quarter-mile from where the explosions occurred. He returned to the apartment to find Anna and Tugi waiting. "Ready?"

Anna mumbled, "Never a dull moment."

"We'll take a couple of extra hot coffees with us."

Strapping on her weapon, Anna said, "Come on, Tugi, let's go for a ride."

Placing a gentle arm on David's arm, she said, "Wait a minute, Davey. If they were watching the mine and Naidvar, do you think they might recognize you?"

"I don't think I was outside long enough in either place for that to happen. Besides, who cares? We're running this show, not them. Best to leave Eric with Gerel for this trip."

Some 40 minutes later, they saw two men on the side of the road frantically waving for them to stop.

As a cruel tease, David drove past them, as though he hadn't noticed their waving arms, looped around, and with deliberate slowness, returned to where they stood. When he pulled next to the men, Anna rolled down her window. David pushed the button to roll down the rear window where Tugi could stick his head out.

"What happened?" Anna asked innocently, in English.

The men looked at each other, then back at Anna and somewhat fearfully at Tugi, not understanding. She repeated the question in Mongolian.

"Teyrïn cono," (wolf) one man whispered to the other.

"Our ger caught on fire. We lost our truck, too," answered one of the men, who stood some four inches taller than his partner.

"Really, that's terrible. Let's go see," she said, handing the men two cups of hot coffee they had brought. "We have some extra," she said, without going into explanation.

The men gratefully took the coffee and the five walked back to the site of the explosion. With Tugi on a leash, she listened to their story, as the shivering men eyed the wolf, hoping he wouldn't do more than sniff and growl. David sifted through the ruins to find parts of the drone. He found the burned license plate from the truck, saw it was a Chinese plate, threw it down and said nothing. Within moments, he held up a piece of propeller. "What's this?"

"We were playing with a flying machine," said the shorter man, which Anna translated.

"Playing how?" asked David.

"Only playing," said the taller man.

"All right," David answered, innocently. He walked away to make a call. Mandalgov had a cell phone tower and he hoped he was close enough to reach it. The call went through. Sandoval answered. He told his friend all that had happened and asked if Shorni could make a hot meal for some guests he would be bringing. He and Anna had already eaten.

"It will be our pleasure to honor them in our household and perhaps ask them a few questions; that is, if you, Anna, and Tugi, of course, would like to keep us company," Sandoval replied, with an emphasis on the dog's name.

An hour later, with the guests comfortably seated, eating, and warming in the ger with a well-used glass of vodka in front of each of them. Sandoval asked, "Where is your home?"

"We are from Bayannur," the taller one said.

"That's wonderful. My parents are from Beijing," Anna declared, in Mandarin.

The men's faces lit up and the three engaged in friendly conversation for several minutes, with occasional laughs. She explained to the others in English that their captives' Mandarin was street dialect; not upper class. Worse, their accents strongly suggested they had learned it as a second language, therefore, they were lying. She believed they were native Mongolian. Even so, she had wanted to engage in small talk to relax them and asked Sandoval if he had any questions. Shorni remained silent and played the dutiful wife, leaving control of the household to the man, until she decided to speak to them in her native tongue to ascertain their linguistic skills, or lack thereof. Soon enough, she confirmed their native Mongolian heritage.

David said to Sandoval in rapid-fire English, "These guys couldn't have had anything to do with the truck because they lost their communications before we came here. The only person who knew we were coming was Batu."

"Unless you said something about it in your home and it's bugged," Sandoval said.

Tugi laid head on paws, watching, waiting

for an order. The TV was off. A single soft 40 Watt light bulb glowed above the door.

The shorter man finished his drink, gave a slight burp out of courtesy to indicate he had enjoyed the offerings and said, "We were supposed to fly our machine here and into the round city to the south," he said.

"Why here? Why there?" Sandoval asked, taking his own drink, proving it wasn't poisoned. Friends drinking together.

The shorter man received a quick look from his partner, when he said, almost lightheartedly, "We were only following orders to watch both of you, but everything caught on fire"

Flabbergasted, a wave of emotions swept through Anna, from shock to embarrassment, to anger, to rage, until she recalled something her father had once told her: "Always smile in the face of adversity. There will plenty of time to cry later."

Anna laughed, "Why us? Why me? I'm nothing to you."

The bigger man said, "Not to us, to others. You're outsiders. We're told you don't belong here. You ask too many questions. We only follow orders," he repeated.

She'd had enough of being friendly. "Tugi, ready," she ordered.

Instantly, the wolf rose to its feet, looking first at her and then at the men. Six people and an animal froze in time. A flip-flop of emotions instantly occurred, from warm friends to bitter enemies. Good cop bad cop.

"Who sent you?" she spat, staring hard at the men. Tugi eagerly waited for a taste treat, awaiting the command to rip flesh.

Sandoval said, quickly, "Not in here, Anna. Take them outside. Remember all the blood the last time he tore up somebody."

Shorni blurted, angrily, staring at her husband, "Yes, and it took me days to clean up everything and to purify the home again."

The taller man said to Anna, as though he were passing the time of day, "We were told you both need to go away."

Go away? Anna felt fury beyond any emotion she had ever known. She was a citizen. She melded. She spoke the language and taught at their schools. She belonged. The man made her feel as though he had a vested interest in her demise. Well, she admitted to herself, maybe it's about time real passion went two ways.

"What do you want to do with them, Sandoval?" David asked, interrupting her thoughts.

"I going to load them in the back of the pickup and drive them over to Mandalgov. The people I know there will be interested in further interrogations."

"It'll be a cold ride," David added.

"Yeah."

Shorni felt dirty. These evil men had cast an evil omen inside her home. She would have to spend a considerable amount of time engaged in rituals to ensure the complete absence of their spirits. She announced those words out loud.

"No," Anna shouted, taking command. She was adamant, with fire in her words. At that she stood. "I'm going to take them outside and feed them to Tugi." The giant wolf stood, waiting a single command word.

"All right with me," Sandoval said, knowing he had lost control over Anna.

"Okay with me too," David added, knowing the same thing.

"Me, too," Shorni threw in, siding with Anna.

"Outside, both of you," Anna commanded. She opened the door to let in a blast of cold air. "Come, Tugi."

"You shouldn't tease the wolf," Sandoval said, in a way the men understood.

"Who's teasing," Anna blurted.

David knew she wasn't. The hard set of her jaw, the narrowing of her dark eyes, the throaty way she said the words, all sent a chill through him, along with a sense of pride. She had finally come into her own. She would have allowed Tugi to have his way, but for the fact they needed these men alive.

"Who gave the order?" Sandoval asked.

Fearfully, the men stood and the shorter one blurted. "The order came from somebody from the Mongolian Department of Interior. We don't know who. Our boss never told us."

"Who's your boss?" David asked.

Clearly feeling the drink after a day of thirst and starvation, the shorter man gave the name of his Chinese boss.

"What does he do down there?" Anna asked.

"He's the head of processing for the biofuel project," the man replied. "He's the one who was ordered to get rid of both of you, one way, or another."

Anna reflected on his words. At the same time, she reflected on those of Shorni. Suddenly, everything made sense. Bad omens are negated by the sign of the cross, by crossing ones fingers, by American Indians' concern for spirits. Omens were a need, a belief, something to provide comfort and sanity in the face of irrationality or the misunderstood.

When she evaluated her own life in those terms, the path made perfect sense. Upset the path and upset the spirits. One must escape from bad circumstances, not because of their outcome, but because the spirits will cast omens upon you, like smoke following a moving vehicle. It was easier for her to understand omens. She had no clue as to whether any of this related to gut feelings, 19th Century beliefs in cosmic teluric influences, or miasmic properties of the spring air, vague references to put blame on the universe.

She briefly pondered the differences in humans who followed their personal need for spirits, demons, gods, omens, beliefs, the occult, the need to identify with the bright side, the dark side, or the desperate need to worship. Finding herself in the midst of it, she made the decision not to pursue a vaporous line of thought.

Like a kite following the breeze, Anna attached herself to the ever flowing and all pervasive current of omens. After over-intellectualizing everything, she decided to omit all the folderol and follow common sense.

Let others decide whether these men should be tortured or eaten. She abstained from asking Tugi for his opinion.

Chapter 12

Anna still bemoaned her choice of giving up chemistry for social sciences. Her true skills lay in mathematics and she loved the analytical aspect of science. In that vein, she couldn't come up with a reason why something about this entire bio-diesel project bothered her. She couldn't argue about the altruistic motives, or the desire to move away from coal as much as possible for environmental and health purposes. Some little thought poked at her, like a bubble under pressure waiting to rise to the surface.

She ran the numbers through her head. Two full years of production-yields from ponds, versus number of vats, percentages of oil recovered, gallons vs. barrels, costs, Btu (British thermal units) per liter yield. She only needed a few more pieces of information. Going online, she compared the heat energy produced by coal compared to biofuel and heating oil, finding the latter two about equal. After mentally processing the data, she wrote it all down to show David.

By the time Anna had finished, she had pages of calculations detailing the amount of energy needed to heat all the gers in Ulan Bator for a year, in terms of tonnages of oil recovered from the algae produced over that time.

In her estimation, the fuel would have to be refilled in numerous containers for storage within or outside each ger, or perhaps supplied weekly in, say, a 15 gallon container. Unlike coal, however, biofuel is explosive. That fact, unto itself, could lead to unheard of problems such as explosions, fires, numerous deaths, and, as always, bad press. Fortunately, those issues did not directly concern them. Theirs revolved around production.

She also discovered something else. "Honey, can you look at something with me?" she asked, late one night, having gone over and revising her figures several times. She had put their son to sleep an hour before with Tugi laying by his bedside for protection. His vocabulary had increased so rapidly, it had become obvious the child was precocious.

David put down recent vat production reports to make space for Anna to seat herself next to him on the sofa. When she showed him the figures, he put a finger to his lips, as if to indicate silence, and said, "Honey, I don't want to look at this now. What I really want is some late night coffee and dessert." He nodded his head toward the door.

Anna picked up his cue and replied, "That's sounds wonderful. Let's go."

In the 24-hour commissary, each grabbed a cup of coffee from an urn and a warm jelly roll from beneath a lamp heater. Taking their seats, David spread out the papers she had given him while she explained the data. When he had finished, she said, "In summary we're 4% of where we need to be."

"That's all?" he asked. He had long suspected a problem, but spent most his time on management and overall production efficiency.

"Okay, maybe 5%," she said.

David stroked his recently trimmed beard to ruminate, "This place is supposed to be the end all."

"Given two full years of operation means that maybe 20 million gallons, or about half-a-million barrels of oil, plus or minus, are in storage somewhere. Even under the best of conditions, we could only produce a tiny fraction of what we need. Do you see any way Naidvar can increase production another 20-25-fold?"

David pondered and said, "No. And if whoever made the deal was approached, he might shrug and say that at least it's a guaranteed contract. Furthermore, Naidvar is supposed to be a trial run to see if the government can pull off the operation. Now that they can, I would assume they can scale up production elsewhere."

"Yeah, like where?" she asked. "Honey, first,

have you heard of any other sites being considered for the huge amount of oil we need; and second, were you able to separate the monies earned from the indoor vs. the outdoor operation?"

"No, again," he replied. "To my knowledge. there is nothing else being planned, otherwise I would have been told about it, or at least, should have been. I do know that the algae we get from the vats are shipped off to China separate from the ponds, because it's not mega-seaweed, but a single celled species, so it's processed differently. The whole arrangement sounds like a co-mingling of funds, the kind of thing that gets attorneys disbarred. I need more time with the paperwork."

David held up a finger, "Oh, small point. The cost of biofuel ranges from $140-$900 a barrel with most of it hovering around $350. Petroleum hovers around $100, or less."

Anna said, "It sells for that much? There must be a fortune wrapped up storage. A half-million barrels at $350 per barrel comes to a couple hundred million dollars. Maybe somebody should check to see if it's all there."

"Good point," David said. "We can ask Batu if he knows of someplace that will store that much fuel and if he has any thoughts on the subject."

"As much as I love him and Gerel, are we sure you want to let them know we might be onto something?" she asked, realizing how contrary it must sound when not long ago, she had chastised David for not wanting to tell them about the platinum discovery.

David suggested, "Let's wait before bringing them in on this. Bob is arriving in a few days. We'll talk to him first. When we do speak with them, we'll gently start talking about the amount we produce vs. the amount we need to see what they say."

The following evening, Anna's radio squawked. "Anna, where are you?"

"Gerel and I are out looking for Tugi," she said. "It's freaking freezing cold and windy. We have to find him."

"You've been gone for three hours," he told her. "I already picked up Eric from day care. Come on back."

Anna added, "We were taking our morning excursion outside the crater and you know how we let Tugi run free? Each time he goes farther and farther away and this time he didn't come back."

"Well, you'd better come home. A storm's coming in," he said.

"I know. The temperature must have dropped 50 degrees in the last half hour. I kid you not. We're in the car now. We have to find him," Anna said.

"Honey, he's a wild animal. He'll come back on his own. He knows the way. He also knows how to find shelter. Now come on back," he insisted.

"All right, all right," she moaned, resignedly.

Anna turned to Gerel and asked, "How is he supposed to get inside the buildings once he returns?" She wouldn't let it go.

Gerel responded gently, placing a hand on Anna's arm. "He'll find a spot out of the wind and curl up, just like when you found him. At home, the ground itself is warm."

Reluctantly, Anna turned the big car and slowly headed back to the crater, scanning the vast expanse of land surrounding them as she did so, wondering how she was ever going to sleep with visions of how she might have lost her first child.

She did not well sleep that night. Eric fussed, possibly missing his baby sitter, needing frequent diaper changes, while Anna tossed and turned, waiting for the morning light that wouldn't occur until 9:00 am. David took over the baby sitting duties at some early hour, permitting his wife to regain her own fitful sleep.

After checking the clock countless times during the night, Anna quietly slid out of bed at 6:15 am. Finding her husband and son asleep, she padded down the Berber-carpeted hallway in her pink fur-lined slippers and robe she had purchased from the company market. The dull sounds of TVs belonging to those who had just gotten off the graveyard shift served as background noise.

She reached the back door of the building where the howling wind could be heard, but not felt. Reluctantly, she opened the door to find her beloved Tugi, asleep, curled up in a manner that made her jealous of his comfort, except for the top shoulder that was gashed open three inches, with another wound to the hip, both decorated with congealed blood.

At that moment, she saw herself as a soft toy in a glass machine grabbed by mechanical arms to deposit her into an alternate universe with survival as their only common denominator.

She laughed out loud, tempted to vocalize the words an elderly citizen might say upon close examination: *Mirror Mirror on the Wall. What the hell went wrong?*

Chapter 13

Farmer held up two miniature transmitters. He said, "Everybody makes them. These two were made in China. I retrieved one from your bedroom lamp, the other from beneath your sofa. Good thing you went for late coffee."

The reality of the find strained Anna's credulity, not so much David. He'd had his suspicions, as did Sandoval. Somebody thought they were important enough to listen to, and probably record their conversations. He was more concerned about what they might have revealed during their discussions in the main living area. Anna was more concerned about what they had said while in bed. Of one thing both were certain. Neither had mentioned a word about the genetically mutated algae, or more recently, about the platinum, or the moldavite.

Anna suddenly said, "That explains the incident with the cement truck. When you got back home around 1:00 am after your midnight adventure, you said we were going to leave for the

mine in the morning and gave the time. Somebody heard that and had hours to prepare. As
you thought, the two Chinese guys apparently
had nothing to do with the incident."

David shrugged. "If nothing else, call it guilt
by association. I'm afraid I did not expect an attempt on our lives to occur, though." He said it
if it were an everyday occurrence, failing to hide
the concern in his voice. He continued, "Anyway, I think these guys know plenty. Maybe
we'll hear more after Sandoval's friends 'nego-
tiate' with them."

The conference room was frequently used by
administrative and educational personnel, shift
supervisors, scientists, and building managers.
This particular meeting turned out to be short.
Only David, Anna, Batu, Temujin, and Farmer
attended, after the room had been had swept for
bugs. Before Farmer began the sweep, Temujin
told him the last place he would talk about his
secret would be in that room.

Farmer said, "I have a friend in the DoD in
the U.S. who knows somebody in the Ministry
of Defense who has worked with us on several
occasions. It makes for good international relations. I did this without the knowledge of Tomo.
It's not a big deal, but we needed the information about the location of the oil storage tanks."

David asked, "How did you get tied in with
defense so closely, might I ask?"

Farmer shrugged, "In another life, I worked for them—in a manner of speaking."

"You've had a lot of lives," David commented.

Farmer merely grunted. As soon as he connected his cell phone to a projector a picture came on the screen. He explained, "You're looking at where your purified biofuel is stored. These rows of petroleum oil storage tanks are what most everybody uses. In the foreground, a tanker truck is running a hose to the top of one of the tanks, ostensibly filling it. The tanks are white to reduce evaporation and condensation. The big ones here range from 200,000-400,000 gallons each. A float-gauge is inside the tank, much like the one in your car's gas tank to let you know how much is present. The float levels were added up here to give you a total of the amount you projected."

"So much for my theory," said, Anna, tired of it all. She started out as a teacher of English to foreign students, got married and gave birth to a son. Over a short time she had become involved in conspiracies, electronic surveillance devices, and attempted murders. Was there nobody to take the bull by the horns?

Understanding her look of frustration, Farmer had to answer truthfully, "I'm not certain you have a case here against anybody for any wrongdoing. It looks like a dead end."

David said, "Thanks Bob. Somebody help

me here. If Naidvar is a proof-of-concept experiment and that concept has been proven, why aren't other facilities being constructed for production? According to Anna's figures, which I agree with, we need to produce more than 20 times what we do now just to stay even, but from what I can find out, nothing is in the works. Hell, for another five million, we could build our own processing plant and not ship anything down to China. The amount we'd save in overhead would pay for itself in nothing flat and we'd be completely independent. Why rely on them at all?"

Batu asked, "Did you speak with Tomo about this?"

David nodded in the affirmative. "Yes, I did. He told me the political process is slow. This is not a dictatorship. Once the various committees are satisfied with the information we supply, they will make their decision."

"Утга учиргүй, хий хоосон," exclaimed Temujin, the equivalent of "That's bullshit." All eyes turned to him. Only Anna laughed, understanding the strong Mongolian epithet for 'words meant to deceive'.

"Which part?" Batu asked.

"All of it," Temujin stated emphatically, and abruptly left the room.

Chapter 14

Anna left Tugi at home when Farmer flew her back to UB, with David's misgivings. This wasn't about confronting a stylist about a bad hair job, this was thanking a man who had given her and the program she represented national attention. It was also about stirring up the muck to see what crawled out. Of those who knew of her journey, only Gerel supported her. As an employee of Groebels, Anna felt she needed to play the role of investigative reporter.

As for Temujin, although the scientist had never met Tomo, he disliked the man with a passion, if only because his name kept popping up whenever there was trouble, the classic definition of a bad omen. Similar to people of other nations, athletes everywhere, and especially American baseball players, Mongolians were superstitious. Despite Tomo's reportedly smooth façade, some people are a magnet for bad luck. Stay away unless you covet their bad vibes like a vacuum sucks in air. Woe be your life after that. Had he been told about the escapade with the cement truck and the Chinese men who had been tracking Anna's movements, never mind their Bayannur connection, he would have disliked him even more.

Temujin held the unheralded bragging rights for creating rapid-algal growth in both outdoor and indoor facilities. This included two different species, one single-celled, and the other related to seaweed. They were his brainchildren. He'd be damned if somebody was going to ruin his work. Only he knew that his students back home had taken his mutant DNA snippets a step further. At any time he could double or triple their present production rate, but he'd steadfastly refused tell a single soul until this whole mess got sorted out.

For a brief instant, he thought about selling exclusive rights to the highest bidder. It would mean a vast fortune could be his and the world would be a better place; or would it? Rapid growth algae controlled by a single entity would drive up costs for every component squeezed out of the life forms, thus limiting the number of people who could enjoy the benefits.

No, he was a loyalist. If anybody was to reap the benefits, it should be Mongolia. *Should* being the operative word. He'd have to wait until events played out before making a final decision. If the bottom fell out here, he'd have to find an alternate solution, which might include

David and Anna, both of whom he trusted. Despite their ties to Groebels and its shareholders, the CEO did invest in the creation of Naidvar.

If Anna had learned anything from Tugi, it was how to either stand down and wait for further instructions, or immediately go for the meat. In this case, she, alone, would represent the wolf pack. Prepped in private by David, then on the plane ride up by Farmer, she managed to overcome the fear of confrontation to gain a measure of confidence.

Tomo, impeccably dressed, as always, beamed a smile across the desk at the woman. If anything, she appeared more radiant than ever, eschewing the highly colorful tribal wear for a green print collared coat over black slacks.

"What a pleasant surprise, Anna. I heard you got married and have a new son, as well. Congratulations. What brings you here? Please, let me offer you some tea." He made a quick call on his intercom.

Anna took the proffered seat and in a few moments, a woman brought in a tea pot with two cups. She poured a cup for each and quietly departed.

Anna politely took a sip. She began, "For one thing, I wanted to visit the school where I first taught before getting transferred to Darkhan." (She had done so prior to her visit to Tomo's office. She had also contacted Jim and Connie, her old instructors, who had moved back to UB and spent a day with them, getting congratulated on her teaching award while spending the evening at their home before retiring to the hotel. She assisted in the cooking, and, speaking in their native tongue, told them of her work, her family, and the project at Naidvar, leaving out any suggestion of ill adventures.)

"For another?" Tomo asked, politely.

"Look, Anandyn, you have done so much for me I can't thank you enough. I came to see you because I need some advice."

Tomo gave a slight frown. "I'm listening."

"I dearly love David and he is doing a great job managing the program down there. Everyone knows how well he organizes, how efficient he is."

"But . . . "

"The problem is, he's developing conspiracy theories, like somebody is after their secrets and somebody is out to get him."

"Get him for what?" Tomo prompted.

"Oh, for example, we were on the highway going to visit a mine—you know he has a mining background —in the Mandalgov area, and some drunk driver almost ran into us. He thinks it was an attack directed at him. Our baby was with us, for God's sake. You have a family, don't you? You can understand." Anna held back genuine tears.

"Of course. That's terrible. Good fortune

smiled upon you that day and for all of us. You're the face of this program. We can't let anything happen to you. Go on," Tomo said, showing genuine compassion, caught up her monologue. Evaluating.

"It was a big cement truck from somewhere. It got away. As for the rest of it, he wants to keep me out of it. He says it's safer that way."

"Safer? You were in the car with him when it happened," Tomo stated, puzzled at the logic. "All right, anything else?"

Anna composed herself. "Also, somebody tried to steal a container of something that had a secret formula in it."

Brought out of his doldrums, Tomo asked, "Did they get it?"

"David told me 'no'."

"What kind of container? Help me to understand," Tomo requested. To him, pieces were missing from the story.

"He wouldn't tell me that either, other than it was a small vial and I might had have taken it with me by mistake when I returned back to my teaching before I joined them full time."

Tomo settled himself, "That makes no sense. Anything else, my dear?"

Anna leaned forward, in preparation for home school advantage at an away game, "Yes, he didn't say it in so many words, but I think he's bringing your office or your department into these crazy episodes."

Tomo shot upright. "Me, or my department? There's a big difference." His emotions were swinging back and forth.

"No, no, definitely not you. David considers you to be one of the good guys. He thinks of you as a king. He thinks there's a leak somewhere and maybe somebody in your employ is trying to undercut you and maybe do you harm. He also thinks they will try again to ruin your efforts to make a better city. He's confused. Like I said before, I need some personal advice."

Tomo leaned back in his chair, relaxed, nonchalant, confident, comfortable with her words, thinking. A moment later, he scribbled onto a small piece of notepad paper and handed it to her. "This is my cell number. Please understand, I don't want to cause problems between you and David. I do appreciate your confiding in me. How do I put this delicately? Perhaps, if you don't mind, you can call me for a private conversation, if anything else occurs that you think I should know about." He emphasized the word *private*.

Anna smiled and nodded. "Thank you. You can be assured it will be between us. If there's a spy running around in our network, I'll let you know and keep you up on the latest developments."

"I will do the same here," Tomo said, standing to end the conversation. "By the way," he added, "how did you get up here from Naidvar?"

"I caught one of the planes that frequent Ulan Bator," she said truthfully.

"How are you going back?" he asked.

"David arranged for a Cessna to take me," she replied.

Tomo rolled his chair back to the draped window to pull the cord revealing a dust storm in progress. "Looks like you might have to wait a few days. Where are you staying?"

"Edelweiss Art Hotel," she replied.

Tomo raised his eyebrows in surprise. He expected her to mention something in the $20 range. She had come a long way. He offered, "I'll have one of my people drive you."

Although Anna wasn't totally satisfied with her performance, at least she had given Tomo a few things to think about. As planned, she stayed away from the topics of bookkeeping, processing oil in Bayannur, drones using explosives against Chinese spies, and storage tanks holding a king's ransom in biofuel.

With the storm in progress, it went unsaid communications would be down. Had she been able to contact David, she would have learned that Tugi had disappeared.

Chapter 15

"The storm came up so fast it caught me by surprise," Gerel explained. She looked as though she were about to cry. "We were out for our walk-hunting session. Tugi decided to go into the woods like he does sometimes, when the next thing you know, I couldn't see a thing. I waited for a long time before I had to drive back. I was afraid the storm would bury the car if I didn't leave. That was four days ago and yes, I check around the outside of the buildings every day, including the back of ours."

Anna felt sick. She held her arm tightly around her friend's shoulder and said, "Tugi can take care of himself. I'm sure he's very happy where he is."

Batu said, "Nobody blames you. If it didn't happen to you, it would have happened to Anna had she been here. Then you'd be putting your arm around her shoulder."

The four sat at the table while Gerel served. Eric sat in his booster chair. David said, "The floor is all yours, babe."

Anna explained about her meeting with Tomo and all that had transpired. She had done her part. They had no choice but to go on with business as usual until another event occurred.

That event would come about when Farmer brought down copies of the last three years of ledgers detailing shipment, weights, and payments. Apparently Farmer was well-funded, because he didn't seem concerned that it cost him dearly in bribes to obtain the copies.

It didn't take long to find out at least one accountant was burying the indoor sales of algal oil within the sales of the overall yield to include the ponds, thus siphoning off a small fortune. A small percentage of a fortune is still a lot of money.

David ticked off points on his fingers. "The mass of algae is sent to Bayannur. The refined biofuel is then sent back to UB. That's under contract. The rest of the byproducts are supposed to be sold on the open market. They're not. In fact, there's a separate contract with China that gives them a discounted rate. Compared with their existing biofuel program, this is small potatoes to them, but it's a major loss of income for a dirt-poor country like Mongolia, unless, of course, they are paying more than the discounted rate off the books, but less than the going rate. This suggests that the balance of the money is going somewhere."

Anna nodded, "That sounds like Big Business 101. Aside from that, who is watching the accountants on our end?"

"And how much is Al-Yamani loosing?" David asserted.

A loyalist, and newly devoted company woman to the core, Anna pondered various scenarios. A moment later she said, "Let's play Devil's advocate. What if those tanks aren't really filled with our oil, but are filled with something else?"

"Holy shit. We need to find out," David declared.

"My sentiments exactly," Anna said.

Five sat in attendance in the conference room. David said, "Before we get started, I'd like to know how you got the samples?"

Farmer grinned. "I think we can all appreciate how the logic of third world countries differs from that of the Western world. If it were up to me, it would make sense to build a railroad spur from the main line to the storage tanks in order to transfer oil directly from one to the other. Instead, they choose to transfer from the train to a local tanker truck to make a second transfer. The truck driver is a poorly paid grunt. It was a no-brainer to get somebody to pose as a government representative who was ordered to collect a sample of the oil so the driver and his company could receive a commendation for their good work. We did that twice."

The American chemist held sheaf of papers in his hand and began, "David, we analyzed both samples of oil you gave us from two different tanker trucks. Neither of the new samples match what is presently in use. What you gave us has been cut with ethanol, maybe by as much at 20%."

"Which means?" Batu asked.

The chemist explained, "Biofuel can be mixed with hydrocarbons, such as gasoline, and kerosene. In the States, we add it to gasoline. Your miles per gallon go down because the car doesn't generate the same amount of heat energy, so you have use more gas to go the same distance. You get maybe 40% of the heat from ethanol than from biofuel. On the plus side, it burns cleaner with less pollution. It's also biodegradable."

Temujin said, "Which means that when we start using what is in the storage tanks, we may not get as much heat. Therefore, what is in the tanks is not as pure as what is currently in use."

"Correct," the American replied. "You will get plenty of heat. The question is, will it be enough?"

Temujin said, "We would have to begin the experiment all over again to see if the new mixture will be sufficient."

The American said, "I would expect it to *not* make that much difference. Remember, even the ethanol is now diluted by some 20%. However, from a scientific standpoint, I think we should do the experiment over again. It would be the right thing to do to be on the safe side."

Anna said, "We're not on a schedule. We might as well try to reorganize and restock the same gers we're using now with the diluted batch."

"How are you going to get it from the storage tanks?" David asked.

While the others pondered his question, David said, "Here's another issue. We're receiving the amount we expect to receive, except that it's diluted. I'd like to know what happened to the 20% that's missing. Did the people in Bayannur take the original oil and add ethanol to it in order to give us more than we bargained for just to be good guys? I think not. My guess is that somebody sold the 20%."

Anna mentally calculated and said, "At a half-million barrels in storage and with 20% missing, that would mean 100,000 barrels are somewhere. At a minimum value of $350 per barrel, the total loss comes to $35 million dollars, if not a lot more."

At her words, everyone looked at everyone else knowing they were in over their heads. David didn't have the connections or the resources to conduct a proper investigation without provoking a government scandal. He wouldn't get to first base, once the slightest hint came out that he might open up that Pandora's Box. The biofuel project would come to an abrupt halt and might not begin again for many years, if ever.

"I'm open to suggestions," he offered, presenting a casual air.

The American said, "I'm a chemist because I like chemistry. I'll leave those decisions to minds greater than mine."

David said, "We have evidence, supposition, and innuendos. Where is the hard proof? We have thieves and supposed plots. We all know something stinks. What is the source?"

He thought, with a sense of impending doom, *Al-Yamani is going to throw me to the wolves, if I he finds out I blew up this project. The man can be endearing until you fuck him, either on purpose, or accidentally,*

Chapter 16

David's cell rang. The caller ID read Sandoval. He picked up.

"David here," he said, not in the best of moods. He would prefer to be blowing holes in mine tunnels at the present moment or sticking a dynamite stick in a location of his choice.

"I've got some information for you from our two Chinese friends," came the reply.

"Anything you can give us will help. This thing is getting deeper all the time," David said. The tone of his voice carried his concern.

"These two are hard-liners. They're not the grunts they pretended to be. It took some work to pry loose what we needed," Sandoval teased.

"One of them seemed ready to talk," as I recall.

"Oh, that. He had a bad experience with a rabid dog when he was a kid. It bit his younger brother, who died an unpleasant death. The authorities here in Mandalgov had a special incentive to loosen their tongues. These two won't be operating with all their faculties henceforth."

David suggested, not without a trace of diabolical humor, "As in a substantial pay bonus on the side to aid in the incentives of the interviewers?"

Sandoval chuckled, "Works every time. While we're on the subject, does the name Bat-Erdene mean anything to you?"

Surprised at the name, David explained that Bat-Erdene was presently under house arrest. He related what Batu had told about his former friend, and how they discovered he was implicated in the poisoning of the vat. He concluded by explaining their findings about the dilution of the biofuel and the missing oil.

Sandoval listened intently and said, "Our informants don't know Tomo's background. They do know he is the one who told them to surveil Anna and to let him know her whereabouts. They think he's the brains behind everything that is going on, although they're not 100% certain. If there is money or oil missing, or whatever, you might want to dig into his banking procedures. In fact, our friends tell us Bat-Erdene was the Mongolian equivalent of the county comptroller otherwise known as auditor general. That was when he contacted Batu for a job. Oh, Tomo is somehow related to the guy who is running the processing plant in Bayannur. If you want, I can bring down a couple of guys who wouldn't mind making extra pocket change to talk with your prisoner. We might need an isolated place for that, though."

"I don't get it. I can see the money part. Why Anna?"

"Hell, I don't know. Maybe he hates women. Ask your guy," Sandoval said.

"I'll definitely take that under advisement and let you know. I want to see if we can get some background on him first, then I'll give you a call."

"Sounds good. You owe me another case of vodka for this," Sandoval teased.

"Only if you share."

"Damn, there's always a catch," Sandoval groused.

Chapter 17

Only a few evenings later, Anna, dressed in jeans, white sneakers, and a short-sleeve green and red floral blouse, left the apartment to walk the hall to check the rear door stoop, again. There she saw her precious Tugi. He looked up from his curled position when she opened the door and stood, wagging his tail. The couple greeted in their own way, the animal dutifully following his master back home.

Eric had not yet retired for the night and lay on the sofa in his father's arms getting read a Mother Goose bedtime story when Anna led his best friend in the door. The child immediately scrambled from his father's lap. His vocabulary embraced the words "Tugi, you're home," which he repeated with delight, running over to the animal, to receive slobbering kisses.

The dog appeared leaner, with no evident wounds, the old ones barely visible. Anna found a large portion of uncooked and uncut meat in the refrigerator. She cut it into portions she thought might be suitable, musing all the while that the portion size was her concern, not his. She opened a lower kitchen cabinet, pulled out his old bowl, and placed handfuls of meat into it, then put the bowl on the floor. He immediately devoured the meat along with a second portion, ensured the bowl was sufficiently licked clean, then drank a copious amount of water from a second bowl Anna had placed next to the first.

David watched the scene unfold before he, too, welcomed the guest, who licked hand with delight. David spoke to him gently in welcoming gentle terms, watching the tale wag more; males bonding. Now sated, Tugi took time to sniff the air always rife with the scents of foods being prepared in other units by those who worked various shifts and who preferred their own foods to those served in the commissary. Typically, the scents of sage, basil, fennel, marjoram, thyme, and onion permeated the airways of the building to a greater or lesser extent, spices used for virtually all varieties of meat dishes. Indeed, going back to biblical times, much of the world's spice trade ran through the area now known as Mongolia.

David, dressed in his own jeans, T-shirt, and sneakers, opened the door at the knock to greet Batu and Gerel. Tugi immediately went to Batu looking for his usual treat. Surprised to see the dog's presence, both guests traded greetings with the animal, while Anna surreptitiously slipped a treat into Batu's hand, who gave it to the animal.

Too excited to go to bed, Eric insisted on staying up to play with Tugi while the adults talked. David kept a close eye on the playmates. The pet had been gone for some time and might not be as domesticated, as much as they might like to think.

After the guest had taken their seats on the sofa and holding their proffered drinks, David and Anna sat in two cushioned table chairs.

David opened the conversation by saying, "This mystery has too many moving parts."

Batu asked, "How can stealing something have a lot of moving parts?"

Anna laughed, "David isn't talking about stealing. He means there are a lot of other things going on at the same time, sort of like a machine."

"Oh. You people and your endless idioms," Batu complained, slapping his forehead lightly in mock frustration.

"Like you don't have any. Right? Anna retorted.

"Of course. At least ours make sense," Batu came back.

Anna laughed. "You're thinking of a proverb."

"What's the difference?" Gerel inquired.

Anna explained, "An idiom is specific to a particular culture or a group. If I said 'you are talking goat' it would mean you are an argumentative person in Mongolian society, or 'a beauty cannot give you milk tea', it's your way of saying you cannot tell a book by its cover. One of ours is, 'You can't put lipstick on a pig.' If I said, 'A man fails seven times and rises eight times', this is a Mongolian proverb everybody can understand. Another example, 'He who drinks, dies; he who does not drink, dies as well'."

David swung his crossed leg in restlessness. He was not in the mood for casual banter. He had called for a business meeting. Interrupting, he said, "Look, guys, I'll keep it simple. Going back to my original statement, this puzzle has a lot of pieces and they all seem to be moving.

"We know Bat-Erdene coerced someone to poison the vat. Maybe he is responsible for the theft of the vial and he may be possibly tied to other actions. He worked as the head of financial services for the county before Batu hired him to come down here to do the same job. We have a possible issue with a fortune in missing oil. I don't understand a lot of it."

Gerel offered, "Greed is an incurable disease. It knows no bounds and eats away at the soul. Are you saying we need more evidence for everything?"

David shook his head. "Yes, and where is the missing oil, assuming all the storage tanks are diluted? And why would Bat-Erdene try to sabotage the program by trying to poison a vat? I can see him trying to steal the vial so they, or somebody, can copy our success. But why is somebody trying to stop a program when they're making a fortune?"Caught up in the flow, Anna queried, "Maybe more than one person or faction is involved and they're working at cross-purposes."

David said, "There has to be duplicate set of books somewhere."

"If Tomo is involved, why ruin your source of income when you have plans to run for the presidency?" Batu stated, flatly. "I'd leave him out of it."

Anna conjectured, "Unless there is already enough money in the bank to cover what you just said."

"Overall, I see nothing wrong with the program, in general," Gerel offered.

"No argument there, David threw in. "This whole mess is what Americans call a Chinese Fire Drill, or a three ring circus without the rings."

Literate in the English language as they were, their guests looked at one another, stupefied. Neither had been to a ringed circus or knew the meaning of a fire drill as pertains to the Chinese.

David saw his lapse in judgement in speaking in the vernacular and said, "We need more information. I'll leave it at that."

"I'm thinking about taking a shortcut," David said, after the guests had departed. He had caught himself blabbing too much and forced himself to put the brakes on. At this point everybody could be a suspect and if he didn't trust his friends with news about the ore find, why should he compromise himself by telling them everything on his mind so they could tell others?

"I'm listening," Anna said, with a suspicious sidewise glance at her husband.

This time David nodded. "Two possibilities come to mind. I have an offer from someone to drive down here to pick up our prisoner and take him to a secure location over in Mandalgov for a little chat in a soundproof room. It'll cost me, though."

He thought about acquiring a case of the best Russian vodka, but at least Sandoval would share. He might leave his wife at home on that occasion. From what he'd seen, she might outdrink them both, like the beginning portion of Raiders of the Lost Ark when Harrison Ford's future partner in adventure is seen drinking enough shots in her own Himalayan bar to put her contestant under the table. He tried to ignore the fact that the bar caught fire afterward.

Anna gazed off into space for a moment before saying to David, "Before you do anything, dear, I have couple of ideas. First, let's go online."

Chapter 18

It didn't take Anna long to find what she was looking for. Several past articles lauded the democracy of Mongolia, exemplified by Anandyn Tomo. His lineage was that of generations of sheepherders, yet he 'earned' the right to attend Harvard School of Law in Boston, Massachusetts, USA, and who now served as Minister of the Interior.

The second piece of information proved to be just as valuable. Under Tomo's direction, he brought the vast Table Top strip mining operation to full operational mode, after he had secured a joint operation with China, an operation worth many millions to his native country.

The next morning, David put his cell on SPEAKER, while he spoke with Farmer, who said, "You're not going to get any information from Harvard about his finances. Those are locked. You might need a presidential order for that. Besides, they would only show he was good for the money. They don't care where it came from. If that were the case, the school might close tomorrow. Hell, I can think of one or more past American presidents and scores of politicians worldwide who wouldn't have made it in."

"Including rulers of other countries, no doubt," Anna added, sarcastically, thinking about their present circumstance. "Let's see if we can find out where the money came from." She mumbled, almost rhetorically, her senses probing the ever flowing vaporous current of her feelings.

Not wanting to bother Gerel, Anna put Eric in daycare. The couple donned heavy coats and scarfs, led the prisoner, wearing only a bathrobe and house slippers, outdoors. It was still dark, with only the stars as witness to the procession. "Careful, don't let your crutch slip on the ice," David advised, sliding open the door to the large storage shed. He pushed their captor inside.

Anna held Tugi's leash tightly, although she dearly wanted to let him finish the job. It might happen before the evening came to an end. David hit the switch to turn on a single 1000 watt spotlight to illuminate the tractor, drone, band-saws, drill presses, and a score of hand tools from rakes to shovels to trowels, all neatly parked. The drone lay in its own corner niche.

David saw Bat-Erdene looking at the drone. When he looked back, David winked.

No chairs were present. The couple stood

with their backs to the light. The prisoner faced it.

"You may not be able to sleep after this, baby," David said, without concern for silence.

Anna replied, smugly, "On the contrary, I should be able to sleep better than ever after we watch Tugi do what he does best." She was weary of the intrigue. She was fed up with the attacks against her person and her reputation. She was a citizen. What happened to crimes against the state, should an attack against her be made, as Tomo had once said?

Local rumor had it that it is better to be tortured by a man than a woman. When the man gets what information he seeks, he will either kill you or let you go, while a woman will continue with the torture even after gaining the information. Anna took over. She said, "Bat-Erdene, you live at 362 Baatar Ulaan Street, right?"

The prisoner nodded, shivering, his eyes shifting from Anna to Tugi. The immediate future looked glum.

"Yes. We know that's where your wife and children are right at this moment. Who ordered you to poison the vat? We want a name. We have ample evidence to prove in court that you and Tomo are in this together. You're everybody's accountant. Where is your duplicate set of books, the set that details the amount of stolen oil? Tell us what you know and maybe you'll live. On the other hand, we can guarantee abject poverty for your family. They are already shamed by your behavior. Both shamed and destitute at the same time is a bad combination. If you refuse to talk, we will leave you and Tugi alone together."

Cold frost issued from her mouth when she said, resignedly, "What the hell. I might as well do that anyway, whether you tell us or not. That's the mood I'm in." She remembered about how some countries torture suspects, then let them return home to think about what they went through before any interrogation began. She was already in a foul mood. The welfare of an entire country was at stake she didn't need permission from anyone and wasn't about to let anybody talk her out of it. All the signs were aligned. *Why not?* She thought, making up her mind.

"Tugi, attack," Anna commanded.

Like a Jack in the Box, the dog shot forward, his teeth ripping into Bat-Erdene's left arm, before he had a chance at any self-defense, easily biting through the robe. The hapless victim shrieked and flew back against the wall of the shed, blood soaking through the robe, dripping onto the concrete floor of the shed. David smiled, not surprised.

"Tugi stop," Anna commanded, pulling back on the leash.

"Don't pull him back, now, let him go for it all," David said. In his view, she needed the experience, if they were to be a team.

"Who stole the vial?" Anna shouted.

"What vial? I don't know anything about any vial. I swear," Bat-Erdene cried. "Look, Tomo told me I could have a percentage of the profits. He wanted all the money he could get."

"Where do you keep your duplicate books?" she inquired.

The wounded man knew the game had ended. He was dead meat either figuratively or literally. He was hoping it would be the former. "The books for Naidvar are locked in the lower drawer of my desk with the key in the top drawer. The books for the oil are in the same location in my home."

David immediately made a call.

"Next question. Where is all the money? Not just what you stole from us with the sale of the oil, but also from the coal strip mining operation, and how much is it? Anna demanded."

Bat-Erdene looked surprised that she understood the extent of the graft. He had no choice. "It's all buried within the Table Top account in the National Bank of Mongolia," he answered.

"Account number?" David demanded.

Bat-Erdene told her. Anna recorded it on her phone. "How much is in there and who has access to it?"

"There's $120 million in the account for our share, some $37 from the oil and the rest from the coal."

"Keep going. How much has he paid you?" she insisted.

"Around $3 million so far," the captive replied.

"Bank and account number?" Anna demanded.

Bat-Erdene watched Tugi begin to lick the blood dripping onto the concrete slab of the shed floor, now mixed with the pee of the prisoner. He supplied the information.

"Once Tomo is indicted, that money will be returned to the national treasury, don't you think?" Anna asked her husband.

"If it's within our power," David replied. The way things were going, he could only hope. The corruption usually starts at the top.

"Who put the transmitters in our house?" Anna used a local term to mean dwelling.

"I did," confessed the condemned.

"Nice confession. Where did you place them?"

"One beneath the bed and one beneath the sofa," came the reply.

"Who gave them to you and ordered you do that?"

"You know who."

"Tugi ready."

"No, no. Tomo, it was all him." Bat-Erdene was a broken man, a dying plant torn up by the roots. Rubbing the tears from his eyes and the snot from his nose, he said, "I swear I don't know where he got them from. I'm so sorry."

Anna spat, "Yeah, I know. Everybody is sorry after they get caught. Do you give a damn about the false hopes you gave to millions and the suffering you permit them to endure because all you want is money? You disgust me." She didn't give a damn about his feelings, her sense of humanity coming to the fore. In her mind, now that they had beaten the slithering tail of the snake, the time had come to crush the head.

"What is Tomo's relationship to the Chinese guy who runs the oil processing in plant in Bayannur?" David inquired.

"They're related. The guy is Tomo's uncle. His father had two brothers," said the prisoner.

"What's the name of the guy who is running the plant in Bayannur?"

After hearing it, David remarked, "That sounds like a Chinese name."

Anna said, "A lot of natives living in Inner Mongolia have Chinese names. That doesn't change anything except to say this whole thing looks like a family enterprise."

Chapter 19

David scratched his head with one hand and scratched Tugi's ears with the other. "How did you figure it out? Every time I tried to wrap my head around the issues, one morphed into the next."

"Same here," Batu said, patting his wet lips with a napkin in an entirely Western fashion.

Anna said, "It was the only thing that made sense, the common denominator that encompassed all the parameters. Tomo wanted to maintain the appearance of being a good guy by making the China deal—the public didn't need to know the details—and he wanted to be absolutely above-board with the Naidvar project; support for me, TV, the promotion of experimental gers, development of the ceramic oil delivery system, the whole thing. I'm starting think that my Teacher of the Year award was a sham too.

"He needed money to plaster the country with his picture and pay top dollar for TV ads when it came time for him to run for president. He already had a deal going with China to sell them the best grade of coal we had, with them getting most of the ore. He didn't care if the trash went to his own people. Greed is a self-perpetuating disease.

"He was backed by the Chinese all the way. They wanted their boy in the presidency to repeal the environmental protection laws. That would enable them to rape the country of mineral resources at will.

"Not only would he appear to be a hero by signing the Naidvar deal with Groebels, he used me to be the face of it. David warned me about it early on. With my husband heading the project, everything appeared to be totally legit, while Tomo stole from Naidvar too."

Gerel asked, "Then why try to ruin Naidvar by getting Bat-Erdene involved with the thefts, the attacks, and the surveillance?"

Anna said, "For a lot of reasons. For one, he knew Naidvar was doomed to fail, witness the lack of preparation and lack of money invested in infrastructure to supply the needs of the people. With the help of his Chinese friends in Bayannur, early on he had run the numbers. There was no way Naidvar by itself could come close to providing what we need.

"Second, Tomo had made enough money from the theft of the oil to feel comfortable enough to shut us down. And third, he was heavily invested in the coal business, an investment that would provide him enough money to do what he wanted for the rest of his life, which included running his own country into the ground. By the time anybody was the wiser, Naidvar would die and he would be president."

The group sat in silence, making an effort to digest a heavy meal.

"Is there any good news out of this?" Gerel put one palm to her cheek in a universal gesture of worry.

Batu said, "Absolutely. I think our current president might direct all the new-found wealth coming into the country to construct our own oil production facility after confiscating the profits made by these two dark souls."

Completely in her element, Anna added, "Considering the level of graft involved, it might be smart to renegotiate the coal contract with China. My sense is that, once this is exposed, they will express a willingness to cooperate, denying all wrongdoing, of course."

Anna tried her best to say it the right way, lest nobody be offended. "I have one favor to ask. As a simple teacher, I would like somebody to let me know right before the authorities come to pick up Tomo. I have his private number. He asked me to call anytime. I will do that. I will wish him the best of health, because in a few minutes, he will be arrested for treason. In this country, I believe those persons receive the death penalty."

David said, "Before we do anything, I need to write a complete report and submit to Al-Yamani. This is his call, not ours."

"Tugi's gone again," Anna lamented, watching her son walk from room to room calling for him.

David nodded, solemnly, "I have a feeling he came by to pay his last respects before joining a pack. The good news is that Khaled is coming here."

"Al-Yamani is coming to Mongolia?" she said, genuinely surprised.

"Yes, to Naidvar, in fact. After I sent him a coded and secured condensed version of the latest events, he got back to me later and said he is going to take the corporate jet to the air force base in UB, pick up Farmer, and come here for the grand tour."

"That is exciting," Anna smiled. She had heard endless tales about this man from her husband. Suddenly, she frowned. "Do you think he's the one who paid off my debt to TAB? Should I ask him about it?"

David grunted, "Personally, I'll leave that question up to you. If he denies it, you won't know whether he is avoiding the issue for his own reasons, or he doesn't know. If he says 'yes', what are you going to do, get mad or thank him? If nobody had paid it off, you might still be teaching and this country would be in a world of hurt. Anyway, the way he talked, it sounded like he might have another assignment for us."

Closely watching Anna's reaction, he added, "Apparently, we're both supposed to get some kind of presidential award. He wants to be here to see it. I guess Farmer is going to take back the drone too."

"Oh, come on, Davey, I don't want or deserve a presidential award," Anna shot.

David said, "I told him you'd say that. I told him I didn't want it either. He told me to suffer. I did ask him to bring a case of quality vodka with him because I owed someone a favor. He laughed and said he'd bring several. That should make Sandoval happy."

"Knowing you, if any of it even gets to him," she quipped.

"Not with you around," he returned, giving his wife a great loving hug with Chopin playing in the background and little Eric still looking for Tugi.

Chapter 20

Khaled Al-Yamani sat at the head of the conference room table, accompanied by Farmer, David, and Anna. In front of each lay photocopies of David's lengthy report detailing everything he and Anna believed to be relevant about their mission. David couldn't remember when he'd last seen his boss wearing casual clothing. It made him look even thinner.

"Aside from the man in the hospital, your two friends here, and the couple in Mandalgov, who else knows the extent of this?" asked the CEO of Groebels.

"No one, as far as we know," David answered.

Al-Yamani turned to Farmer and said, "Bob?"

Farmer said, "Anna, we need you to do something for us. This job isn't finished."

He held his hand up when he saw her about to protest, and continued, "You might think it is, but we need an airtight case. That said, you'd be surprised what a wad of dollars will do to assist a secretary to forget that a phone repairman wanted to fix something in her boss's office. In a word, your upcoming conversations with Tomo will be recorded.

"You said you have his private cell number, right?" When Anna nodded, waiting for the other shoe to fall. Farmer said, "Tell him David is making you crazy. Now he is planning to go down to Bayannur in the next couple of days. He wants to inquire about some kind of records. We want to see who he calls after that and what he says. Can you do that?"

"No worries," Anna grinned.

Farmer said, "Good. I'll make a few calls to set it up. Plan on doing it tomorrow."

The next day, when Anna made the call to Tomo, she said, "Good morning. This is Anna. I hope I'm not disturbing you."

"No, no, Anna. I'm in my office. What can I do for you?" Tomo replied, cordially.

Anna said the appropriate words, and then asked Tomo for advice. "What should I do? He wants me to go with him."

Each time she spoke she put the phone on speaker for the others to hear. The conversation was already being recorded.

Tomo paused in his reply, finally advising, "Why, go with him, enjoy yourself. Enjoy the city and the plant. See the operation. I'll even call ahead to let them know you're coming."

"Oh, would you? That's so kind, Anandyn.

I'll call you when we get back," she replied, hoping she hadn't overplayed her hand.

"What time are you leaving from Naidvar," he inquired.

"In about two hours, around 11:00 o'clock."

"Very good. I'll let them know," Tomo concluded.

Farmer turned on the speaker connected to the bug planted in Tomo's landline. The tones were heard when he punched in numbers and somebody picked up on the other end. To everyone's great surprise, Tomo spoke in Mandarin. Anna's eyes widened in shock. The call lasted 20 seconds when a voice at the other end said, "We'll take care of it."

Al-Yamani, Farmer, and David looked at Anna, who flopped back in her chair. Mustering her strength, she took a deep breath and said, "Once we're in Chinese territory, he wants us both dead and the car burned to make it look like a single-car accident."

Before the others could remark, the speaker picked up tones for another call being made, this time to Bayannur. Once again the conversation was in Mandarin.

At the conclusion, Anna translated, "Two troublemakers are coming to see you to look at our books. I have taken steps to ensure they won't get there. In case they do find their way to you, shut down your computers and tell them you have experts working to fix the problem.

You don't know how long it will take. Then, give them the tour."

The connection ended, the number recorded.

"That's all we need," said Farmer.

"What now? They all go to prison?" Anna said, expectantly, looking at Farmer and Al-Yamani.

Al-Yamani said, "What happens to the bad guys is not up to us. Nor is what happens to this project. Everything is going to be in limbo for some time, perhaps years, until all this gets sorted out."

Anna said, "What's going to happen when we don't show up anywhere?"

Farmer replied, "Let him call you. Tell him you had car trouble and David put off the visit."

David said, "Wait a minute. Does that means everything gets shut down? I mean the vats, the ponds, the oil recovery, everything?"

Al-Yamani looked grim when he replied, "Yes, in all likelihood."

Not long ago, Anna would have cried. Now the feeling didn't strike her. She remained stoic, pondering their future.

David said, "Khaled, you have an investment here. You must have a say in what happens."

"A say is all I have, I'm afraid. Put yourself in their shoes. First of all, no arrests have been made. The package is being put together. Nobody is the wiser. Second, this will be a lasting national scandal lasting. Third, the conspiracy will have to be sorted and the monies recovered. There may be more players involved. Fourth, presidential and other elections are on everybody's mind, and so forth.

"On the plus side, Temujin tells me he has a better, faster growing strain than the last one, so if, and when, they want to move forward, we'll be the first to know. I'm scheduled to meet with the president the day after tomorrow.

"Until they want to move ahead, I have another assignment for you both. You'll leave in a couple of weeks, shortly after you receive your awards."

"Things could get ugly fast. It's best you both disappear. You know, go on an extended vacation," Farmer said.

The family sat on a love seat facing the corner windows looking out at the complex. The sun was well above the eastern ring of the crater and the crystal clear sky presented a picture suitable for a 1000 piece jigsaw puzzle. Eric sat on his mom's lap while she and David explained to him that Tugi is a dog and he wanted to live with other dogs.

Anna remarked, "Davey, I want to test out of chemistry."

He looked at her in full understanding of her meaning, but prompted, "Go on."

"I had only one more year to go at USC. I've gone online and seen examples of finals for the courses I had left to take. I've been studying and I feel confident I can pass them. As far as the lab work, I'm also comfortable with the instrumentation and the other procedures we do here.

"Temujin is a full professor of chemistry. Maybe he and the other chemists can write a letter as to my level of competence and we can send that in with a request for the chemistry department to put together an online final exam for me to take. I want this all done honestly with no political string-pulling. What do you think?"

David nodded agreeably, "Honey, I think that's a terrific idea. It's definitely worth a try. The recommendation, if you get it, will go in with your cover letter. It can all be done online. Why wait. Let's go see him now."

By the end of the following day, glowing recommendations were emailed to the chair of the chemistry department at the University of Southern California along with a well-prepared cover letter. With the future of Anna Chan Alday uncertain, at least online testing was a possibility. Given her nascent ability to read omens correctly, it would come about.

Subsequent to her emailed request, a cascade of events occurred: Al-Yamani, Farmer, and their prisoner, Bat-Erdene, returned to UB; Al-Yamani and Farmer held a lengthy meeting with the president and his heads of security; Tomo was arrested in a simultaneous raid on Bat-Erdene's home to retrieve the accounting books detailing their nefarious activities; Bat-Erdene's bank account was frozen, along with Tomo's account in the National Bank of Mongolia; a firestorm of news releases occurred (which, curiously, omitted the names of David and Anna); and through quiet diplomatic channels, the head of operations in Bayannur was arrested to permit his head technician to take over operations; and Al-Yamani flew to Morocco for several days to oversee the phosphate mining operation headed by David's father and Draco Harwood.

Accustomed to making hard decisions, Al-Yamani found this one particularly interesting. It had nothing to do with opening or closing a mine, hiring or firing, or forcing another company out of business. This one concerned the closure of an existing operation in order to seek a fortune in a different dimension at the same location; that is, trading biofuel for platinum. In the end, he made his decision.

Finding free time to write on his flight back to his headquarters in Germany, he sent a lengthy email to David and Anna, which read as follows:

D & A: For the first time, the president has been made aware that existing production cannot meet future needs and believed closing the entire operation might be in everyone's best interest, especially since the head of production in Bayannur was arrested by Chinese authorities. Dr. Farmer and I offered him an alternate plan of action. We continue to let our investment grow. So far, all that has occurred is only a speed bump in the growth of an enterprise.

Instead of losing our investment, we double down on it. We build our own processing plant at Naidvar itself, but until that construction is completed, we continue to use the operation already in place in China.

A project like this takes a lot of heat energy. It makes no sense to cause further pollution to a city that one is trying to get rid of by burning more coal to do so, however, natural steam is already present in Naidvar. As you know, the TSR (Trans-Siberian Railroad) runs through Bayannur near Naidvar and carries the oil northward to UB. We will transport our own oil by tanker truck to tanker cars when the TSR stops near the community. The TSR, which always stops at UB anyway, will then decouple at the tankers, to be picked up by another engine to take them to the storage facility on a spur we will build. There are alternate ways of doing this, but we feel that this is the most economical.

There are two caveats to this: First, the test market must be increased and the logistics of fuel delivery and storage must be worked out. One idea to construct safe kiosks located in strategic locations to enable the public to refill their own fuel supply.

All of this will take time. Given our cooperation, the president will use this plan to promote his re-election, which looks like it should go smoothly.

The second is this: The president is adamant that both of you head the operation, with Anna working in concert with Batu in chemistry and David overseeing the entire project. (He had an ulterior motive for awarding you the medals, which you are slated to receive in a few days.)

Because many events are occurring simultaneously, you

are both relieved of your work. I will contact you regarding new assignments to which you will attend, until such time as reconstruction of Naidvar can be completed. I will be in contact regarding those assignments shortly.

K

The couple stared at the letter and reread it, without saying a word for some time. Didn't the man ever sleep? For them, the time was 7:30 am, or 12:30 am in Germany, seven hours behind.

"It was a good run while it lasted," Anna muttered, when a ding occurred. Another email had arrived.

Anna opened it to find a final comprehensive exam covering four years and seven different chemistry disciplines. The time limit of five hours was given. She would take the exam under supervision at a time of her choosing to ensure strict adherence to the time limit.

She made a superficial scan through the 14 pages of material, but had no urge to look at the questions at that moment, although she saw it was heavy in math, her mainstay. "From the frying pan into the fire," she declared, cheerily, as though she had already won a contest, throwing her hands into the air. She shot up from her chair and marched around the room talking to herself, waving her hands around saying, "I got this, I got this."

David scratched his beard trying to remember Farmer's words. They were something like,

"Hey, she's yours, not mine."

Anna scheduled the test to be taken in their apartment three days hence. She knew how this went: get good sleep, carb up for energy, answer the easiest questions first to warm up, take regular short breaks, go over everything when the test is completed and only change an obvious error, because the first response is usually correct.

She had never felt so empowered. Even in school, the classes were something she enjoyed. She had never felt driven or had to work hard. She embraced this unusual feeling as though she was finally returning to a comfortable place in her mind that circumstances had pulled her from.

Gerel babysat Eric in the compound play area, while Batu and Temujin kept her company, watching the clock, calling for a five minute break each hour, while otherwise reading on their own in silence.

She completed the test 40 minutes early, including the go-over, and made that announcement. The men noted the hour, signed the form that requested signatures from witnesses, and Anna return-emailed the exam. Done.

Two events occurred via email another three days later. The first was from the Department of Chemistry, University of Southern California. It read:

Dear Mrs. Alday, We have reviewed your test and have

graded it at 93%. This is an exceptionally high score. Many of the questions pertain to classes offered at the Master's level. We are pleased to inform you that you will be awarded a Bachelor's Degree in Science with a specialization in Chemistry.

Furthermore, the reviews we received in your behalf speak of your expertise in the chemical extraction of biofuels for a particular species of algae and your receipt of a presidential award for your work in Mongolia. We are extremely interested in this same field of endeavor and, as such, invite you to write a thesis on your work to be submitted for approval. If such approval is given, and the thesis is accepted by our committee, you will also be awarded a Master's Degree.

Furthermore, once this degree is awarded, we would be pleased to invite a person of your talent and acclaim to join our research staff at the university. If you chose this path, the door will open for you to work on your doctorate. Please inform us of your intentions.

Signed, R.J. Cunningham, Chairman, Department of Chemistry, University of Southern California.

David looked at his wife and said, "Damn, baby, who would have thunk . . . "

The couple was pleasantly stupefied at it all, preparing to rejoice, when the computer dinged. Another email arrived. It came from HQ and read:

Dear D & A: Groebels has a significant stake in a very large project presently underway in the Mojave Desert that dwarfs what you experienced in M. In this facility, the end-product is received. The goal is to produce pharmaceuticals from the algae. I believe you both have the knowledge and organizational skills to assist them in their assays and more efficient extraction of the product. I have been in contact with the corporation in charge of this operation and they are eager to meet you. (And congratulations on your degree, Anna!)

Dr. Farmer will pick you up during his next trip down to Naidvar on the 15th. Arrangements will be in place for your flight back to Southern California.

Good luck.

K

Anna's first thought was that getting transferred to Mojave would put her close to San Diego where she could keep a close eye on her money, perhaps put more into particular investments her father, now she, had a stake in. Why dam up a perfectly good river? She refrained from asking about Al-Yamani's knowledge of her pending degree, figuring it would be a rhetorical question, as they all were, when pertaining to this mysterious man who seemed to have a finger in every pie.

From forty below zero to as much as 130 above. Nice contrast, Anna mused. Out loud, she said, facetiously, "Sweetheart, would you go so far as to say we are at a crossroads."

The comment struck David as facetious, causing him to break out laughing so hard, she got caught up in it. If Tugi were here, he would have licked the tears from their faces.

Suddenly, a distant thumping shook the windows to interrupt their laughter. The noise increased by the second. They hurried to the corner window to see the landing of Sikorsky UH-60 Black Hawk military helicopter, capable of holding up to 11 troops. "What the hell?" David muttered.

The couple hurried outside in time to see four men emerge, three of them wore military uniforms with side arms. This was not a social call. The fourth was Robert Farmer. David approached the group and said to Farmer, "Damn, Bob, how many hats do you wear?"

"Too many I'm afraid." He turned to the man standing next to him, a hard looking broad-shouldered man, a look that bespoke of too many missions. "David, Anna, this is Captain Batbayar with the Mongolian Defense Forces. Captain, this is David Alday and his wife Anna."

The three shook hands. The captain said, "So you are the famous couple. I would ask you both for your autographs, but unfortunately I am here on business. We are seeking a man by the name of Batu Gansukh and his wife, Gerel."

"Batu?" David and Anna uttered in unison. David felt like a leftover. Supposedly, he headed the project, yet he had not been forewarned of this matter. At that moment, he realized the truth he had been hiding from himself. He was only a simple pawn, as were they all.

Farmer read his thoughts and said, "Sorry, old chap. Orders, you know. How about if we go inside where it's a little warmer?"

"Anna, please take the gentlemen to the people they're looking for while I talk with Bob," David requested.

The pair entered Admin where they located an empty office. David closed the door and each man found a seat. Farmer explained, "It's interesting how people get a conscience after they're caught, especially when getting put to death is the only thing they have to look forward to."

David twirled his finger with impatience, waiting for the rest of the story.

"Tomo gave Batu a lot of money to steal the culture vial and put it in Anna's pack. It was meant for the Chinese."

"What kind of money are we talking about, a thousand, ten thousand?" David was curious as to how much money it took for a man to give up his soul. He already knew men who would do it for a free meal.

"Would you believe $100,000?" Farmer said.

David exclaimed, "That's crazy, man. Batu must have held out for a long time for that much. Batu told us the three grew up together. I guess those two were tighter than we thought. Still, 100 grand won't get you anything in the States, or in many Western countries. It would work in India or right here in a nice house."

Farmer said, "We checked his bank account.

The money was transferred just as Tomo said on the date he told us. Batu, had endless opportunities to take the culture, but he had no way to get it into foriegn hands, until my plane was the only one coming and going. When Anna came down for a short visit, he saw his opportunity.

"The single simple act got him up on charges for theft of government property, conspiring to defraud the national government, conspiring with a terrorist to overthrow the government in concert with a foreign power, and a dozen other charges."

David grunted, "Beats my worst bad day. I'm curious, how does Gerel enter into this, if at all?"

Farmer shrugged, "Somebody had to take care of the bank book at their house. If it was her, then she knew about the deposit, unless Batu hid the money somewhere without her knowledge. She'll need to be questioned."

"Speaking of our friends," David said. He waved his hand to indicate the passage of five people outside their room; two of whom were officers. They accompanied Batu and Gerel, both in handcuffs, who were simultaneously and vociferously arguing their case with Anna, the only one willing to listen.

The two men exited the room and met up with the group, following them to the helicopter, where the prisoners were helped onboard. Farmer turned to the couple and said, "I'm starting to rethink where I want to go when I retire. There is too much action for me around here." At that, he climbed aboard, and the pilot, who had remained behind, spooled up the rotors and in a few moments, the windows of the compound began to rattle as the machine took to the air, rotated 180, and flew northward back to Ulaan-Baatar.

"I don't know whether to cry or laugh," Anna confessed, watching the helicopter clear the southern rim of the crater."

"If it makes you feel any better, with Batu out of the picture, you might want to apply for the job opening," David teased.

Anna began to chuckle. I know it's a little early, but if you've got any of that vodka left, I sure could use a little taste."

"Only if you're nice to me," David offered, leading his wife inside.

"Yeah, I was nice to you once and look what it got us. Just ask Eric." Anna squeezed David's hand and led the way. The signs were pointing in one direction: inside where it was warm. If she had her way, it would soon be hot outside and air conditioned inside.

The couple stood holding hands, watching the plane taxi down the runway. As if to mark the moment, a lone wolf howled.

About the Author

Mark Sneller, PhD, is a former professor of microbiology and medical mycology. He lives in Tucson, Arizona, where he operates Aero Allergen Research, a company specializing in indoor air quality and the identification of mold in contaminated buildings. He is the author of several health-related books, as well as the Jeffrey Shenero series of adventure novels.

* 9 7 9 8 9 8 8 1 5 8 8 0 6 *